# THE WOLF THRONE

SOPHIE L. HART

# CHAPTER 1
# JAZZ

My car's engine sounded like a dying animal choking on gravel instead of its usual combustion-engine hum.

On this Tuesday morning, the sky in Tallow was the same color as wet cement. That's what you got for living in Maine. This gray, sleet-like filter was one of the many permanent fixtures of this place.

There was a reason they called this place "Sleepy Tallow." The grayish skies and the pine trees all around it made it feel like it was a ghost town, or a place where people just slept most of the time. Imagine Forks from *The Twilight Saga*; it had that kind of vibe.

Right now, my car was fighting for its life as I held on to the steering wheel tightly, my knuckles turning white as I urged this heap of metal to move forward. My body shook violently against the frayed vinyl of the driver's seat. I lovingly and accurately called this car "Heap." It was a 1998 Ford Ranger that had gone through a lot of winters and so many logging roads that I had already lost count. Its clutch had started to slip, and it was about to break down completely.

I knew exactly where I needed to go. Ashford's Garage.

It was the only place on the edge of town that could fix engines that were too old or too complicated for the chain stores near the highway. It was also the last place anyone in their right mind would want to take their car if they didn't have to.

Ashford's was right where Tallow turned into the wilds. The hills and thick woods where the local stories began, and where I had heard that Damien Ashford and his family lived in a commune that was off the grid. There was a lot of gossip in Tallow, and the Ashfords were always the most interesting people to talk about. People whispered about their wealth and strange, private lives.

My palms were sweating profusely, making it harder to grip the steering wheel. It wasn't the four-figure repair bill that made me anxious; it was the man I was about to meet.

Damien Ashford.

I hadn't officially met him, but I had seen him before. Everyone in Tallow did. He looked like someone coming out of a myth, a man who looked like he was made out of stone and shadows. According to some, he was quiet, rude, and very protective of his shop and privacy. Every woman in Tallow aged eighteen to eighty said he was "the most ruggedly handsome thing to ever exist in this dreary little town."

"Just get me there, Heap," I said quietly, pushing down on the gas pedal.

The road turned, and at last, the garage came into view. The building was big and useful, but it was also dull and gray. There was a chain-link fence around it, and it was surrounded by barbed wire on top. It didn't look welcoming for a garage. It didn't even look open at all. From outside, I could see broken-down trucks and old cars scattered across the wide lot. I could even smell the oil, cold metal, and pine sap from here.

I stopped by the big bay door and turned off the engine. The truck coughed one last time, shaking violently, before going quiet. Thank God.

I sat on the worn-out seat for a moment, trying to hype myself up. *You're Jasmine Snow, a twenty-four-year-old high school library assistant, always calm, logical, and put together.* I was definitely afraid to walk into this garage, feeling like I was about to face a top-of-the-food-chain predator.

I pushed the door of my truck open, and the rusty hinges squeaked in protest. It was eerily quiet as I stepped outside, rain immediately falling on my skin. It was only a drizzle, and it wasn't surprising. It was always drizzling here in Tallow. I looked around the yard, but the only sign of life was a big, black, custom motorcycle parked near the entrance. It was a far cry from the broken and worn-out engines that were scattered in the area. This was how I knew that Damien was here.

Next to the main bay was a smaller door that led to the office. I knocked, and the sound was hollow and echoed.

No answer.

I turned the knob. It moved.

As I walked in, I was surprised by the sudden change of atmosphere. It was wet and cold outside, but when I stepped in here, I immediately felt warm. It was clearly because of the dimly lit orange lights.

There wasn't much in here; just a big metal desk with papers scattered all over, a computer, and on the wall was a yellowed clock and a calendar with a classic car model and a woman in a bikini. The place smelled like coffee and motor oil.

I was just about to leave when I saw him.

He was coming out of a back door that clearly led to the main workshop. He was wiping his hands on a rag.

No matter how many times people talked or whispered about Damien Ashford, they couldn't convey how real he was.

He was enormous. I stood five feet five inches tall, and I felt small standing across the room from him. He had to be at least six-foot-five and built like a tank. He wore a dark, faded gray t-shirt that pulled tight across his chest and shoulders, as if he was too big for the fabric. His arms were thick and very muscular, and his tanned skin was peppered with grease.

His face was very serious. He had chiseled cheekbones, a jawline that could cut glass, and dark, thick hair that needed to be cut but somehow made him look even more wild.

When we locked eyes, I was taken aback by how beautiful they were. A deep amber, almost gold, and they stared deep into me, as if seeing through my soul. The way he stared at me held no interest or judgment; it was something raw, with unblinking focus.

And then I felt it.

It felt like a bludgeon, and I wasn't sure if that could be categorized as just attraction. Something vibrated deep inside me, a low hum that spread outward, making my skin tingle and my stomach tighten. I was suddenly feeling so drawn towards him.

Suddenly, my brain started to scream.

*Mine.*

It wasn't my conscious self. It was like a deep roar that echoed inside my head. I took an involuntary step back, startled, and looked at his face to see if he had said something.

No, he hadn't. His lips were pressed together in a thin line. But his golden, predatory eyes were burning, peeling off layers of who I was. I didn't feel calm, nor did I feel like myself in my clothes. I wasn't Jazz Snow, which begged the question.

Who was I in the presence of this man?

I made myself talk, but my voice came out breathier than I wanted it to. "Hi, my name is Jasmine Snow. I... I have an appointment."

He stayed still. He just stared at me, chewing on the inside of his cheek. His eyes went from my face to my knees and back up again. It felt less like someone was looking at me and more like they were claiming me. It felt both exciting and scary at the same time.

"Didn't call," he finally said. His voice was a low baritone with that slight rasp. It made the hair on my neck stand up.

"I... I know. I tried calling the main line, but it always went to voicemail." I pointed vaguely toward the door and added, "I know you're busy, but I really need your help. They said you were the only one who could fix old cars, and I need a miracle. My truck is already dying out there."

He finally let go of the oil rag and dropped it on the desk. He took one slow step closer, and I instinctively stood my ground, fighting the urge to back away.

"What seems to be the problem?" he asked, in a rough yet soft voice.

I started explaining everything, from the moment the engine started to stutter, to the clutch already slipping easily. His eyes never left mine while I talked, and it took all of my willpower not to shy away from him or stutter. I saw the muscle in his jaw tighten and then loosen. His nostrils opened up a little, as if he were taking a deep breath of the air around me.

Shit, did I smell bad?

Once I was finished, his eyes flickered outside to where my car was parked. "A '98 Ranger," he mumbled, and the corner of his mouth turned up just a little, showing a tiny bit of amusement. "Then it's a real piece of junk."

"It's my baby," I said defensively.

He made a short, rough noise that could have been a laugh. "Come on, show me."

He quickly turned around and left the office without checking to see if I was following. I rushed to keep up and suddenly became clumsy. Outside, the drizzle had already stopped.

He walked around Heap slowly, stopping for a moment to look at the woods with his big hands resting on the chain-link fence. Even though he was facing away from me, it felt like his full and heavy attention was still on me.

"Open the hood," he said.

I did what I was told, and the hood let go with a groan of its own. I stood awkwardly by the fender, trying my best not to ogle at his size, bent over my sorry excuse of a car.

"The transmission's toast," he said after a few minutes. I almost expected it would take longer for him to check everything. He tapped the oil filter with a dirty finger. "There's no clutch pressure plate anymore; it probably took the bearings with it. It might also be the flywheel. Could be the whole thing."

Being close to him was driving me crazy. I could smell him now, the strong smell of the garage and something that was just him: warm skin, something musky and clean, like rain on hot asphalt and pine needles. I leaned in closer just to smell it, which was a silly, lizard-brain urge.

"So...a bill for four figures," I said, running my hand through my hair.

He stood up straight and turned his full height back toward me. The movement was quick, which scared me. He was close enough that I had to look up to see the fine stubble along his strong jaw.

"It's five," he said, his amber eyes dropping to my mouth and then back up to meet mine. "Maybe six. It depends on whether I need to make parts."

I felt my heart sink at the money, but at the same time, I was dizzy from the realization that he was standing too close to me. My body was letting me down. It felt like every nerve ending was pulling toward him and asking for contact. It was just a strong, terrifying need.

He must have seen the look on my face and had mistaken it for financial worry. His jaw tightened again, nostrils flaring.

"Look, I can take a look," he said, his voice dropping an octave. "But it will take at least three days. I have a full schedule, and I charge fifty dollars to get it on the lift."

"Fifty is fine," I managed. "Can I leave it?"

"Yes. Put it here." He pointed to the space near my truck and added, "Outside the gate. Don't block the bay."

"Okay." I was stupidly upset that the conversation was coming to an end. It was like pulling a splinter out of my heart: painful but necessary. "Thank you, Mr. Ashford."

"I'll call you in three days with the full estimate," he said in a flat voice. He then held his hand out, palm open, and I was almost convinced he was asking for a handshake until I realized he needed the keys to the car. I wanted to slap myself for thinking so.

I pulled them out of my pocket and dropped them in his hand, and he was quick to wrap his fingers around them. His long, veiny hand. As I looked up at him, he was still staring back at me.

I knew he was watching me without having to look back. I could feel the heat of his gaze pressing into the middle of my back all the way until I turned the corner, and the chain-link fence of Ashford's Garage disappeared into view.

The strong feeling I had for the mechanic made me forget about the man waiting for me at home.

# CHAPTER 2

# DAMIEN

I lied when I said I would give her the estimates in three days. The Ranger's transmission still lay disassembled on the floor, and the clutch assembly was waiting for parts that wouldn't arrive until Friday or Saturday. But the truck wasn't the problem. *She* was the problem, and I was wasting time I didn't have going back to our interactions and imagining what it would feel like if I had been able to smell and touch her.

Her smell still pervaded the garage.

There was a sweet, soft smell that stuck inside the office. I couldn't bring myself to clean the place up. I didn't want to lose her scent.

I was twenty-eight years old, six feet five inches tall, and ready to fight. As the Alpha's son, I learned about the Codex, being responsible, and the strict rules of the Wolf Throne. I was next in line to lead the pack. But when Jasmine Snow came into my garage, the place that was once dull, quiet, and filled with grease and oils, the place felt a little lighter, warmer.

*Mate.*

The thought popped up in my head suddenly and stayed affixed there, as if a beast had burrowed under my skin. My wolf snapped into place, possessive and so sure when I smelled her scent. It was strong, sweet, and entirely addicting. The primal recognition was tearing me apart; the wolf in me wanting to take her here on my desk and claim her right then and there, even though I knew it was the most unprofessional, territorial, and reckless thing I could do.

I didn't call her today. I was too afraid. I was supposed to be busy with my own duties, like checking if everything was in order in the pack, keeping an eye out for any threats. But instead, I was in my garage, not even fixing anything. I was just pacing the concrete floor and twitching my hands because it was too quiet in here. I loved how she smelled.

My thoughts were interrupted when the office door creaked open.

I was bent over my desk, pretending to go over some papers. I didn't need to look up to know it was her. My wolf turned rapt, and I could feel my muscles tighten right away.

"Mr. Ashford?" Jazz's voice was soft and shaky, like she was scared to come in here. She should be.

I looked up at her with the same blank expression I gave everyone else. I needed to keep up the nonchalant, closed-off, and mysterious guy that lived on the outskirts of town persona to drive any unwanted visitors away. But deep down, my blood was thick and hot, flowing through my veins.

She had dark hair that was slightly damp, and she was wearing a light jacket that didn't do much to keep her dry and warm. Her beauty was strong enough to handle the harsh conditions.

"Speak up, Snow."

I said as I left my seat, going around the desk and leaning against it. I watched as she took a step back, wringing her hands nervously.

"I just came to check on Heap," she said as she hugged herself. She tried to act calm. "And to see if you have any news about the estimates and how long it would take."

I crossed my arms over my chest. "I told you three days at the least. It's been one. Did you really think I could just pull a new transmission out of nowhere?"

I watched as her cheeks heated up in embarrassment. Then, her eyes looked defensive. "No, I thought maybe it would be better if I came to check on it again today, see if there's even a bit of progress."

"Snow, this isn't a dealership," I said, using her last name as a weapon. "I'm just one person. It takes three days to look at the timeline. Come back on Thursday or Friday."

She bit her lip and looked around the shop. The place was filled with old iron and stains of grease, a reminder of my own dangerous, lonely world in the woods.

"Can I...wait?" she asked, looking straight into my eyes. She was proud but also desperate. "I came here on foot. It's too far to walk back before the next bus arrives. I can just stay out of the way. I brought a book with me."

I was having trouble breathing. The idea of her sitting five feet away from me for hours, breathing the same air as me, and letting her scent fill the garage was the most tempting and the worst thing I could think of.

*Yes. Stay close to her. Keep her scent in here.*

*No. Get her out. You'll go crazy.*

"Fine," I growled. "But stay inside the office. Don't touch anything."

She smiled with a grateful, innocent smile that felt like a punch. "Thanks, Mr. Ashford."

"Damien," I said without thinking. I couldn't stand how stiff she was.

"Damien," she said again, and my name sounded heavenly leaving her lips. I turned and went to the garage before my wolf would do anything I might regret.

She moved quickly. I watched her for a full minute through the small, dirty window. She moved around, sat down in the hard metal chair by the desk, and pulled a book out of her bag. Not following her and inhaling her scent was hurting my muscles.

I was supposed to be working, but all I could do was lean against the tool bench and rub the oily rag between my hands. The way she turned her head, the way she flicked her wrist as she turned a page, and the way her chest rose and fell with each breath all made me pay attention.

*Mate.* My mind whispered. A soft, human-smelling mate with wide, innocent eyes and a strong spirit.

I walked back into the office. She looked up, surprised, and pulled the book into her lap.

"Is something wrong?" she asked, blinking up at me.

"No." I leaned one hip against the cold metal edge of the desk and added, "Just waiting."

It was almost too much to be so close. I could feel the heat from her skin despite the generous distance.

"What are you waiting for?"

"For parts. To get a good cup of coffee. For the rain to finally stop in Tallow."

She laughed, and it was a short, musical sound. "No wonder you live on the outskirts. You're going to bring people down with your mood."

I grinned, surprised at how comfortable she already was with teasing me. "Or maybe my real home isn't this dirty, greasy garage, sweetheart."

I saw her think about it, her lips pursing and her eyes staring off, wondering.

"What's it like out there?" She asked, pointing in the general direction of the woods. "I guess it's already known that the Ashfords don't mix with the locals. You probably can't blame them if they think you're closed off."

My whole body got stiff. This is where the falsehoods started. I said in a flat voice, "We keep to ourselves. Land for the family. More privacy."

"Must be nice, quiet." She thought.

"Quiet," I said, snorting a little. "It's never quiet. There's always something—or someone—that needs your attention. Something is always trying to take what you've kept safe."

I pushed myself away from the desk and slowly walked to the door of the workshop. I think I've already scared her enough.

"What about you, Jasmine Snow?" I asked. "Librarian assistant. It looks like a calm life."

Her cheeks turned red. "Yes, it is. It's quiet and safe. I like being safe."

"Safety is an illusion," I couldn't help but retort, and she looked up at me with confusion.

"Do you?" I pushed back and got closer. The air between us was suddenly heavy. "That doesn't sound very safe, you know. Driving a ten-thousand-dollar wreck to the most dangerous, out-of-the-way shop in town, knowing I was the guy who ran it."

Her light blue eyes were clear and strong when she

looked back up at me. "Sometimes you have to risk everything for what you need," she said simply.

What she said hit me like a punch in the gut. She didn't know what she needed, but her gut told her what it was. She needed me.

I had to put a stop to this. I had to say no to her now and end things before she got caught up in the coming slaughter. I needed to make her hate me and go.

"I don't think you know what you're risking," I said in a low voice that sounded like a warning. I put my hand out to rest it on the door frame, but my fingers touched the edge of her collarbone instead.

The contact was a live wire.

All the walls I had carefully built, my duties and responsibilities as the next alpha, the Codex, and the other packs trying to threaten my own, all came crashing down. The humming in my body got louder and more frantic, feeling the violence. Under my touch, her skin felt soft, warm, and just right.

She gasped, her eyes widened, and she tilted her head back, showing the weak curve of her throat. I could feel the demanding shift in my core, the wolf rising, wanting to taste her, bite her, and mark her.

I pulled my hand away like it was on fire. I backed up three steps and hid behind the desk. My heart was racing in my chest, threatening to come out of my skin.

"You need to go, Jasmine," I said, and my voice shook a little.

She stood up, and she looked just as shaken as I was. "Let me pay the fifty-dollar fee, at least."

"Don't give me your money," I said as I put the papers away. No matter what happened, I wanted her to leave before I threw her over my shoulder and carried her into the woods.

She walked over to the desk and said firmly, "No, let me pay."

The only thing that kept us apart was my messy desk. We looked at each other again. The tension inside the office was so heavy and loud that with one wrong move, I don't think I'd be able to stop myself from pouncing on her.

I leaned over the desk and said in a low, threatening voice, "You owe me. And you don't even know how much it costs yet."

"Then tell me," she said, leaning in as well. I was shocked by how brave she was. She was a librarian's assistant, but she was a warrior at heart. *My warrior.*

I stopped because I knew I couldn't say no to her right now. My wolf would break my hold. But I also couldn't tell her the truth. Not about the Wolf's Throne. Not about the threats coming from the other packs.

I said, looking at the corner of her mouth, "The price is going to be high. It might shock you."

She stood her ground for a little longer, her chest rising and falling quickly. She was having trouble breathing, just like me. The air felt thick and hard to breathe.

Finally, she let out a breath. She felt like she had lost, but not broken. "Friday," she said, her voice low.

She left. There was a loud click when the office door closed.

I didn't move until I heard the bus leave the main road. I finally let go of the breath I didn't know I was holding. It was a rough, deep breath that sounded like a man and a growl.

I was sure I wouldn't wait until Friday. I needed her tonight. I had to test the bond, taste the inevitability, and see if the promise was as bad as the reality. And then, after I had taken her completely, at least in body, if not yet in spirit, I would have to send her away and keep her safe so that the wolves of Tallow could never get to her.

But I would find her tonight. Tonight, I would be selfish. The Alpha of the Ashen Ones would give up his job tonight to protect the mate bond. He would deal with the bloody aftermath the next day, whatever it may be.

# CHAPTER 3
# JAZZ

I only lasted seven hours.

After leaving Ashford's Garage, or more like stumbling away from Damien Ashford, I got home and stared blankly at my computer screen. I couldn't focus on any of the cataloging questions. The office in the high school library was too bright, too quiet, and too normal.

I didn't have a problem with how much I might be spending on the truck; I had already started scrambling my savings accounts and was ready to accept the financial ruin. The problem was that the world I thought I lived in was safe and predictable, but it turned out I needed something that would bring me out of my comfort zone. Damien Ashford was there, waiting for me to get out of it, to finally give in.

*Mate.*

The silly, basic word that my mind had made up in

front of him kept banging around in my head. I didn't like how animalistic it felt. I hated that a man who was rude, scary, and always looked like he was ready to fight could make my body sing with a harmony I had never heard before.

Then there was Vincent. My real-life boyfriend. I avoided his calls all afternoon. It was as if Damien's presence had completely erased Vincent from my mind, making him seem far away and unimportant.

By seven o'clock, mist and darkness had completely covered Tallow. I told Vincent that I had a bad headache and needed to be by myself. I ate a sad meal that had been microwaved, walked around my small apartment, and tried to talk myself out of it.

*Go back there.*

*Stop being silly, Jazz. You can wait until Friday.*

*He is waiting.*

I took off my work clothes and put on jeans and a thick, burgundy sweater. I wanted to be comfortable and safe. It didn't help. There was some kind of physical pull, pulling me toward that cold, greasy metal box on the edge of the woods. I made up a reason: I had to pay the $50 deposit. I had to sign the repair order in person. I had to...make sure that what I was feeling when I was near him was something I didn't make up.

I called a taxi and paid the driver a lot of money to take me right outside the garage's chain-link fence. I didn't want anyone to see me come back. This felt like a confession of guilt, something I couldn't tell anyone.

I was alone in the dark after the cab left. The air was colder and sharper, and I could smell the damp earth underneath the soles of my shoes and the pine trees just hovering several meters away from where I stood.

"Damien?" I called out, but the darkness around me quickly swallowed my voice. I suddenly felt so stupid. I should have stayed home.

I walked to the door of the office. It was now locked.

I said to the locked door, "Damien, I just came to pay the deposit. I'll just leave a note and some cash under the mat."

*What was I doing?*

I reached down to feel for the welcome mat, which definitely wasn't there.

A loud, heavy clank came from inside. My heart jumped into my throat. The noise was too loud and too heavy to be rats or something else. There was definitely someone inside.

I stepped back from the office and turned to look at the main bay doors. And then I saw it: a small sliver of light coming through the bottom corner of the door.

"Hi?" I called again, this time louder, fighting the urge to run away.

There was silence. Then, the sound of a lock bolt being thrown, which sounded like grinding. The big metal door creaked open just enough to show the bottom half of a man.

Damien.

*Mate.*

He had on a pair of old, greasy work pants that hung low on his hips. His chest was bare, and it was all sculpted, tan muscle. In the dim light, sweat shone on his torso, following the deep lines. He was breathing heavily, and his chest was moving up and down as if he'd just finished a hard workout. Or maybe a fight.

He didn't say anything. He just stared at my feet in the crack of the door. Then he slowly lowered his head and crawled out from under the bay door. It was unsettling to see him move with such slow, animal grace. He stood up, towering over me.

"You came back," he said, his voice not a question but a statement.

I couldn't help but look at his chest because of how broad he was. "I...I had to pay. I don't like owing money."

"I knew you'd come," he said, stepping closer and closing the distance between us at an alarming rate. "I didn't think you would wait until Friday."

His eyes were just like I remembered: bright, predatory, and glowing. They looked almost all gold in the dark. I could still smell the same heady mix of rain and oil, but now there was a raw, musky smell of sweat and pure male heat underneath it.

"Why are you here? It's the middle of the night," I said, my voice coming off small and weak.

"I was waiting," he said, sounding like an admission. He then closed his eyes. "I couldn't breathe because I knew you were out there. I had to see you again. I needed this."

*Belong*. The word made my spine tingle. It was possessive, and at that moment, completely, devastatingly compelling.

He reached out and put his calloused hand on my cheek. His fingers were rough and smeared with engine grease, but his touch was surprisingly soft, which was scary because it was so different from the raw power of his body. The humming in my body that had bothered me the day before came back, but this time it didn't just vibrate; it roared. It felt like the center of my body woke up all of a sudden and wanted to be so close to him.

"This is going to cost you everything, Jasmine Snow," he whispered, and his voice shook. "You can't go back if we're going to do this."

"I don't care about the cost," I said, lying with a weak and careless voice. The logical part of my brain was gone, and all that was left was the crazy, primal need to close the last few inches between us. "I just...I have to know what this is."

He didn't say anything. He dipped his head and kissed me, taking my mouth that was nothing like the gentle, careful love I was used to from Vincent. This felt raw, hungry, and complete.

He tasted like smoke and coffee. His arms wrapped around me and pulled me hard against his bare, sweaty chest. His body was so big that it was crushing, but for the first time in my life, I felt grounded. Every molecule in my body knew his, and the long, awful ache of being empty was finally going away.

He picked me up with ease, my feet leaving the ground, and carried me back through the small opening under the bay door and into the workshop.

He put me down on the workbench, and the cold steel hurt the back of my thighs. This was very different from how hot his skin felt against mine. He didn't stop kissing me. My hands, guided by an instinct I didn't know I had, got tangled up in his thick, wet hair and pulled him closer.

This was more of a basic need than a loving hug. Every touch was possessive, like a claim of ownership that I suddenly wanted. He broke the kiss only to lightly brush his teeth against my jaw and breathe in my scent.

"*Mine*," he growled, his hot breath hitting my ear. The sound went straight to my core and made me moan.

I gasped when I heard fabric being ripped, and cold instantly met my chest. I looked down and realized that he had actually ripped my sweater open. I looked up at him, and his eyes were wild, almost animalistic. Before I could react, his fingers were reaching behind me, unclasping my bra in one swift motion, and my breasts spilled from the cups that used to hold them.

A moan left Damien's lips before he leaned down, taking a nipple with his mouth and sucking on it.

I arched my back and cried out in pleasure, letting Damien lick and bite on the sensitive nubs, his hands squeezing them and pushing them together.

"You're beautiful, you know that?" He whispered as he reached up to kiss me again, hands playing with my nipples, flicking and pinching them in between his fingers.

"Damien, please," I pleaded, feeling my wetness pool in my panties. His nostrils flared, and he growled.

"You smell so fucking good. I...I need a taste."

I could only nod, and with my consent, he held onto my pants and pulled them down, bringing my underwear with it. Cool air greeted my bare legs, and I shivered, but Damien's body close to mine brought warmth and comfort with it. He kneeled, his face level with my vulva, and his hands gripped my thighs to open me wider.

"Do you taste as good as you smell?" He asked, his amber eyes meeting mine, and I could only bite my lip. I watched him take a good whiff of me, his eyes closing as another satisfied, belly-deep groan left his lips. Before I could react, he was on me, his mouth breathing hot breath on my pussy, and then kissing it.

"Damien!" I gasped, my hands going up to grip his hair.

His tongue shot out and licked more of me, tasting my juices and playing with my clit. He slipped his tongue inside my hole, feeling and tasting my walls, and the soft, thick feeling of his tongue moving inside of me was pushing me closer to orgasm.

"You taste so fucking good. Where were you all this time?" He said, his lips against my drenched warmth as he said it, the action sending more pleasure to my core. He continued to eat me, his mouth and tongue doing wonders down there that I was so close to breaking and coming.

"That's right, Jasmine. Come for me," he said as he pushed one long finger inside of me. I gasped again, his finger stretching me a little and hitting that sweet spot inside of me.

With several more licks and his finger thrusting inside of me, my orgasm came like a tidal wave, my whole body shaking and spasming as I cried out his name over and over again.

He didn't stop licking me until I was pushing his head away from the sensitivity. I watched with hooded eyes as he stood back up with a grin, his lips glossy with my juices. I couldn't help the blush that crept up to my neck and cheeks.

As I looked down at him, still in his jeans, I could clearly make out the huge, thick outline of his cock begging to be released. My fingers carefully reached for his zipper, and his breath hitched when he realized what I was about to do.

As his jeans fell to the floor, he took out his cock from his boxers, and my heart raced at the sight of him.

He was *huge*.

Thick. Veiny. Leaking of pre-cum. The head was painfully red, as if begging me to release it from its struggle. I licked my lips involuntarily when I heard Damien chuckle.

"Want a taste?"

He didn't have to ask me twice. I jumped off the desk, kneeling in front of him, his enormous member waiting to be touched and sucked, throbbing anticipatively. Damien gripped himself, the tip of his cock teasing my lips as he nudged me with it.

I opened my mouth, tongue sticking out, taking it as an invitation for Damien's cock to slip inside. The moment it touched my tongue, heat pooled in my stomach, and I moaned out at the feel of his hardening cock filling my mouth.

"Fuck, Jasmine. Your mouth feels so good." He sighed, his head thrown back. I swallowed him up, sucking every inch of him that my throat could take, and I gagged at the sheer size of him. I bobbed my head up and down, my hand going up to grip the base of his cock that couldn't fit in my mouth.

He was a moaning and panting mess in front of me. His hand gripped my head, his fingers digging deep in my scalp as he gently tried to push my head further to try and get more of his cock inside. I did my best, and as I did so, I used my tongue to lick the underside of his cock, and he twitched inside of me.

"Jasmine, sweetheart, you're ruining me." He cried out, and he immediately pulled away, his cock leaving my lips with a *pop* and a string of saliva still connecting us.

"You can't make me come yet, baby. I still need to feel myself inside you." He said, and he brought me up, pushing me back down on the workbench again.

He spread my legs open, his fingers flexing against my skin as his other hand caressed the inside of my thigh soothingly, as if warning me of what was going to happen next.

The moment the tip of his cock brushed my clit, I gasped, my back arching as my legs opened wider, begging him to put it in already. As if sensing my desperation, he chuckled, licking his lips as he thrust inside, the head of his cock stretching me already. We both gasped at the feel of it, and he slowly pushed himself further inside, inch by painful inch.

I squeezed my eyes shut and bit my lip. It stung. I didn't realize how much it was going to hurt.

"Breathe, baby," he whispered, feeling his fingers caress my cheeks. I opened my eyes, and his amber ones stared right back at me, pupils blown wide. He looked like an animal in heat.

I did as I was told, and I breathed in, in the same

moment he thrust further inside until every last inch of him was inside.

I cried out in pain, but as soon as it did, it was then replaced by overwhelming pleasure. My body adjusted to him inside of me, stretching out my walls, touching the parts of me that not even my own fingers could reach. It was mind-blowing.

His thrusts became deeper, faster, sloppier. I couldn't contain the moans leaving my lips while Damien whispered my name against my neck, over and over again. The proximity of our warm, sweaty bodies and the thrill of him taking me over his work-bench was enough to push me to my orgasm.

"That's right, baby. Come for me, I can feel you getting tighter." Damien groaned, and with one more push, I was coming, my release coming hot, fast, and overwhelming. I could see stars. Damien caught up with me, and with several more thrusts, he spilled his seed inside of me, feeling his cock pump every last drop of his cum.

We stayed like that for a long time, with only the sound of our breathing in and out in a rough, steady rhythm.

"That was..." I breathed out, and Damien chuckled as he removed himself from my embrace, his cock slowly pulling out of me, and I hissed in the slight sting.

"You were amazing." Damien sighed as he helped

me up and kissed my forehead. "When can I see you again?"

I raised a brow, a smirk forming on my lips. "You'll have to promise me to fix my car first, then I'll consider."

He laughed, a sound that was so carefree and relaxed you wouldn't believe that it came from the same man who people in Tallow believed was a mystery.

"I promise. But I'll have to take you out to dinner first."

# CHAPTER 4
# DAMIEN

Thinking about her had hurt physically. It was like finding out I had lost a limb until she walked into my garage. Taking her on that cold steel workbench was the most reckless and necessary thing I've ever done. I had walked away from the heat of her body, but the smell of her sweet scent was now stuck in my mind, making it hard to think clearly.

I should have been back in the Ashen Ones' territory, with the pack elders around me, talking about strategy. The political power in the packs was bad enough already, and most likely all of them were full of ambition and challenge. Every day I was away from the compound, Elford and the Dravens got stronger and got closer to challenging my pack's authority. But the thought of duty and the harsh reality I was going to face seemed far away compared to the warm, bright reality of Jasmine Snow.

After I dropped her off at home after that sweet intercourse, I watched her go, and my wolf, the possessive and commanding part, had won me over. It wasn't finished. It couldn't be. I sent the one text that she'll likely read when morning comes.

*Be ready tonight. Seven.*

She replied with a single emoji, but it already felt like a blood pact.

I spent the whole day in the garage, but the tools were just for show. I was so worried about how the meeting would go that I couldn't think of anything else. I wasn't able to drive my truck. Tallow was small, and my black pickup was too easy to spot near the apartment district. This made it easy for Elford or any of the Shadowfangs to track me down and ruin my evening with this beautiful girl.

No. I needed something louder, faster, and difficult for anyone else to recognize.

I finished work early and cleaned up. I drove my old Ford back to the commune myself, even though the guards were worried and frowned at me. I went straight to the secret hangar where my dad kept his most private things. The chopper, a custom black-on-black machine made for tough transport, was an extension of my shift. It was small, but it was fast. Graceful.

I threw a leg over, and the heavy engine roared to life with a sound that shook the hangar's walls. The noise was loud and aggressive, overpowering the smell of woodsmoke in the commune.

It was easy to pull strings. Jasmine's apartment had a helipad at the building's rooftop, and when I asked the owner if I could land my chopper there for a short while, he was more than happy to accommodate me and even offered to let it stay overnight.

I was up in the sky in minutes. It was going to be a quick journey to Jasmine's, but I was going to take her on a ride before we had dinner. I already had our night planned.

I landed the helicopter on the rooftop, exactly at seven. I turned off the engine, and the silence that followed was deafening, broken only by the loud ticking of the cooling metal.

Before I left, I already told Jasmine where to meet me. She must be confused.

I didn't wait long. I was leaning against the chopper, light dust from the trip covering my old leather jacket and boots. I looked up and saw her leave the elevator, her face lit up by the golden glow of her apartment. Her curious blue eyes got bigger right away when she saw the machine and then me waiting. Her shock was the perfect mix of fear and excitement.

"Damien, what's all this?" she asked, her tone slightly excited yet curious.

"I told you to be ready," I said, pointing to the passenger seat.

She walked toward me and looked at the chopper

for a while. "Ready for what, exactly? I was thinking about dinner, maybe. Not...this."

"We don't get second chances," I said as I pushed off the door and opened it. "We get tonight. And tonight, we take off."

She got inside, and I helped her get settled, and in the small, cramped space, I could clearly smell her scent and her heart ramming against her chest. Her presence was intoxicating. I had to hold myself back from skipping dinner and taking her right there on the chopper's leather seat.

The strong engine lifted us off the ground.

We flew low over the thick Tallow woods, and the dark canopy stretched out below us. I could feel her breath catch in my neck because of how fast, how high, and how daring the flight was. I was showing her my world without her knowing it. It was the feeling of total, ruthless freedom that came with having complete power and being able to rule the land that was mine by birthright. I turned the chopper's nose toward the sea, away from the center of the commune that was filled with political predators.

As I glanced towards her, I could see the wonder in her eyes, her smile bright as she looked below, clearly unafraid. The wind blew back her dark hair, and her blue eyes sparkled with the moonlight that shone above us. She was ethereal.

After several more minutes, we landed on a private land near town where I had reserved us dinner near the docks. The Rusty Anchor. It was a well-known local dive, the kind of place where I could talk without worrying about anyone with enough pack knowledge to matter hearing me.

I turned off the engine and swung my leg over. I reached back and put my hands on her waist, waiting for her to slide off. When she hit the ground, her legs shook, but her eyes were bright, shocked, and happy.

"You have a helicopter," she said, her voice full of awe and disbelief.

"It's easier than driving when the woods are full of trouble," I said, taking the gear off her head. Her hair was messy and wild. I ran my rough thumb over her cheekbone. I reached out and took her hand, threading my fingers through hers. It already felt so natural.

"Let's eat," I said, my voice dropping back to the rough command she was learning to follow. "I need to talk to you, Jazz."

The Rusty Anchor was cheap, smelled a little like old beer and salt, and was thankfully empty except for the grumpy bartender, who was too tired to care about whoever came inside. We sat down in a booth by the window that had been damaged.

I still held her hand and rubbed my thumb in circles over her knuckles. She was my own selfish anchor that reminded me that something good, something that was mine, still existed, even though my life was falling apart. Since we got here, I hadn't let go.

Jasmine started, her voice low and her eyes wide as

she traced the rough scars that crossed my forearm. "Why do you hate Tallow so much?"

I had already ordered ahead for us, and when the waiter spotted me, he easily went back inside to get our food. While waiting, I let the "Bad Boy" side of me take over. This side of me told half-truths with a lot of confidence. "I don't hate Tallow. I can't stand being watched. My family built everything we have here, but it wasn't cheap. They want things from me that are outside of what is normal for me."

I stopped and stared her straight in the eye. I needed her to know that I was dangerous, not a nice date. "The business isn't just about engines. It's about land. And loyalty. The more you go into the woods, the fewer rules there are. The Ashfords are in charge out there, which means that for the rest of my life, people will test my strength and try to take what's ours."

"What kind of things?" she asked, her voice soft with real interest.

"Demands. Problems. Obligations that last for generations," I said, keeping the words simple but heavy with meaning. "The reason my store is on the edge of town is so I can keep one foot in the civilian world and the other in the woods, the territory I'm sworn to protect. It's a lonely way to live, but that's how it has to be. People expect me to be tough and do whatever it takes to protect what the family has built, even if it means cutting myself off."

She paid close attention, and I could see her face

soften with understanding. "That sounds like a lot of stress, Damien. It looks like you have the whole woods on your shoulders."

"Maybe I do," I said with a slight, bitter chuckle. "And that weight means I can't choose safety. I can't choose what will happen. My path is set, and it's not safe."

I leaned over the table and whispered. "When you came into my shop, I saw everything I never thought I could have. You're safe. You're light. Jasmine, I could be bad for you."

I looked her in the eye, and there was no denying the truth in my eyes.

She only stared at me, and despite the seriousness in my tone, her eyes held a bit of mirth. "You can just call me Jazz, you know that, right?"

I couldn't help but chuckle. "Okay, *Jazz*. I told you, I'm going to make another mistake. I couldn't stay away. The pull is too strong. There's something about you, Jazz. Something I can't fight, even though I know it's going to break us."

The air was charged. The admission that our connection was involuntary and incredibly strong had broken the last of her calmness, as if those words were something she had waited to hear. She was shaking a little.

Our food arrived, and we ate in silence. Even though the place was not the kind to have a romantic, intimate dinner, it seemed that it didn't matter to either of us. I told her a little bit of my life outside of this dreary town, and I told her that there was something between us that we couldn't deny.

She even looked like she was in a rush, ready to leave. I was worried that I had scared her off, and I already realized that this was a bad idea.

"Take me home," she finally said when she wiped her mouth.

I nodded once. We got on the chopper without saying a word, and I flew us back, landing on her apartment's rooftop.

The change was instant when we walked into her apartment. Her room was small, warm, and clean, and it smelled like cinnamon and old paper. It was everything mine wasn't. I stood in the middle of her living room, a giant inside a cramped space filled with books, trinkets, and plants.

She walked right up to me, closing the gap I was trying to keep. She reached up and took the leather jacket off my shoulders. "Stop talking, Damien," she whispered. "Stop giving warnings. Not yet."

Her lips crashed into mine, and it wasn't as desperate and urgent as last night. This time, it was slow, careful, and full of understanding. We didn't have to rush. We had the place to ourselves, and we were hidden from sight. No one can get us here.

I gripped her thighs and lifted her off the floor, her legs instinctively wrapping around my torso as we blindly navigated her bedroom. Luckily, it was already open. I gently put her on her small bed, something in the back of my mind worrying that if I moved too aggressively, I might break it.

Our clothes were gone in seconds. The kisses became sloppier, deeper, more urgent, and before I knew it, my cock was already teasing her folds, already wet with her juices. Her scent and arousal were so strong that I was fighting the urge to release my orgasm right then and there.

I pushed inside, her soft walls enveloping me, and I was surrounded by the loveliest warmth known to no other man than myself. We moaned in unison, breaths heavy as I slowly thrust in and out of her, giving her the time to adjust to my size. A lone tear escaped the corner of her eye, and I kissed it away.

She breathed deeply and nodded, permitting me to move more. My eyes rolled back as I thrust deeper, faster, Jazz's moans filling the quiet room as her tits bounced underneath me.

"Damien, I'm close," she gasped, her hands gripping my shoulders.

"Yeah? You want me inside of you?" I teased, and she moaned in response. Her pussy was squeezing me so painfully that when she came, my own orgasm followed. I was easily filling her up with my seed.

I held her tightly and buried my face in the curve of her neck, breathing in her scent until my wolf was satisfied for a while.

For five minutes, I was just a man, not an Alpha, a

leader, or a target. I was going to be her mate. We were destined for each other.

As I looked up at her, she had somehow fallen asleep. Soft snores left her lips, her arms still wrapped around me, my softening cock still buried deep inside of her. I carefully slid out, my cum oozing out of her vagina, and it took all of my willpower not to get hard again and fuck her even when she was asleep. She was beautiful even when unconscious.

I got dressed in the dark, quiet room, putting on the leather that felt more like my skin than the human body I was wearing. I leaned over and gave her forehead one last kiss. I didn't turn around. I snuck out of her apartment, my mind clearer, setting my priorities straight.

Before the first hint of gray light appeared on the Maine horizon, I was gone.

# CHAPTER 5

# JAZZ

The first few days were a blur of blinding happiness. I was drunk. Not love, exactly. I couldn't put into words what I felt for Damien Ashford. I had the best sex of my life.

I walked through the high school library's hallways, and the smell of cinnamon and old paper wafted through the air. And yet, all I could smell was him. Oil, leather, and that musky heat. I was glowing. People noticed. My coworkers joked that the weather in Tallow, which is always gray, must finally be good for me. They had no idea that I was feeling the effects of something that happened on a mechanic's workbench and in my own safe bed.

The guilt about Vincent was always there. Vincent was nice, predictable, and completely, deeply boring now. He felt like a ghost of a life I was already trying to get away from. I stayed away from him by pretending to be sick and staying up late at the library. I couldn't look him in the eye without remembering Damien's gaze, his rough hands, and the growl that came deep from his belly right before he broke me.

I kept waiting for the text, the call, heck, even the sound of a helicopter. Damien promised he would call me on Friday, or maybe later. He had said that he couldn't stay away, that the pull was strong.

The happy high began to turn into anxiety by Thursday.

Every five minutes, I looked at my phone. The buzzing and humming of the library turned into a heavy silence that grew even louder with every minute that passed. The only last name I had for him was Ashford, and the only way to reach him was through the garage's broken landline and the temporary cell number he texted me from, which now only rang once and went straight to a generic voicemail.

I tried to make sense of it. Damien was the "bad guy". He still had so many secrets with him. Maybe this was just how he did things: once the fun was over, he was done with it. He said the cost would be high. Maybe this was the price: the sudden, painful feeling of being left behind.

*He got what he wanted, Jazz. You were a brief distraction. A release.*

It was the safest way to explain. It kept me sane. It meant that the problem was just a man with bad morals and not a major problem with the universe as a whole.

On Thursday, I drove myself to work in my neighbor's old Corolla. She was kind enough to lend it to me for the day, considering that the car barely left the parking area since she was getting too old to drive. The following day, as promised, I was going to claim Heap back. He should be as good as new again.

Heap was parked neatly in Damien's yard.

My old Ford Ranger was spotless and shining in the dark. The paint looked a little newer, the tires had just been cleaned, and when I opened the door, everything was quiet.

I walked around it, running my hands over the smooth, waxed hood. I opened the door, and the inside, which usually smelled musty and like spilled coffee, was clean and smelled a little like a new car. It still had a hint of that deep, musky smell that screamed Damien.

My heart raced against my ribs like crazy. He must have written a note. An explanation. Anything.

I saw my own keys hanging from the ignition. I looked around, but there was no note on the dashboard, no message hidden under the wipers, and no text explaining the huge favor he had just done that cost thousands of dollars.

I looked at the odometer. He had driven it for exactly five miles. Just enough to see if the new transmission works. Just enough to give it a drive and then back again.

This wasn't the kind of behavior that happened in a simple ghosting, sex-and-run story. A jerk would leave a voicemail and a bill for twenty thousand dollars. Damien had given Heap a second lease on life and hadn't billed me for a single dollar.

For the next twenty-four hours, I was frantic, trying to get in touch with him.

On Saturday morning, I went back to the garage. Heap was a delight to drive. But as I got there, the office was dark, the fence was locked, and the bay doors were closed. There was a poorly taped sign on the main gate that said, "Closed."

My heart skipped a beat. I was slowly growing anxious.

I took out my phone and dialed the number he used to message me during our date. It went straight to voicemail. I tried for the next ten minutes. No answer.

My anxiety turned into anger. The logical voice in me said, "*See? He left. He doesn't like to commit. He knew the sex was too intense, so he paid for a fixed transmission to get out of it. This was the simplest story. It hurt, but it was possible to get through it.*"

But then I remembered when he explained how difficult and unsafe his life was in the woods. I couldn't understand everything, but his voice held the truth about the dangers he had to face there, and how much he needed to protect. I still had so many questions for him that were left unanswered.

My body was the first to feel it. A deep, cold ache settled in my stomach. It seemed like an organ was missing. My whole nervous system was on edge, looking for him and wanting to be close to him. Why am I feeling this way? I have never felt this way with anyone before, not even with Vincent.

I kept looking at my own hands. They felt strange and useless now that they couldn't touch the rough calluses on Damien's. I remembered how he growled on the workbench. That was possession. That was a promise. And now he was gone.

I went back to my apartment feeling lost. I couldn't eat. I could hardly sleep because I kept having broken dreams about amber eyes and the sweet smell of his skin.

Vincent finally caught up with me that evening.

He came over with Thai food, which was my favorite kind of takeout, and stood in my kitchen looking worried and a little hurt.

"You've been ignoring me all week. I know the car has been stressing you out, but it's fixed now, right? Your neighbor said it runs like new. Talk to me, please."

When he put his hand on my shoulder, it felt like nothing. It felt cold. I forced a small, strained smile, but inside, I felt horrified and scared.

"I know," I said. "Sorry. This week has been hard."

He began to tell me about his day, which was a boring story about a new client and a software update. His voice was calm and steady, and it didn't have the same pull that Damien's did.

Vincent was clean-shaven, wearing a sensible Oxford shirt, and worried about how stressed I was. He was the ideal guy for the life I thought I wanted.

But all I could see was Damien. His skin covered in engine oil and sweat. His eyes the color of volcanic heat, and his words with a touch of authority that made me want to obey him. I couldn't take back what I did with Damien.

The smell of the Thai food made me sick to my stomach. I suddenly felt sick about the gentle, easy comfort Vincent offered. I didn't want safety; I wanted danger. I wanted the terrifying, all-consuming fire.

I suddenly stood up, which made the chair screech as it moved back. "Vincent, I can't do this right now."

His face fell, and his eyes were filled with confusion. "Do what? Have dinner? Are you feeling alright? That Damien guy didn't mess with your car and scammed you, did he?"

Even Vincent saying Damien's name made me feel possessive, which was completely out of place and very unfair to the man in front of me. To the man I said I loved for a year.

"No," I said, lying. "Nothing happened. He made the car work again. Everything is okay. I just...I need some time alone. I need space."

"Jazz, I might be able to help. Tell me what you need." He pleaded, the worry lining his forehead. He was just about to reach out to me again, but I reeled. The hurt in his eyes was evident.

"Vincent, please. You need to leave."

I watched as the hurt in his eyes turned into realization, and then anger. Without saying anything else, he sighed, left the apartment, and slammed the door shut. I was shaking. The logical side of me was worn out from the quiet.

I wasn't just alone; I made my partner leave. And everything in my gut told me that Damien wasn't just ignoring me; he was in trouble. I needed to do something.

I looked out the window at the dark outline of the woods, where I knew his commune was hidden. For the first time, a tear rolled down my cheek. It wasn't because I pushed Vincent away, but because I suddenly lost what felt like a primal half of myself that I didn't even know existed a week ago. I didn't know how to fix myself without him.

# CHAPTER 6
# JAZZ

One week.

Seven days, no calls, one perfectly working Ford Ranger, and a heavy silence. I really did try to get back to normal. I put the fiction section in alphabetical order twice, started getting ready for meals for the next month, and even sat through a whole dinner with Vincent, even though my skin crawled the whole time, and I fought the urge to scream at him to stay away from me.

The truth was that the ghost of Damien's touch was still vibrating in every cell of my body, and not having him around was a real, physical pain. I was in a state of confusion and hurt, sure that something bad had happened to him or that I was the bad thing that had happened to him.

The air in my apartment felt heavy on the eighth day, which was a Wednesday. I was standing by the window, looking out at Tallow, the mist not going away. I drank coffee that tasted like ash, and that's when I heard something loud yet so familiar.

It wasn't the deep sound of the chopper. It was his black pickup truck, making a low rumble. The truck I saw the day I dropped off Heap, a truck that matched its owner's personality down to the smallest detail. It came to a quick stop at the curb, and its tires sprayed a bit of rainwater.

My heart jumped in my throat. Hope filled me, and it was so strong that it felt like a hallucination. For a moment, I allowed myself to be happy. He was here. He was still alive. He came back.

I opened the door and flew down the stairs, tripping once before grabbing the railing to stop myself. I ran out onto the sidewalk, my hair flying, wearing an old pair of sweatpants and a T-shirt, not caring about my appearance.

He was still huge and dangerously beautiful, leaning against the driver's door. But there was something wrong with everything about him. The gold in his eyes that had both scared and excited me was gone. Instead, it was cold and flat. His leather jacket was zipped up to his neck, making him look distant.

I stopped ten feet away, and my breath caught in my throat. The magnetic pull was still there. It felt like unbearable pressure. At the same time, it felt like it was pushing me away.

"Damien," I whispered. Then, a little louder,

"Where have you been? The store is closed. I've been trying to get in touch with you for a week. I thought—"

"Stop," he said, cutting me off. His voice was flat and harsh. It was the most chilling sound he had ever made.

He didn't move a muscle, but his predatory focus was still on me.

"I came to get my tools," he said, pointing vaguely to the back of his truck. There was a big, heavy-duty toolbox in the bed that was strapped down tightly. "And to let you know that this is over."

The words hit me hard and so suddenly. They seemed vague, like a sentence in a language I didn't know.

"Done? What are you talking about, Damien? I..."

"We had sex," he said, cutting me off. "That was all it was, Jazz. A physical relief. You were helpful. There was a strong attraction, but that's not the same as being committed. I told you it would be dangerous."

I could feel the blood drain from my face. My head was spinning as I tried to make sense of his words and the confessions he told me at the bar.

"No," I said again, moving closer, wanting to break through him. "No, you can't say that. You told me you couldn't stay away. You-you took a helicopter to my house! You fixed my truck. That's not just 'physical relief', that's—"

"It was a mistake," he said again. His voice was so cold and firm that I flinched. But they sounded so wrong coming from his lips.

He looked like he was at war with himself. As if he lied on purpose with every word he said, trying to hurt me as much as possible so I would never look back.

Or was I imagining things?

I shook my head and whispered, "You don't believe that. You're not telling the truth, Damien. Something happened, didn't it? Is it your family? I don't care how dangerous it is; you can't just walk away after we—"

"I can do whatever I want," he said angrily, his voice finally losing its control. He stepped toward me like a predator, and I got ready for him to push me. "And what I want is for you to forget my name, stay in your boring, safe life, and move on with that loser boyfriend you have. Jazz, I'm not made for softness. I'm in danger myself. And you are a risk I can't take."

The words were mean, but they didn't break me. If anything, they made me want to fight back.

"Is this how it is now?" My voice was sharp because I was so angry and because I knew deep inside of me that he was lying. "You think I'm weak? You think I'm so easy to get rid of that you can buy me a fixed transmission and then leave? Damien, tell me the truth! Look at me and tell me you don't feel this connection anymore!"

He did look at me. His eyes were full of pain. His

jaw was twitching, and his hands were shaking with tension. He was fighting with himself. He opened his mouth, and for a second, I thought he was going to tell me everything. Tell me that he was lying and that he couldn't bear to end things between us.

Instead, he looked away, shoved his hands deep into his pockets.

"I made my decision. Please don't come looking for me again. Stay away from the shop. Stay away from the woods. You don't belong there."

He turned quickly and slammed the door on the driver's side. Everything felt final, but something in me told me to fight for this. To fight for *him*.

I stood there, shocked, watching as he started his truck. The roar of the engine brought me back to my senses.

"Damien, no!" I yelled and ran toward the truck. I hit the passenger window hard with my palm. "You owe me more than this! You have to tell me the truth!"

He didn't pay any attention to the noise or me. He put the truck in gear and sped away, leaving a trail of smoke behind him. And just like that, he was gone again.

I couldn't let him leave. The idea of losing him was worse than death. It was like my soul was completely left behind.

I turned around quickly and saw Heap, which was sitting innocently in my parking space. My truck that is always there for me and now works. The truck he fixed up as a last, cruel gift.

I rushed to the driver's seat and fumbled with the key to start the car. The engine roared to life right away, which was very different from how it sounded when it was dying a week ago.

I turned the wheel hard and pulled out into the street. I immediately saw the taillights of Damien's black pickup truck disappear around the first bend.

He's not telling the truth. He's going to leave again. I'll follow him. Everything didn't make sense; it was just a gut feeling.

I pushed the gas pedal down, making Heap go faster than I had ever dared. I drove carelessly, going through the quiet streets of Tallow and ignoring the sound of a horn as I cut off an old Buick. I was completely focused on the black truck and the man inside who was ruining both of our lives for a reason he wouldn't tell me.

I followed him out of town, past landmarks I knew, all the way to the edge of town, where the dark, thick forest awaited me. As if daring me to go inside. The road got narrower and bumpier, and the trees crowded in, making the asphalt very dark and hard to navigate.

Damien drove like a crazy person, taking the turns with the ease of someone who knew the road and the area well. I kept up, and with every mile, something was telling me that I was going in the right, unavoidable direction. As if it were fate.

He finally passed the tall chain-link fence around Ashford's Garage, but he didn't stop. He quickly turned off the main road and onto the gravel path that led into the woods' deepest part. I knew this path led to his real home.

I slammed on the brakes and pulled Heap off the road, where it was partly hidden by a group of pines. I didn't want him to know that I was following him. I had to follow him to find out where he was going and what was making him so avoidable, the "world" that wanted him to own everything.

I got out of the truck and started walking. My heart was pounding against my ribs, and my breath came out in short gasps. I walked as fast as I could toward the tree line, following the new track his tires made in the wet gravel. The air here was very different from Tallow's. It was colder and wilder, and the smell of pine and wet earth was too strong.

I walked and walked, too high on adrenaline to worry that I was in the middle of nowhere. Then, the gravel path led to a clearing where I saw the edge of a group of buildings. This must be where he lives.

The hair on my arms stood on end. I felt a deep, primal sense of danger wash over me, stronger than any fear I'd ever felt. I felt so exposed out here, so vulnerable. I was suddenly very aware that I had stepped into another territory, and I was somehow trespassing. If anyone saw me here, they would probably kill me on sight.

But I moved forward. Pushing the fears and worries to the back of my head, I focused on finding Damien again and following the magnetic pull that's been tugging at me ever since I met him.

# CHAPTER 7
# JAZZ

I stood behind a wall of pine trees, just a few feet from the gravel road, and watched where Damien's black truck had disappeared into their commune. My heart felt like it was tearing itself out of my chest, trying to follow him and clawing out to get closer to him.

He had said that I was a risk. He had made fun of how safe and boring my life was. He had turned me down with a cold cruelty that didn't care that he was breaking my heart. It was the end of everything. But I couldn't move. I could see the raw pain in his eyes. I could see the stress in his hands, the way his jaw was clenched in desperation, and the way his eyes were full of pain as if it was hard for him to say those words to me. He was running away.

*"This was a bad idea."*

Those words were said in his cold, flat voice.

And now I was in his world. It was dark, lonely, and demanding. The atmosphere here felt like a wall of invisible pressure that pushed me back toward the safety of Tallow. I knew I couldn't just walk in and ask for answers. This wasn't a library. This was the land of a man who looked like he was made of shadows and mysteries.

Instead of going home to cry and call Vincent, my grief and anger turned into a desperate urge. I turned my back on the gravel path and ran into the deep woods.

It was a foolish choice that hurt him.

The tall, old pines blocked the weak Tallow sunlight, so the woods here were dark even during the day. The air was thick and cold, and it smelled like damp earth and rotting wood that had been there for hundreds of years. The ground was dangerous, with slippery pine needles, sharp rocks hidden under thick moss, and roots that snaked through the earth.

I ran. My lungs hurt right away, and a burning heat spread through my chest. My legs screamed with the new strain. Branches hit my face and arms hard. It left cuts that hurt and were jagged. The pain didn't even register; I was distracted. It was nothing compared to the pain of being rejected that was tearing me apart from the inside.

As I ran, the only sounds I could hear were my ragged breaths and the frantic beating of my heart. The clothes I was wearing got snagged and torn, clinging to my skin with sweat and the forest's damp-ness. I ran until I was completely lost, miles from the safety of Tallow and deep into the forest. The farther I went, the thicker and heavier the air felt.

It wasn't a gentle stop when my body finally gave up. I hit the ground hard on a bed of rough pine needles under a huge, old, three-trunk oak. The blow knocked the air clean out of my lungs. I rolled into a ball, buried my face in my knees, and rocked back and forth. Then I unleashed the scream I had been holding back since I saw the cold, fatal look in Damien's eyes.

It wasn't a human cry of pain or fear. It was a scream of deep anger and sorrow, pure and raw, tearing its way out of my throat and echoing through the quiet, indifferent forest. I screamed until my throat was raw and my whole body shook with the force of the sound. How desperately I wanted Damien to turn around. I screamed until I was too exhausted for anything else, leaving only empty, shaking breaths.

*"Why did you go? Why did you lie?"*

When the noise finally stopped, my broken, shud-dering sobs took their place. The silence that followed was different. It wasn't the dead silence of the woods. It was a silence that listened. A silence that was tense, aware, and fiercely angry.

I slowly raised my head, my eyes gritty with tears and sweat. The sun was slowly sinking for the last time, deepening the shadows until the trees turned

into a menacing blackness. The temperature plum-
meted quickly, and a deep, cold fear settled over me.

And then I could feel them.

The eyes.

Even though I couldn't see them clearly, I knew
they were watching me. Not harmless animals, but
something intelligent, calculated, and dangerous.
Once more, the air felt sharp, but this time it was more
intense. The chaotic static I'd felt after Damien left
was now shifting into a sharp tension, making me feel
like the only outsider in a native environment. Of
course, these creatures knew exactly where I was; I
was their prey.

I scrambled backward on my hands and knees,
looking frantically into the dark gaps between the
trees. I thought I saw something move. A flash of dark
fur and low shoulders that disappeared behind a
thicket of ferns. Then one more. And one more. They
were quiet, quick, and moved like deadly shadows.

Adrenaline rushed back, chilling my blood and
replacing my sadness with pure fear. This wasn't just
the woods; it was the edge of Damien's world, the
place where he had warned me about "ruthless
survival".

I struggled to my feet, my legs shaking uncontrollably. I tried to get my bearings. Which way was
Tallow? Which way was the commune? It didn't
matter. Every direction looked equally perilous.

This time, a much closer, low, guttural snarl broke

the silence. It wasn't a pet dog. It was rough, deep, and resonant, utterly without mercy or doubt.

I tripped and fell back, staring into the darkness. Slowly and deliberately, they emerged from the trees and into the clearing.

They were wolves. Not the thin, shy gray wolves you see in nature documentaries. These were massive, powerful animals with coats of burnt umber and midnight black. They were huge, with low-slung heads and massive shoulders. When they curled their lips back, they revealed their long, terrifyingly sharp, yellow-white teeth. The dark, wild beasts from the forest stories were now real.

First there were three, then four, and then five. They moved quietly and in coordination, forming a wide semicircle around my fallen body. I was surrounded, every exit blocked, their hostile energy making the air feel colder.

And their eyes. They weren't Damien's amber color. They were a cold, malevolent yellow that reflected the last bits of fading light. They looked hungry. They looked murderous.

I backed up until I hit the rough bark of the oak tree. The fear immobilized me. I was trapped, completely alone, staring into the faces of predators.

Damien had tried to keep me safe from this. This was the price he had to pay to exist in his world. These were the things that demanded total loyalty and tolerated no mistakes.

The largest black wolf, clearly the leader, walked onto the bed of pine needles, placing its huge paws down. It didn't growl; its yellow eyes simply fixed on my throat. I knew, with the horrible certainty of prey, that this wolf wanted to kill me. It was calculating the best way to strike.

I tried to scream again, but all that came out was a pathetic, strangled squeak.

This is it. I'm going to die here. Eaten by wolves in the woods of the man who rejected me. The thought was strangely calm, a final, hopeless acceptance.

The huge wolf coiled up, readying its leap. I closed my eyes and braced myself for the crushing weight and the pain that would tear me apart.

But when the fear reached its peak, something extraordinary happened.

A heat hotter than any fever and more intense than Damien's most desperate touch shot through my veins. It felt like my bones were screaming, changing shape against my will, the sound muffled by the blood pounding in my ears. It was painful, terrifying, and necessary. My teeth ground together with agonizing force.

The sad, human scream was replaced by a loud, deep, and powerful howl that seemed to come from nowhere. It wasn't my sound, yet it tore out of my lungs with the force of a newly awakened animal.

I didn't understand the noise. I didn't understand why the fire was consuming my body. But when the black wolf leaped at me with its mouth wide open, my eyes flew open. The last thing I saw was the attacking wolf's muzzle frozen in mid-air, its cold, yellow eyes widening not with anger, but with shock and recognition.

My howl stopped it instantly. Then the world shattered into pain and the terrifying sound of bones breaking, followed by the furious, blinding smell of familiarity as Damien's truck roared back into the clearing.

# CHAPTER 8
# DAMIEN

I drove the pickup hard, the vehicle's black paint a dark, angry shield against the Tallow darkness. I had to lie when I uttered each word of the rejection: liability, mistake, and convenience. Every phrase felt like a knife turning in my stomach. I had seen the destruction in Jazz's eyes, and that was the only thing worse than the frigid silence of the pack waiting for me.

I slammed the truck to a stop beside the main Ashen Ones hangar, not caring that the guard looked astonished. The pack's cruel, organized strength kept this place quiet and secure. But since the wars, that calm felt brittle, ready to fracture at any moment due to Elford's rising ambition and the quiet anarchy in the five clans. I got out and felt the heavy, nauseating weight of my leather jacket, the *Alpha's mantle*. I knew I was back where I belonged, shackled to my duties.

The beast inside me was a vicious, caged prisoner. It wept at the separation, struggled against my control, and begged to have its mate returned immediately. *She's freezing. She's lost. Fix it. Take her.* I proceeded through the compound to the council hall, trying to bury the emotion beneath reports and plans. I passed the main fire pit, which was still cold and murky from the morning fog.

I chose the throne over the mate and the pack over the primal command. To survive, I had to become the cold-blooded animal I needed to be; the man who didn't look back at the light he had just extinguished. When I opened the council hall door, the boom resonated in the empty chamber.

"Damien, you're late." It was Kai, one of the senior Betas, looking worried. "The Dravens sent a report. Another planned breach. We think Elford is trying to push us into an early conflict."

I grunted and walked to the far end of the table. "What is it this time? Cattle? A marker on the border?"

Kai shook his head and pushed a scratchy, hastily scrawled paper across the smooth oak. "They report that one of their scouting units spotted an unauthorized woman trespassing deep in the restricted zone, near the old triple oak." He paused. "They claim she's armed and a danger to the pack's security, so they've surrounded her and are waiting for permission to eliminate her."

I lost my focus. "Someone?" I spoke in a low growl.

No sane person would do that. Only utterly desperate people. Only the grieving. I had just aggressively shoved away the only one. The phrase *unclaimed human female* hit me like a physical electric charge, shattering the Alpha control I had worked so hard to build.

The mate bond, which I had tried to shatter with cruel forethought, screamed one dreadful word that tore through my mind: *Jazz*. She had come for me. The fool had chased me deep into the territory, straight into the danger I had sought to keep her away from.

I didn't need to wonder why Elford was there. He was always there, hunting for any opening to strike at me. He knew that my father was getting weak and was in hiding. And now he had found the perfect, lethal flaw: my mate, who was still standing in his line of fire and smelled like a human. I grabbed the note and crushed it in my hand.

"Clearance for elimination!" I yelled, my blood boiling with anger. "He's trying to provoke a war. If someone dies on my land, my pack gets the blame. It disrupts the peace that is already so fragile."

I threw the letter onto the table, the Betas looking at me in shock as I changed my mind. I had lied about my responsibility, and now my deception was going to get her killed.

"Damien, we need to discuss the response," Kai said, standing up from his chair. I was already halfway out the door. The argument was slow. The debate was legitimate. My wolf didn't argue when its mate was in danger.

"No time," I muttered, my voice deepening and cracking as the beast rose. "I'll deal with the intruder." I didn't care about the truck as I sprinted out of the council hall.

I tore off my leather jacket and boots as I raced toward the back of the compound. The triple oak, deep in the territory, was already in my mind's eye. I didn't need a map or someone to guide me, though. The mate bond was a hot, stinging laser pulling me directly to her. Every beat of my heart was a frantic drum demanding I come home.

I moved effortlessly, and the shift was a welcome end to the control and anguish I had been holding onto for the last hour. My Ashen Ones wolf's massive, black body hit the ground running, smashing bones and exploding muscles. I didn't have time to consider the transformation. I was too busy smelling the terror and the intoxicating, unique scent of her. It was a mix of library and snow that was so strong and distinct it made me feel drunk. It was mingled with the heavy, aggressive odor of the Dravens.

I arrived in seconds, tearing through the last cover of pine needles. The sight froze me in my tracks. Five huge, dark, yellow-eyed wolves, the Dravens, stood in a semicircle. Elford was at the front of the group, a smug look on his face as he began to shift back into a man.

Jazz was in the center, rocking against the oak tree. She was bruised, terrified, and looking up at Elford's pack with her throat exposed as a last, defiant challenge.

Then I heard it: a loud, high-pitched *howl* that tore from Jazz's throat and made the Dravens freeze instantly. The sound was wild, primal, terrifying, and intensely familiar.

That was no human.

It was the sound of a new Snow wolf. I watched Elford, the Dravens' leader, look at Jazz with a horrified, dawning expression. My mate wasn't human. She was one of them. And my denial had forced her first agonizing shift, putting her directly in the path of my enemies.

I plunged into the clearing, the sound of my Ashen Ones challenge drowning out all else. My sacrifice meant nothing. She was now fighting for me. I couldn't save her innocence in time, but I could save her life.

My wolf, the massive black beast now charging into the clearing, recognized the sound instantly: *Snow*. The realization hit me like a battering ram, knocking aside the terror and the Alpha control. All that was left was a white-hot, all-consuming fury.

My mate wasn't human. The lie that was supposed to save her, my sacrifice, and the agony of rejection...all of it was for nothing. She was one of the five clans, and my deliberate cruelty had induced her first, most perilous transition, putting her straight in the open jaws of my enemy.

I didn't slow my charge. I leaped at the nearest Dravens scout, a large, brown-grey creature still stopped mid-lunge by Jazz's howl. I bit down hard on its side, snapping bone in a calculated wound, not a kill. It was a clear, immediate signal that this territory and this prey were now mine. The scout dropped to the ground, yelping and thrashing, which gave me a few seconds of clarity in the midst of the chaos.

Halfway through his shift, halfway between a man and a wolf, Elford shouted in disbelief and anger. Jazz's body was shaking violently against the triple oak, making him lose focus. Her skin was straining over widening bones, and her fine hair was thickening and sticking to her damp clothes. She was immobile, weak, and in excruciating pain.

*Cater to the shift!* The instinct was immediate and correct. Every wolf in the clearing understood that a novice shifter was completely helpless during their first transition.

I rammed my massive black bulk into Elford's changing form before he could advance. The impact was enormous, meant to distract and protect Jazz. Elford yelled, half-man, half-wolf, the voice deadly with sorrow and recognition. "Ashford! You break the peace for some pathetic human whose name you don't even know? And she's a *Snow*?" He spat and then frantically tried to stand up again.

"She is *claimed*," I growled, the sound shaking my chest. I knew he realized the gravity of that. He knew I had been sniffing around the borders of Tallow, hunting for a weakness, but he also knew that my relationship with her carried a strong, dangerous scent. He tried to make my mate the ultimate curse.

"You rejected her! You tossed her aside for my pack to find!" Elford roared, spitting out blood and pine needles.

Before I could rip out his throat for the confession, the air filled with unfamiliar sounds. Jazz's pained call was answered by a chorus of screams, familiar but far distant.

"The Snows," I heard Elford croak out, his sneer twisting into fury. "The peaceful ones have arrived."

The clearing erupted. Five more figures burst from the opposite side of the territory. They were sleek, beautiful, pale gray wolves. They were lighter, faster, almost spectral. They weren't built for the brute force of the Dravens or the massive muscle of my own pack; they were built for stealth and speed. But they all moved toward the same point, their attention immediately focused on Jazz, the one who had called. This was her lineage. Her pack. Her family.

The Dravens instantly broke their circle around Jazz and turned their entire, yellow-eyed rage on the newcomers. It instantly devolved into a messy, three-sided brawl. The Snows lived up to their name and were fiercely defensive. They moved quickly and cooperatively to keep the Dravens away from Jazz, but they weren't fighting to kill. The Dravens fought to shred and tear, while the Snows fought to contain.

I capitalized on the chaos, holding Elford down a moment longer before shoving him away with brute force. He got up fast and squinted, assessing the fight. He saw the Snows and my protective fury over Jazz. His shifting features made it clear that he recognized the political disaster I now represented: an Alpha claiming a Mate from the neutral, powerful Snow pack.

I stood in front of Jazz and the main conflict with my large black body. Jazz was the only thing I could think about. She was alive, she was shifting, and she was surviving. The calm, predictable life I gave up for her was a cruel fiction I had manufactured. She was Snow. She was a shifter. She was my mate. And now she was officially in the middle of the pack war.

I looked up and yelled my challenge again. It was a deep, earth-shaking sound that made every wolf in the clearing pause. It was a clear warning: "Get closer, and I'll tear you apart."

Blood and pine needles covered the fighting lines. The Snows had arrived, Jazz was changing, and the fragile peace was shattered for good.

# CHAPTER 9
# JAZZ

The pain was the first thing that got my attention. Like most injuries, the pain wasn't dull and localized. Instead, it was deep and systemic, as if my bones had been ripped apart and reassembled with crude tools. Every muscle fiber in my body screamed in protest; my joints were hot, swollen, and too heavy to move. I felt like I had been hit by a train and then immediately forced to run a marathon.

I was lying down. Not on cold pine needles, but on something soft, familiar, and heavily scented with lavender.

I needed to see. Heavy curtains over the window blocked most of the light, but even that little bit hurt my head. I was in my own bed, in my small Tallow apartment, which usually felt clean, safe, and calming.

The sense of security was immediate, but then a huge wave of confusion hit me.

The woods. The dark wolves. The terrifying yellow eyes. Damien's truck roaring back into the clearing. Then the heat. That intense heat had made a vile, gurgling sound tear from my throat and slam through my body.

When I tried to sit up, a searing pain shot through my left side. I gasped and collapsed back against the cushion, my breath coming in short, shaky bursts. I looked at my arms. The cuts from branches, which had left long, sharp lines during my frantic escape, were gone. In their place, the smooth, pale skin was covered in large, ugly, red bruises that indicated internal damage, not just surface wounds.

Not long after the pain, I noticed a terrible scent.

My room should have smelled like cinnamon and old library books, but instead, it carried strong, strange odors. I could faintly smell the clean, pleasant lavender soap my mother made. But beneath that was the heavy, wild, smoky scent of pack. Of large, warm bodies. Of power and stress.

I realized I wasn't alone.

Two figures sat in the corner of my room, in the dark silence. They were my father, Elias, and my mother, Eleanor. Their faces were drawn, their eyes heavy with a look that felt like a mixture of worry and shame.

"Jazz. You're awake," my mother said, her voice

coarse. She sprang up too quickly and rushed to the edge of the bed.

My father followed. His usually calm, tall frame looked tense, and he clenched his hands worriedly behind his back.

"What happened?" I managed, though my voice felt raw. My tongue felt too big and heavy in my mouth. "The woods... the wolves. Mom, I think I hurt my ribs."

My mother sat on the edge of the bed, not touching me. Her blue eyes, like mine, were brimming with tears.

"Dear, you're home. You're safe now," she said in a soothing voice.

"No, I'm not," I countered, my body tense. "I was surrounded. Mom, those things were huge. They meant to kill me. And then I felt like I was going to explode. What was that?"

Looking at their faces, I didn't see loving parental concern. Instead, I saw a terrifying level of knowledge and betrayal. They knew. They weren't surprised by my story.

"Where is Damien?" The name came out as a demanding scream. The only things that felt real were the memory of his strong, protective presence and the pain I felt right before I blacked out. "Did he help me? Did he—"

Finally, my father spoke, his voice strong enough to cut through my mother's quiet distress. "Damien

Ashford is gone, Jasmine. He's back with his people. We brought you home. You have been asleep for almost two days."

Two days. Two full days. The rejection landed again, fracturing my heart. He came back to save me, but this time he didn't even wait for me to wake up before leaving.

"He left me," I whispered, full of shock.

"Yes, he rejected you," my father said quickly. "Given the circumstances, it was the only logical thing for him to do. He cannot afford a mate from a rival pack."

"Rival pack?" I just stared at them, the words making no sense. "What are you talking about? He's a mechanic. I work in a library. We aren't in a military feud! What packs?"

My mother finally reached out and laid her cool hand on my forehead. "Oh, Jazz. It's time. We can't hide it any longer. Not after what happened."

I had never seen my father take such a hard stance. He moved to the foot of the bed, planting his feet wide, a strong, defensive posture that made my stomach churn, just like Damien's.

"Jasmine," my father said, his face grave and sad. "Everything you think you know about us, yourself, and this town is a lie fabricated to keep you safe. We are not merely human. We are shifters."

I closed my eyes and waited for the punchline and the nervous laugh. It never came.

"Jasmine, we are werewolves," my father said. "We are part of the Snow pack. When you ran into the woods and howled, you weren't hurting anyone. You had your first shift. You are now a new shifter."

The room spun. Wolves. Shifters. Lies. The words hit me all at once like a string of bombs.

"No," I said softly, shaking my head vehemently. The movement jarred my body again. "No, that's not real. That's fiction. That's what I read to escape the real world, Dad! It's not possible."

"The Dravens and the wolves that surrounded you are very real," my mother countered, her face pale. "They are the most violent of the five clans. They were trying to kill you because you smelled human in a place you shouldn't have been. Your Snow wolf's howl was a distress call. That's how we knew to be there so quickly."

"Five clans?" I repeated, my brain too overloaded with the bizarre information to keep up. "Who besides the Ashfords and the Dravens?"

My father sighed and ran a hand through his hair. "Damien's group is The Ashen Ones. There are the Shadowfangs. The Grimvales. And us, the Snows."

He walked to the dresser and pulled out a large, rolled-up chart I had never seen before. It was a map of Tallow and the surrounding territories, divided into five harsh, jagged colors.

My father pointed to a small, out-of-the-way section near the coast, far from the central hills where Damien's commune was. "The Snows," he stated. "We are the pacifists. We are a small, quiet pack. We maintain political neutrality. Because of the constant fear of conflict and the laws of the Codex, we chose to raise you without knowledge of the shift, hoping you would live a normal, peaceful, human life."

The truth was not just shocking; it was a deep, fundamental violation. My stable career, my predictable routine, my sweet human boyfriend Vincent...all of it was a lie. The people I trusted most had built a cage around me.

"You lied to me," I said, my voice losing its last bit of composure. "My whole life was a lie. You let me date a human. You never told me I had this thing inside me that could get me killed!"

"We were protecting you!" Mom burst out, her eyes finally overflowing with tears. "The shift is usually genetic, but in our pack, it often skips generations. We hoped you wouldn't shift and would be free to live your life the way you wanted. Right up until you met Damien Ashford."

I thought of Damien again, his beautiful gold eyes, and the strange, powerful pull that had made me drop all my defenses. The mate bond. He wasn't a protective, bad-boy mechanic because he'd found his next lover.

"Damien... he knew," I realized, and everything clicked. "That's why he was fighting me. That's why he rejected me. He smelled the pack on me, but he thought I was human, didn't he?"

"He felt the bond," my father confirmed, raising his voice. "But Damien is the Ashen Ones' Alpha. He is the future Wolf King. While we are neutral, he is fiercely territorial. The Codex, the law governing our species, states that two packs vying for power cannot ally, not even through a mate bond. If he claims you, it is a sign of weakness. The Throne immediately sees a political target."

I looked at the clan map, absorbing the harsh reality he had kept from me. The intense, burning anger I felt was about more than just the deception. It was about the injustice of the rejection. Damien had left me not because I was disposable, but to protect the Wolf Throne and to keep me safe from the conflict that was about to erupt.

"And you," I challenged, looking directly at my father, "you just let him go? You let your own daughter, a member of your pack, be rejected because of an old rule?"

"We are pacifists, Jasmine," my father told me, his jaw set. "We do not get involved in the political fights of the Throne. We maintain our borders and live in peace. Damien's pack saved you from the Dravens, and we brought you home. Thank God you're alive."

In the woods, I had felt a huge, terrifying surge of power rush through my veins. It was anger, the need for vengeance, and the desire to tear apart the attacking wolves. That raw, visceral feeling was far more real than the library ever was.

"But I don't feel lucky, Dad," I muttered, my anger swelling in my chest. "I feel weak. I feel betrayed. This wolf inside me says we shouldn't do anything. If Damien is my mate, you shouldn't stay out of his fight for the throne. You were willing to sacrifice my identity and our relationship for your peaceful lie."

Despite the sharp pain in my side, I tried to sit up again. The muscles in my back obeyed. Finally, I swung my legs over the edge of the bed, planting my bare feet on the cool wood floor. Moving was agonizing, but it was necessary. I wasn't a liability. I was a Snow Wolf, and being hurt had woken me up. If my family were too afraid of the Codex to help me, I would fight for my life, my identity, and my mate.

My father took a wary step back, seeing the bright, golden light that must have been in my eyes. He turned away from the librarian and looked at the Snow Wolf instead.

"You need to rest, Jazz," he said. "You need to learn control. You are too dangerous right now."

"No," I stated, standing up, swaying slightly but remaining upright. "I need the truth. I need to know why my life was taken and how to get it back. If my mate is fighting for the crown, the Snow pack cannot remain peaceful for much longer. If you won't fight, I will."

# CHAPTER 10
## DAMIEN

Still, blood was on my hands, but it wasn't mine. I had wounded the Dravens' scout to buy time for Jazz's family to retrieve her. My large black body moved through the thickest parts of the forest, the rush of energy slowly giving way to a cold, profound fear.

I knew my life was over the moment the Snow Wolves, her family and pack, appeared, gliding with the terrible, coordinated ease of true shifters. My frantic efforts to keep us apart had failed. The danger wasn't just about protecting Jazz Snow, a newly turned shifter, from a powerful, neutral pack. I had just forced my mate, the one I was meant to cherish, through her first agonizing shift and into a clan conflict.

I changed back into a man in the private bathroom near the hangar. It was a relief to have an action to focus on, rather than the storm of anger inside me. When the shift was complete, I was breathless, my body covered in sweat and grime. I pulled on my new Alpha uniform, dark clothing that felt like a familiar weight. The thick leather jacket felt like a shield. I looked in the mirror. My eyes were still too bright around the edges, and my jaw was rigidly set. I had just failed at the most crucial task of a protector.

The main hall already held the leaders of my pack. The Ashen Ones' council. These wolves had held the pack together since my father's "accident." Their demands were for clarity, order, and power. That's what I was going to give them.

I threw open the doors to the room. It was dark and sharp, lit only by a single lantern over the long wooden table. The three older Betas were seated around it: Kai, the cold, logical mind; Roric, the skeptical, grizzled warrior; and Lyra, the sharp-eyed historian. They didn't look like nervous advisors; they looked like a jury preparing to deliver a verdict.

I moved to the head of the table but didn't sit down. The room was dominated by my size and the strong, angry scent of the recent conflict.

"Report, Damien," Kai growled, his voice tense with frustration. "Patrols confirm a fight at the border. Dravens versus Snows. You engaged a scout in the middle of it. Elford is seeking any opportunity to shatter the peace. Explain."

I put my hands on the table and met Kai's eyes.

"The Dravens were the aggressors. Elford positioned a kill team at the triple oak. Their target was a trespassing young Snow."

"A young Snow?" Roric's voice was heavy with skepticism. "Seriously? Five Dravens wolves against one of the peaceful ones? Why? They haven't shifted in decades; they're harmless."

"Not harmless," I stated, injecting cold certainty into my voice. The name Jazz was too heavy to utter. "She had just shifted. A first shift is always completely unstable. If the Dravens had killed her on our land, Elford would have claimed the ground was weak, and the Ashen Ones would have been left to manage the resulting chaos. I stabilized the situation, pushed the Dravens back, and left the Snow pack to deal with their own. It was a preemptive move to halt a full-scale confrontation."

Lyra, the eldest, spoke last, looking directly into my eyes. "What about you, Damien? The Snows are difficult to keep out when they smell their mate link. Elford will learn that you claimed the woman. He will use this, Damien. He will exploit her."

The accusation felt like a physical blow. I let the angry 'no' from my wolf bleed into my human expression as I met Lyra's gaze. "Elford is guessing. I rejected the Snow. There was a temporary breach of order, which was instantly corrected. This territory was secured, and a war was averted for now. I cannot break my duty to the pack."

The lie was so potent it forced a moment of silence. The room's atmosphere shifted from fear to grim acceptance. I had to be strong and ruthless for them. They didn't care about the messy details of an illegal mate as long as I cut the thread cleanly.

Kai's demeanor went from cautious interest to intense seriousness as he moved the reports on the table. "The Snow girl is irrelevant now," he said, his voice low and dangerous. "You did right by prioritizing the core threat. The dangers are escalating, Damien. It's time you knew the full truth of this mess."

He paused, letting the statement sink in during the silence. "Your father, the Wolf King, did not die in a logging accident."

The words weren't a surprise. My wolf had smelled the planned violence and murder when the body was brought home. Hearing the human confirmation, however...the harsh, political finality of the news, hit me like a blow to the chest.

"He was assassinated," Kai whispered. The revelation fouled the hall's air. "The records state a structural collapse, but there is clear evidence of a strong, forced shift that would have killed him regardless of his injuries. Someone staged a death that looked like an accident to weaken the throne without leaving a clear target. They want the five clans to fight each other, rather than unite against a common enemy."

Roric slammed his hand on the table, his face a mixture of pain and rage. "The King is dead, Damien.

There was no immediate challenge, which proves this was calculated. They want the flaw to show. They are hoping you fail."

Lyra pushed several documents across the table. These records, land deeds, and surveillance reports were compiled by the Ashen Ones' secret network, not the police. "We have tapped into all communications. Over the last two months, the Dravens have been moving rapidly and deliberately. There has been a high volume of activity near the edges of residential Tallow, which borders the Snows' territory. Reconnaissance. Watching."

The documents were difficult to read, the words blurring on the page. The timing was now perfect.

As memory flooded back, the events of the past few days seemed chillingly interconnected:

My father is gone. The throne is empty. The clan is exposed.

The Dravens are moving near Tallow.

Jazz Snow enters my shop, and she's apparently my mate. She smells human, but carries the distinct scent of our mate bond.

Elford. Elford had been there all along.

He had orchestrated the entire plot, not just my father's murder. The Dravens were monitoring the Snows because they were the smallest pack, mostly isolated, and located near the water. If Elford could provoke the Snows out of neutrality, he could effectively isolate the other packs or force them to take sides too quickly.

But why focus on the Snows? Unless...

Unless Elford's plan required the Snow pack to move. The Snow pack was considered peaceful, but if I, a strong Alpha-mate, claimed a seemingly human Snow, it would create absolute chaos. My pack would instantly be at odds with everyone else for violating the Codex by interacting with humans and breaking the neutrality treaty. It would immediately discredit me as a leader and a potential king.

I now understand the real purpose of the Dravens' report. Elford didn't just want a confrontation. He wanted to eradicate any proof of my involvement before I could claim her. He wanted her dead to either hide my weakness or punish me by seizing the Snow land.

The agonizing rejection, the helicopter escape, the final harsh words, all were part of my desperate, protective plan to save the only innocent person in Elford's intricate revenge scheme. I thought I was freeing a loved one from a political war.

The truth was a heavy burden: I had been trying to destroy the mate who was at the center of everything.

"The Snows are pacifists," I said, the truth hardening my voice like steel. "They are the only pack that does not seek the Throne. They had nothing to do with this assassination."

"Perhaps," Lyra replied, her face strained. "But

because of your connection to Jazz Snow, the human woman, they are now easy prey because they are linked to you." She added, "Her quick shift can be a huge asset or a huge liability."

I finally sat down, gripping the arms of the chair so tightly the old wood groaned. This was no longer just politics; the fight was real, and it was about the woman I loved and rejected.

I knew I had to secure the crown and reclaim my mate. Elford's cruel plot had merged the two goals into one. The rejection had been clear. But the mate bond was now a secret, unspoken pact to go to war. I would be the ruthless Alpha and take the throne. Then, I would go claim my newly awakened Snow mate from her quiet corner of the universe.

"We move forward with the Challenge preparations," I said, standing again. The Alpha was in control now. "I will not fail my father, and I will not lose my claim to this land." I added, "Elford is preparing for the endgame, and I will meet him there. However, the Snow pack territory is to be considered a neutral zone. No hostile patrols. And say nothing to Jazz Snow. The pack needs to believe I messed up with her."

The lie sounded like a sacred vow. I would fight for her always, but first, I would have to be against her.

# CHAPTER II
# DAMIEN

Without a ceremony, the Wolf King's funeral was somber, brutal. There were no outsiders. Only the pack leaders and the Ashen Ones. The Maine sky was chilly and indifferent. Beneath its gaze, the Alpha rite took place deep in the Ashen Ones' domain.

My father, the legendary Alpha and King, was prepared for the fire by having his body covered in white burial cloth. Our family returned their dead to nature, submitting them to fire and air. No burials. Around the clearing gathered the entire Ashen Ones pack, a sea of solemn faces and dark leather. They were silent, a sign of their sadness. We were all broken, crying, and waiting for retribution at the moment.

As the person closest to the pyre, I carried the burden of their collective grief, as I was the new Alpha in all but name. I was dressed entirely in black for the funeral, which contrasted with my father's white attire. My muscles ached to a level I had never experienced before, and it was a tangible manifestation of the lie I was leading.

The great leader was my father. I was supposed to be sad. But my thoughts were consumed by two unpleasant realities, revealed at yesterday's council meeting: Elford murdered my father, and my mate became the weak point in Elford's scheme.

The pack's stench was a potent mixture of dread, grief, and ravenous loyalty, all directed at me. I sensed their fears, their silent prayers that I would protect and avenge them, heightening my own anxiety and amplifying the sense of isolation that came with their dependence.

I looked beyond my pack's circle. Past the statue-like soldiers at the periphery. Into the ruthless, black line of the forest. Miles away, in Tallow's quiet civilian area, my new mate Jazz Snow was waking up to a world she didn't comprehend. I had drawn her into this society, then vehemently turned my back on it. It tasted cold and harsh. I tried to get rid of her by calling her a liability, but later I saw that she was essential to Elford's strategy.

A mate from another pack. My right to the Challenge was revoked since it was political suicide and a sign of weakness to assert such a link during a time of power, according to the Codex, the old code that governed the five clans. If I went to fetch her, I might have given the Dravens control over my people and endangered the stability of my pack.

I forced myself to look back at my father's grave. People recalled him as a powerful, intimidating King who maintained order by controlling every aspect of life. The expense of the throne was known to him. When I was younger, Dad taught me the value of duty.

Kai, the Elder Beta, advanced alongside the flame that would ignite the pyre. With a somber expression on his face, he knelt before me. "Alpha," he uttered, referring to the title that was mine by blood but not yet legally. "Revenge is yours to take. We're waiting on your orders."

I reached for the torch. The iron felt heavy, as if it would wreak a lot of havoc. I glanced at the council, Roric's dejected expression, and Lyra's astute, cunning gaze. The boy was being watched to determine whether he was capable of wearing the crown.

I raised the torch, catching the cold, flickering light. The flames embodied the Ashen Ones' power.

"My father," I began, my voice reverberating through the hushed pack. "We lost the King to a coward's treachery. It wasn't an accident. It was murder."

A growl of fury rolled through the pack. The official lay dead.

As I continued, locking eyes with the pack, I found betrayal, fear, and searing hunger for justice. "The traitor thought cutting off the head would wither the body," I said. "They expected the Ashen Ones to scatter. They believed I would break."

I dropped to my knees and placed the torch on the floor. I bowed my head over my father's pyre. I uttered a last, solemn promise, one only I and the King's ghost could hear.

"I swear," I snarled, my voice brimming with rage, "that I will find the traitor who started all of this trouble. I'll take revenge for the King. I'll defend our rights to this territory and this pack. I will not give up until the person who did it is torn to pieces, and I will pay the blood price."

I got up and took up the flame once more. "We'll receive justice. The son will murder the assassin of the King. The challenge will be accepted. We shall inherit the throne."

I swung the torch down with purpose. Dry wood and ceremonial oils erupted, sending up a roaring plume of smoke and heat. The searing blast pressed on my chest. As the Ashen Ones howled in grief and unity, I stared into the blaze, seeing only Jazz's wild innocence and glimmering gold eyes.

I walked away. Away from the wailing flock and the pyre. Into the empty, chilly council chamber. The Betas arrived next. Their attitude had changed; they had vowed to exact revenge.

"The Challenge will be brutal," Roric declared, placing his palm on the ceremonial dagger's hilt that was concealed within his belt. "Elford is strong. The Shadowfangs are intelligent. The Grimvale family is cruel. Alliances are essential."

"I have the Ashen Ones," I said as I removed the surveillance's maps and data. The documents concerning my father's passing were placed aside, and I turned my attention to the Codex, an ancient collection of leather-bound rules that established the guidelines for the Challenge and the clans.

"We need a strategy for the Snows," Lyra murmured. "Jazz Snow is a new shifter. Claiming her is forbidden. She's unstable, dangerous. Elford will argue you're unfit, wielding the mate bond against you."

The idea that Elford would use her existence and name as a weapon was intolerable. Heat flooded my face at the thought. An overpowering urge to protect Jazz clashed with a terror of what exposing our bond would do. I clenched my fists, fighting the desperate impulse to rush to Tallow and pull her into safety. Confessing the bond could save her, but exposing it would cost me everything, maybe even her life. The fear was suffocating, and every second I spent away from her was a battle between longing and self-restraint.

I responded, "Jazz Snow is a liability that has been neutralised." The words had a heavy, metallic quality. She has been rejected by me. My pack believes that I have shattered the bond. We maintain the deception. I refuse to allow a transient vulnerability to undermine the Challenge.

The lie couldn't be true, I realised. Turning off the mate link was not an easy task. It was an unrelenting, excruciating pull on my whole being, pleading for her presence and safety. The temptation to find her was something I fought every second I spent organising the war.

Seizing the laminated map of the five regions, I traced the small coastal hold of the Snows and the shadowed land of the Ashen Ones.

As soon as I stated, "We focus on the assets," my voice returned to its Alpha command. "The sea routes and a sizable portion of Tallow's civilian population remain under the Snows' control, despite their benign nature. They also have a solid, long-standing ancestry. Elford will be unable to manage the local economy and supply chains if he is unable to break the neutrality. We have to guarantee that they remain neutral."

"And what if she tries to get in touch with you?" Roric asked.

"I don't think she will," I said, my chest heaving with a terrible sense of certainty. "I made sure she understood the extent of my rejection of her. She believes that I am a predatory Alpha who abused her and discarded her, making me a monster. Her defence is that of contempt. I'll tell the fib again if she approaches me. To win the throne and exact revenge on the King, nothing—not even a fated mate

—will stand in the way of my commitment to this pack."

I was aware that by depriving myself of the one thing that made my gloomy existence happier, I was committing myself to months of suffering. The knowledge settled like ice in my gut. The grief of losing my father and the anguish of pushing Jazz away combined to turn into an inescapable burden. Still, I would endure it all, refusing to let Elford seize the Wolf Throne and take her, stained as it was with my father's blood.

The next step was obvious: become the crucial Alpha that the pack needed, ruthless. Take the fight. Then and only then would I demolish the political barriers, discard the Codex, and reclaim the Snow Wolf that had suddenly entered my life.

Up until that point, my greatest vulnerability and secret, illegal weapon was Jazz Snow. And I would stay as far away as I could to protect her. Until I could ascend to the throne and become her King, I would hide and protect her with all I had.

# CHAPTER 12

# JAZZ

Three days had passed since I woke up to the impossible truth of my existence, and my apartment had transformed from a sanctuary into a cage.

My parents, Eleanor and Elias...really, just Snow pack members assigned to watch me, were suffocating. They acted like I might explode if I saw sunlight or heard a loud noise. I was stuck in the apartment "for my own safety" and "to manage the transition." Mostly, that meant drinking herbal teas that tasted like wet dirt and listening to my father talk endlessly about breathing exercises to keep the beast inside me quiet.

But the beast didn't want to breathe. It wanted to run.

I paced my small living room for what felt like the hundredth time that night, my bare feet quiet on the hardwood. My body felt strange. The deep ache from the shift had faded quickly, replaced by a buzzing energy, like I had swallowed a lightning bolt. My hearing was painfully sharp; I could hear my neighbor's bass three doors away and even a mouse moving in the walls.

The worst part was the smell. Everything was overwhelming: stale garbage from the alley, the sharp scent of cleaning spray in the hallway, and the fear that seemed to come from my own skin.

And underneath it all, a gaping, howling emptiness where Damien used to be.

"You need to sit down, Jasmine," my mother said gently from the kitchen island, where she was chopping vegetables with unnecessary precision. "Pacing triggers the predatory instinct. It simulates the hunt."

"I'm not hunting, Mom," I snapped, my irritation flaring up fast. Another side effect of the wolf. "I'm bored. I'm angry. And I feel like I'm just waiting for something bad to happen."

"The other shoe dropped when you howled in the woods," my father muttered from the armchair, not looking up from his book. "Now we just wait for the echoes to fade so we can disappear back into the woodwork."

"Disappear?" I stopped pacing, turning on him. "I have a job. I have a life here. I can't just disappear because the Snow pack is afraid of a little politics."

"It's not just 'a little politics,'" my father said,

snapping his book shut. "This is a war for the Wolf Throne. And you just made yourself a wild card in a fight that usually ends in blood. We're keeping you hidden until the Ashen Ones and the Dravens are done fighting each other."

I opened my mouth to argue, to scream that I didn't care about their cowardly neutrality, but the words died in my throat.

A scent hit me.

It wasn't the stale air of the apartment or the lavender soap my mother used. It was a dark, heavy wave of woodsmoke, rain, and raw, masculine heat. It was the scent of the mechanic's shop, but deeper. It was the scent of the forest floor where I had almost died.

It was him.

My heart pounded so hard in my chest that it drowned out the neighbor's music. The wolf inside me, restless until now, suddenly became alert, head up and tail wagging in eager, almost embarrassing submission.

"Jasmine?" My mother looked up, sensing the shift in my mood. "What is it?"

I ignored her. I walked to the balcony door, my hand trembling as I reached for the lock.

"Don't," my father warned, standing up. He smelled it, too, now. His nostrils flared, and a low, warning rumble started in his chest. "Ashford is here."

"I have to see him," I said, the words coming out wrong as my mind scrambled. "He's outside."

"He is the Alpha of a rival pack during a Challenge," my father barked, moving to block me. "He is dangerous, Jasmine! He rejected you. He left you for dead!"

"He saved my life!" I shouted back, the gold fire flashing in my vision. "And I need to know why!"

I didn't wait for permission or use the door. Adrenaline pushed me to unlock the balcony and step into the cool, damp night. We were only on the second floor—a height that would have scared me before, but not now. I jumped over the railing and landed in the alley below, crouching easily.

I straightened up, scanning the shadows.

He was there.

Damien stood at the end of the alley, just out of reach of the streetlamp's light. He leaned against the brick wall, arms crossed, almost blending into the night. He wore his usual leather jacket, dark jeans, and heavy boots—the classic bad boy mechanic look. But his eyes burned through the darkness.

I walked toward him. I should have been furious, should have yelled at him for leaving me, for the lies, for what happened in the woods. But as I got closer, my anger faded, replaced by a pull so strong it felt like I was being drawn to him by something I couldn't fight.

I stopped a few feet away. The air between us felt charged and heavy.

"You're alive," he said. His voice was rough, like gravel grinding together. It wasn't a question; it was a statement of relief that he was trying desperately to hide.

"No thanks to you," I countered, trying to summon the anger back. It felt weak. "My parents told me everything. Or at least, they told me what they know. About the packs. The Throne. The Codex."

He nodded slowly, his gaze sweeping over me, assessing my injuries, my stance, my new reality. "The Snows," he muttered, a flicker of bitterness in his tone. "I should have known. The scent was too clean to be human, but too soft to be a warrior."

"Is that why you came?" I demanded, crossing my arms to stop my hands from reaching out to him. "To inspect the 'liability'? To see if the mistake had fixed itself?"

He flinched. It was small. A tightening of the jaw, a slight shift in his stance, but with my new eyes, I saw it clearly.

"I came," he said, pushing off the wall and taking a step toward me, "because I couldn't stay away. Because the bond... It's screaming."

He stopped and ran a hand through his dark hair, looking more vulnerable than I'd ever seen. The tough Alpha act faded, and I saw how tired and conflicted he really was.

"I tried, Jazz. For three days, I tried to stay on the compound. I tried to focus on the strategy, on the Dravens, on my father's funeral. But every minute feels like I'm bleeding out. I needed to see that you were real. That you survived the shift."

"The bond," I repeated, testing the word. "My father calls it a political weakness. You called it a mistake."

"It's not a mistake," Damien said, his voice low and rough. "It's biology. It's magic. It's the worst joke the universe could play on us right now, but it's not a mistake."

He took another step, invading my personal space. The heat radiating off him was intoxicating. "When you walked into my garage that first day... do you know what happened to me?"

I shook my head, unable to speak.

"My wolf, the part of me that's all instinct, didn't see a customer. It didn't see a girl with a broken truck. It saw the other half of its soul. It saw the Luna." He looked into my eyes, his amber gaze meeting my blue one. "I felt something snap in my chest, Jazz. Like a cord pulling tight. It's called the Fated Mate bond. It's rare. Most wolves pick partners for compatibility or politics. But this is different. It means we're matched. In strength and in spirit."

"So the 'Mine'..." I whispered, remembering the guttural thought that hadn't been mine.

"That was my wolf claiming you," he admitted.

"Before I could stop him. Before I remembered who I was and who you... Well, who I thought you were."

"And who are you, really?" I asked. "Besides a mechanic who ghosts people?"

He let out a short, humorless laugh. "I am Damien Ashford. Alpha of the Ashen Ones. And since three days ago, I am the primary contender for the Wolf Throne."

He looked away, staring down the alley toward the dark woods. "My father was the King. He ruled all five packs and kept the peace. But he was murdered, Jazz. Killed to create a power vacuum." out as a snarl. "And now, the Throne is empty. The law states that when the King dies, the Alphas of the five clans must challenge for the right to rule. It is a brutal, bloody process. And it requires absolute strength. Absolute focus."

He looked back at me, his expression tortured. "The Codex has rules, Jazz. Ancient rules. It forbids the mixing of bloodlines between rival packs during the Challenge. It's meant to prevent alliances that could create tyrants. If an Alpha claims a mate from a rival pack, especially a neutral pack like the Snows...it is seen as corruption. As a weakness."

"So I'm illegal," I said flatly.

"You are forbidden," he corrected. "If I claim you openly, the other packs, the Grimvales, the Shadowfangs...they will side with Elford. They will say I am compromising the integrity of the Challenge. I would lose the support I need to win. And if I lose... Elford becomes King."

He stepped closer, his hand reaching out to hover near my face, trembling slightly. "If Elford becomes King, the first thing he will do is wipe out the Snows. He hates your pack's neutrality. He hates that you control the coast. He would kill you, Jazz. Just to spite me."

The weight of his words settled on me. He hadn't rejected me out of cruelty. He had rejected me to save me from being a pawn in a war I didn't even know existed. He had chosen his duty to his people over his desire for me.

"So you lied," I said, my voice shaking. "You told me I was nothing, so I would stay away. So I would be safe."

"I told you what you needed to hear to hate me," he murmured. "Because your hate is safer than your love. If you hate me, you stay in Tallow. You stay human. You stay alive."

"But I'm not human," I whispered. "Not anymore."

"No," he agreed, a look of profound sadness crossing his face. "You're a wolf. And that makes everything infinitely more dangerous."

My mind spun. Fated mates, forbidden love, murder. It was all too much. But looking at him in the alley, I felt that pull again. It wasn't just an attraction; it felt right, like he was the only steady thing in the chaos.

"I don't know how to be a wolf, Damien," I admitted, letting my guard down. "My parents want me to hide it, to push it down. But I feel it inside me, always there. It wants you."

His eyes flashed gold. He stepped closer and grabbed my upper arms. His touch sent a jolt through me, even through my shirt.

"Don't say that," he groaned. "Jazz, you have to fight it. You have to stay away from me. I came here tonight to warn you. Elford knows. He saw you shift. He saw me defend you. He suspects the bond."

"So what do I do?" I asked, looking up at him, feeling small yet incredibly powerful in his grip.

"You learn," he said, his voice intense. "Stop listening to your parents about hiding it. Learn to control it. Learn to fight. Because if Elford comes for you—and he will—you need to be able to defend yourself."

"Teach me," I said. The words were out before I could think.

He froze. "I can't. I just told you why."

"You said you couldn't claim me openly," I argued, my new instincts sharpening my logic. "You didn't say you couldn't help me survive. If I'm such a liability, wouldn't it be better if I knew how to defend myself? So you don't have to come rescue me every time I take a walk?"

He stared at me, his jaw tense. He was struggling

with my logic, the Codex, and the urge to just kiss me and forget the consequences.

"Meet me," I pressed. "In the woods. The neutral territory near the stream. No one goes there. Teach me how to shift without breaking my bones. Teach me how to be a wolf."

He glanced at my lips, then back to my eyes. I could see him struggling between following the rules as Alpha and wanting to help the person he cared about.

"If we get caught..." he started.

"We won't," I promised. "I'm a librarian, Damien. I know how to be quiet."

A faint smile appeared on his lips. The first I'd seen in ages. It changed his whole face, making him look softer and less weighed down by grief.

"Midnight," he whispered. "Tomorrow. By the old mill stream. Don't be late."

"I won't."

He paused for a moment, his thumbs tracing my jaw, his touch leaving a mark on me. Then he leaned in, pressing his forehead to mine. I closed my eyes and breathed him in—the smoke, the rain, the sadness.

"I should have left you alone," he breathed against my skin. "I should have walked away the day you brought that truck in."

"But you didn't," I whispered back.

"No," he admitted, pulling away, the cold night air rushing in to fill the space between us. "I didn't."

He backed away, never taking his eyes off me, until he reached the shadows at the end of the alley. Then, moving faster than any human could see, but clear to me, he was gone. I stood alone in the alley, my heart racing, my skin tingling.

My parents were wrong. Hiding wasn't the answer. Damien was right. This was a war. For the first time since the wolf woke up inside me, I wasn't afraid. I was ready.

I turned back to the balcony, thinking about the jump. I had a meeting with the Alpha of the Ashen Ones, and a lot to learn before midnight tomorrow.

# CHAPTER 13
# JAZZ

Climbing up to the second-floor balcony should have been impossible. Just a week ago, Jasmine Snow—librarian, bad knee from high school volleyball, afraid of heights—would have been stuck in the alley, desperately calling her landlord for help.

But the creature inside me didn't care about bad knees or fear. It only understood power.

I grabbed the rough brick wall, my fingers finding holds in cracks that seemed tiny to my eyes but felt deep to my new senses. With a burst of strange strength, I pulled myself up, muscles working smoothly. I swung my legs over the railing and landed quietly on the balcony, barely out of breath.

The scent of the alley, and of him, still clung to my clothes. Woodsmoke, rain, and the sharp, metallic smell of the Alpha. That scent made my blood race, easing my fear and making me more determined.

I slid open the glass door and stepped into the stifling warmth of the apartment.

My parents were right where I left them. My father, Elias, stood by the door, arms crossed and tense, like a bouncer at a club no one wanted to enter. My mother, Eleanor, sat at the kitchen island, gripping a dishtowel tightly.

The silence in the room felt heavy. I could smell lavender air freshener mixed with my parents' fear.

"You saw him," my father said. It wasn't a question. Damien's scent was probably obvious, filling the room and marking me for everyone to notice.

"I did," I said, keeping my voice steady. I locked the balcony door, the click loud in the quiet room. I didn't try to hide. I didn't try to act like the daughter they wanted. That girl was gone, lost in the woods under the Dravens' eyes.

"Did he hurt you?" my mother asked, her voice shaking. "Did he... reject you again?"

"He didn't come to hurt me," I said, moving past my father to the center of the room. I could feel the wolf inside me, restless from their fear and passivity. "And he didn't come to reject me. He came to warn me."

"Warn you?" My father scoffed, sounding harsh and dismissive. "He came to manipulate you, Jasmine. He's an Ashford. Manipulation is what they do. They play games with the Throne while packs like ours get hurt."

"He came to tell me why I'm a target," I snapped, turning to face him. "He told me Elford, the leader of the wolves who tried to *eat me*, is planning a war. And he told me about the bond."

The word hung in the air, heavy and tense. *The bond.*

My parents exchanged a quick, guilty look, like people caught hiding something. That look made anger flare in my chest, stronger than my confusion.

"You knew," I whispered, the truth sinking in. "You knew about Mates. You knew about the Fated Bond."

"It's rare," my mother said, her voice pleading. "It rarely happens in our family, Jazz. We didn't think—"

"You didn't think to tell me?" I shouted, making them both flinch. "You told me I was human! You said I had a blood sugar problem when I got shaky! You let me date Vincent, a human I felt nothing for, even though you knew there was a chance I was meant for someone else?"

"We wanted you to have a choice!" my father yelled, finally losing his composure. "The mate bond isn't a fairy tale, Jasmine! It's a chain! It ties your will to another wolf, usually an Alpha. It takes away your freedom. We wanted you to be free!"

"Free?" I laughed, the sound bitter. "I wasn't free. I was blind! I walked into that garage and felt like my soul was being torn out, and I thought I was having a panic attack! I thought I was crazy! You let me live here, not knowing anything about what I really am!"

I paced the room, feeling the restless energy inside me. "Damien explained it to me in five minutes. In an alley. He told me more truth in five minutes than you have in twenty-four years."

"Damien Ashford is bound by the Codex to destroy you," my father said coldly. "He explained the bond? Did he tell you that claiming you would cost him his crown? Did he say that for him to win, you have to stay hidden?"

"Yes!" I turned to face him. "He did! He told me everything. He told me why he rejected me. He told me about the politics. And you know what? It made sense. It was cruel, and it hurt, but it was honest. Unlike you."

My mother stood up and reached out to me. "Jazz, please. We were protecting you. The Snow pack isn't made of warriors. We don't fight for thrones. We survive by staying unnoticed. By being insignificant."

"Insignificant," I repeated, the word bitter in my mouth. "Is that our family motto? 'Stay small and hope nobody eats you'?"

"It's kept us alive for generations!" my father insisted. "While the Ashfords and the Dravens fight for a title that means nothing, we live. We raise our families. We have peace."

"We don't have peace!" I shouted, feeling anger

burn in my vision. "We have silence! That's not the same!"

I took a breath, trying to steady my shaking hands. The wolf inside me wanted to shift, to challenge the Alpha, my father. It felt stronger, younger, and more dangerous than he was. That thought scared me.

"Damien told me the King was murdered," I said, breaking the silence.

My father froze, his face turning pale. "That is... a rumor. A conspiracy theory."

"It's a fact," I said. "Damien knows. Elford killed him. And if Elford killed the King, Dad, do you really think he'll stop there? Do you think being 'insignificant' will save us when a murderer is on the Wolf Throne?"

My father walked to the window and looked out through the curtains, his shoulders slumped. "If Elford killed the King... then the war is already lost. The Ashfords will fall. The Dravens will rule."

"Not if we fight," I said. "Not if Damien wins."

"Damien Ashford can't win if he's distracted by a forbidden mate," my father said, turning to me. "And we can't fight, Jasmine. Look at us! I'm a high school history teacher. Your mother is a florist. Our pack is made up of doctors, fishermen, and accountants. We're not killers. The Dravens are born for violence. If we join this fight, we'll be slaughtered."

"So we just wait to be killed one by one?" I asked,

my voice shaking with frustration. "Like I almost was in the woods?"

"That was a mistake," my mother said quickly. "You were in the wrong place. If we keep you here, if we keep you hidden—"

"I'm not something you can just hide away!" I yelled. "I'm a wolf! I felt it, Mom. In the woods. When I howled, it wasn't fear. It was power. It felt right. I stopped a Draven wolf with my voice."

I looked at my hands and flexed my fingers. "I can help him. I can help us. But not if you keep me locked up here, drinking tea and pretending I'm human."

"You're untrained," my father said, dismissive. "You've shifted once, by accident. You have no control. You'd be a liability in a fight."

"Then train me!" I begged. "You're my pack. Teach me how to use this. Teach me how to fight."

"No," my father said. The word felt final. "I won't teach my daughter how to die. The Snow pack stays neutral. We don't break the Codex. We don't get involved in the Challenge. And you... You're grounded, Jasmine. You can't leave this apartment. You can't see the Ashford boy again."

I stared at him. The history teacher. The man who taught me to ride a bike and helped me with algebra. I saw fear in his eyes, a deep terror of his own world. He loved me, I knew that. But his love was a cage. He would rather keep me safe and miserable than let me fight for my life.

But Damien had looked at me in that alley and told me to fight. He told me to learn. He invited me to the woods, to a dangerous place, because he respected the wolf in me and knew it couldn't be caged.

Damien saw who I really was. My parents only saw the daughter they wanted to protect.

"You're wrong," I said quietly. My anger had turned into something stronger, a resolve like steel. "Neutrality isn't an option anymore. You can pretend the war isn't coming, Dad. But it came for me three days ago. And it's coming for you next."

I turned and walked to my bedroom door.

"Where are you going?" my father demanded, stepping forward as if to stop me.

"To bed," I lied. "You're right. I'm untrained. I'm tired. And arguing with you is pointless."

I didn't wait for his answer. I closed my bedroom door and locked it. The lock was flimsy, easy for a wolf to break, but it was still a boundary.

I leaned against the door, listening. I could hear them whispering in the living room in low, frantic voices.

"She's changing, Elias. The bond. It's pulling her away from us. I think we just have to wait it out. Once the Challenge is over, once a King is crowned, the bond will settle. She will forget him."

"She won't forget him. You saw her eyes. She is Wolf-born now."

I moved away from the door and sat on my bed.

My room, once a safe place full of pillows and romance novels, now felt small and closed in. I looked at the digital clock on my nightstand.

**9:15 PM.**

Damien had said midnight. *Tomorrow.*

Wait. No. I replayed the conversation in the alley. *Midnight. Tomorrow.*

Did he mean tomorrow night? Or did he mean tonight, effectively tomorrow morning?

*Midnight. Tomorrow. By the old mill stream.*

If he meant tomorrow night, I had twenty-seven hours to sit in this apartment while my parents watched me closely. Twenty-seven hours of "breathing exercises" and herbal tea.

But if he meant... well, usually "tomorrow" meant the next day. But in the context of urgent, secret meetings?

I walked to the window. The mist outside was thick, swirling around the streetlamps. Somewhere out there, beyond the town, beyond the safety of the streetlights, was the old mill stream. Neutral territory.

My body was buzzing. The energy I felt in the alley hadn't faded; it was still in my muscles, making me tense and restless.

I couldn't stay here. I couldn't sit and listen to my parents plan a life where I stayed invisible.

I opened my closet. I pushed aside the cardigans and slacks, my usual librarian clothes, and reached into the back for a pair of dark running leggings and a black hoodie I hadn't worn since college.

My father said I was untrained. He said I was a liability.

He was right.

But he was wrong about one thing: I wasn't going to stay that way.

If Damien was willing to risk his throne to meet me, to teach me... then I was willing to risk my parents' anger.

I sat on the floor and started to stretch. I didn't know how to shift on purpose yet. I didn't know how to fight with teeth and claws. But I knew how to run. And for the first time, I wasn't running away. I was running toward something.

I closed my eyes and tried to find the spark I felt in the woods. It was still there, a warm ember in my chest. I focused on it, and it flared up.

*Wolf.*

The word echoed in my mind, not as something frightening, but as a name. *My* name.

I thought about the map my father had shown me. The Snow territory. The Ashen Ones. The Dravens.

We were the smallest, the weakest, the pacifists.

*Insignificant.*

I clenched my fists.

Elford looked at me in shock when I howled. Not fear—just surprise. Snows aren't supposed to howl like that. Snows don't fight.

That was our advantage.

If war was coming, being underestimated was our best weapon. But only if we were actually dangerous.

I checked the clock again. **9:45 PM.**

I would wait until they fell asleep. My father was exhausted; the stress of the last few days was getting to him. My mother would take something to help her sleep, like she always did when she was anxious.

By 11:30, the apartment would be silent.

And at midnight... well, I would find out if Damien meant tonight or tomorrow. And if he wasn't there tonight, I would go to the mill stream anyway. I would stand in the neutral territory, and I would try to call the wolf out myself.

I lay back on the floor and stared at the ceiling fan turning slowly above me.

"I am not insignificant," I whispered to the empty room.

The wolf inside me agreed.

We were going to war. And my first battle wasn't against the Dravens. It was against the people who loved me enough to hold me back.

I closed my eyes and visualized the stream. The water. The woods. The man with the golden eyes waiting in the dark.

I would be there. And I would be ready.

# CHAPTER 14
# JAZZ

The old mill stream wasn't a romantic spot. It was more like a scar on Tallow's landscape. It had burned down fifty years ago, leaving only blackened stone and rusted gears sticking out of the ground like the ribs of a giant machine. The stream beside it rushed fast and cold over sharp rocks, then vanished into the thick, dark woods beyond.

It was exactly the kind of place you went to meet a secret lover, or to bury a body.

I sat on a large, flat rock near the water's edge, my knees pulled up to my chest, shivering in my thin hoodie. The digital watch on my wrist read 12:24 AM.

Damien wasn't here yet.

I managed to escape my apartment in total silence, slipping out an unlocked window and dropping to the ground hard enough to hurt my ankles, but not break them. I ran the two miles to the stream, breathing easily in steady bursts that proved my new body was much stronger than before. I got there right at midnight, buzzing with both excitement and fear.

And now, twenty-four minutes later, I was alone in the dark, listening to the water rush by and feeling the damp cold seep into my bones.

He wasn't coming.

The thought was a cold, bitter drop of poison in my chest. My father's voice echoed in my head: He is an Ashford. Manipulation is their language.

Had he lied? Had the moment in the alley been just another tactical move? Maybe he told me to meet him here so he could verify that I was breaking my parents' rules, proving to the other packs that the Snows couldn't control their members. Or maybe he just wanted to see if I was stupid enough to show up.

"Stupid," I hissed into the night, picking up a pebble and hurling it into the dark water. It landed with a pathetic plip that was instantly swallowed by the roar of the stream.

The wolf inside me hated waiting. It didn't care about time or politics. It paced inside my chest, scratching at my throat and begging to get out. The energy I'd felt earlier had turned into a sharp pain, pressure building behind my eyes and under my skin.

I stood up, unable to sit still. The silence of the woods felt judgmental. The trees loomed overhead, their branches swaying in a wind I couldn't feel on the ground.

"Fine," I said aloud, my voice sounding small and brittle. "If you're not going to teach me, I'll teach myself."

It was a reckless, arrogant thought. I had no idea what I was doing. My only reference point was the terror-induced explosion in the woods with the Dravens, and that hadn't been a conscious choice. That had been survival.

But the anger at Damien, at his absence, at his rejection, at the secrets, was a fuel source almost as potent as fear.

I walked to the center of the clearing, away from the rocks. I closed my eyes and tried to find that center of heat again. It wasn't hard. It was right there, a simmering ball of magma in my gut.

*Shift*, I commanded it.

Nothing happened.

I frowned, concentrating harder. I tried to remember the sensation of my bones lengthening, of the power flooding my veins. I clenched my fists, tensing every muscle in my body, trying to force the change through sheer willpower.

Shift!

A sharp, stabbing pain shot through my left shoulder, hot and blinding. I gasped, stumbling forward. It felt like someone had driven a railroad spike into my joint.

"Okay," I panted, clutching my shoulder. "That's... something."

The wolf was awake now. It understood what I wanted. But instead of a smooth change, it felt like two people trying to squeeze through a narrow door at once. My human side held on too tightly, scared of the pain, while the wolf side pushed forward, not caring about the damage.

Another jolt, this time in my spine. A sickening crack echoed in the clearing like a gunshot.

I screamed, falling to my knees. The pain was absolute. It wasn't the fluid, magical transformation I had seen in the movies. It was violence on a biological level. My vertebrae were grinding against each other, rearranging themselves with zero regard for the soft tissue surrounding them.

Stop, I thought, panic rising. Stop it. I can't do this.

But I couldn't stop it. I had pulled the trigger, and the bullet was already leaving the chamber.

My hands hit the dirt. I watched in horror as my fingers spasmed, the knuckles bulging and cracking as they elongated. My fingernails blackened, pushing out into claws that tore through the skin of my fingertips. Blood—my blood—dripped onto the dead leaves.

"Damien!" I screamed his name, a desperate plea to the empty woods.

The change sped up as my panic grew. My jaw popped open with a sound like breaking wood. My vision split in two: one side saw in human color, the other in the wolf's gray, heat-sensitive way. Both views overlapped, making me dizzy and sick.

I rolled onto my side, thrashing. My clothes were tearing, the seams giving way as my shoulders broadened and my ribcage expanded. But it was wrong. It was all wrong. My legs weren't changing fast enough. My left arm was a paw, but my right was still a hand. I was trapped halfway, a grotesque hybrid caught in a biological deadlock.

The pain was no longer localized; it was everywhere. My skin felt like it was on fire. My bones were breaking and knitting and breaking again.

The wolf was terrified. I could feel its confusion bleeding into my mind. It didn't know why it was stuck. It lashed out, needing to destroy something to escape the pain.

I—or the thing I was becoming—swung a heavy, furred limb at a sapling near the stream. The wood shattered, the tree snapping in half like a toothpick. The violence felt good. It was a release.

I snarled, a wet, gurgling sound that was half human moan, half animal growl. I dug my claws into the earth, tearing up huge clods of dirt and grass. I needed to get out. I needed to rip this skin off.

I hurled myself at a huge oak tree, slamming my shoulder into the bark to try to force the change. The hit stunned me, and I saw stars in my broken vision. I fell back, twisting in the dirt and snapping my jaws at nothing.

I was losing myself. The Jasmine Snow who organized bookshelves and worried about rent was dissolving into a red haze of agony and instinct. There was only the need to stop the pain. To kill the thing causing it.

And the thing causing it was me.

I raised my clawed hand, poised to rake it across my own chest, desperate to tear open the cage.

"Enough."

The voice wasn't loud. It was a command that hit me hard, pinning me to the ground better than any chain could.

I froze, my claw hovering inches from my own throat.

Damien stepped out of the shadows of the mill ruins.

He hadn't run into the clearing. He hadn't just arrived. He walked toward me with a slow, deliberate calmness that was terrifying in its own right. He wasn't in his gear. He was wearing a simple grey t-shirt and loose track pants, his feet bare on the cold ground.

But his eyes... his eyes were fully gold. They were glowing with a power that lit up the dark clearing.

He didn't look at me with pity. He didn't look at me with fear. He looked at me with absolute, unwavering dominance.

"Look at me, Jazz," he ordered, his voice vibrating in my bones, overriding the pain.

I whined, trying to twist away. The wolf wanted to

submit, but the pain was too loud. I thrashed again, my half-formed body convulsing.

Damien moved. He covered the distance between us in a blur, dropping to his knees beside me. He didn't flinch at the sight of my distorted body, the blood, or the grotesque mix of fur and skin.

He reached out and placed his hands on either side of my face—one hand gripping the human jaw, the other cupping the wolf's ear.

"Submit to the shift," he growled, leaning down so his face was inches from mine. "Stop fighting it. You are breaking yourself because you are holding on to the human. Let go."

"I... can't..." I choked out, the words garbled by my elongated teeth. "Hurts..."

"I know it hurts," he said, his thumbs pressing hard into the pressure points behind my ears. "Pain is the price of power. Accept it. Breathe through it. Give it to me."

He pressed his forehead to mine. A wave of warmth moved from him into me. Not the wild, burning heat of the shift, but a steady, calming warmth. I could feel his slow, strong heartbeat against my own fast one.

*Mine,* his mind whispered against mine. *You are mine. I have you. Let go.*

The permission broke the dam. I stopped fighting the invasion of the wolf. I stopped trying to hold onto the shape of my fingers and the length of my legs. I exhaled a shuddering breath and surrendered to the fire.

The final snap was deafening, but it was fast. My body arched, my spine realigning in one fluid, agonizing motion. The fur rushed over the rest of my skin. The human sight vanished, replaced entirely by the sharp, grey-scale clarity of the predator.

I was a wolf.

I lay on the cold ground, panting, my tongue hanging out on the dead leaves. I was smaller than the Dravens and smaller than Damien's big black wolf form. My fur, visible on my paws, was pale and silvery white, like moonlight on snow.

The pain receded to a dull throb.

Damien sat back on his heels, exhaling a long breath. He ran a hand through his hair, and I saw that his hands were shaking slightly.

"You are an idiot," he said softly.

I chuffed, a small sound of indignation. I tried to stand, but my new legs felt like jelly. I wobbled and collapsed back onto my belly.

"Don't try to move yet," he advised. "The first conscious shift drains your metabolic reserves. You'll be weak for an hour."

He looked at me, really looked at me, his gaze traveling over my white fur. There was a look of profound wonder in his eyes, mixed with a dark, simmering possessiveness.

"A Snow wolf," he murmured, reaching out to

touch the ruff of fur at my neck. "I haven't seen one in a decade. You...you're beautiful, Jazz."

His touch sent a jolt through me. Even with all my fur, I could feel the warmth of his fingers. I leaned into his hand, rubbing my head against his palm. The bond between us was open now, full of emotion. I felt his relief, his tiredness, and the deep fear he had for me.

"You were watching," I projected the thought. It wasn't speech, but a push of intent and image. You were there.

He nodded, understanding the non-verbal communication of the pack. "I was here at midnight. I saw you arrive. I stayed in the shadows."

Why? I demanded, pulling away from his hand. You let me break myself.

"I had to see if you could do it," he said, his voice hardening slightly. "I had to know if the wolf was strong enough to surface without a life-or-death trigger. If you're going to survive this war, Jazz, you can't rely on panic to save you. You have to control the beast. Not the other way around."

You waited too long, I accused. I almost died.

"You wouldn't have died," he said confidently. "I wouldn't have let you. But you needed to feel the consequence of rushing. You needed to respect the pain."

He stood up, looking down at me. "Shift back."

I stared at him. Are you kidding me? I just got here.

"Shift back," he repeated, his tone brooking no

argument. "The sun will be up in four hours. You need to be back in your apartment before your parents wake up. And you can't walk through town like that."

I whined. The idea of going through that pain in reverse was horrifying.

"It's easier going back," he promised. "Focus on your human form. Focus on your hands. Focus on... I don't know, the Dewey Decimal System. Whatever makes you human."

I closed my eyes. I thought about my apartment. The smell of coffee. The spine of a hardcover book. My hands sorting index cards.

The change was swift. It felt like water draining from a tub. The fur receded, the bones snapped back into place with wet, popping sounds that were gross but bearable.

I lay on the ground, gasping, human again.

And completely naked.

The cold night air bit into my skin instantly. I curled into a ball, covering myself with my arms, shivering violently. My clothes were shredded rags scattered around the clearing.

Damien didn't turn away. He didn't make a lewd comment. He simply stripped off his grey t-shirt, leaving him bare-chested in the freezing woods—and handed it to me.

"Put this on. It'll cover the important parts."

I sat up, snatching the shirt and pulling it over my

head. It smelled like him—intense, musky, and safe. It hung to my mid-thighs, swamping me.

"My pants are ruined," I chattered, my teeth clicking together.

"You destroyed a perfectly good pair of leggings," he noted dryly. "Next time, bring a change of clothes. Or strip before you shift."

"Next time?" I looked up at him. He was standing there, shirtless, the moonlight tracing the heavy muscles of his chest and arms. He looked like a pagan god of the forest, unbothered by the cold.

"You called for help," he said quietly. "And you didn't call your father. You called me."

"You're the only one who listens," I said, wrapping my arms around my knees to preserve heat. "Why didn't you come sooner? I waited twenty minutes."

He crouched down again, so we were eye level. "I told you. I needed to see if you were serious. If you were just a girl angry at her parents, or a wolf ready to fight."

He reached out, brushing a strand of sweat-damp hair away from my face. His fingers lingered on my cheek. "You fought. You fought yourself, the pain, the fear. You have the heart of a warrior, Jazz. Your parents are wrong about you."

"Does that mean you'll teach me?" I asked, my voice barely a whisper. "Really teach me?"

He looked at my lips, his pupils growing so wide they covered the gold in his eyes. In a second, the tension in the clearing changed from anger to desire. The air felt heavy with it.

"I can't be seen with you," he murmured, his thumb tracing my lower lip. "But I can't leave you defenseless. Elford will try again. And next time, he won't send scouts. He'll come himself."

"Then I need to be ready," I said.

He leaned in, closing the gap until his lips were hovering just over mine. I could feel his breath, warm and tantalizing.

"Monday, Wednesday, Friday," he whispered against my mouth. "Midnight. Here. We train. We fight. And when the war comes... You survive."

He kissed me. It wasn't wild or possessive like before. This kiss was slow and deep, full of promise. It felt like a pact between two people willing to break every rule to protect each other.

He pulled back before it could go further, though my body screamed for him to stay. He stood up, offering me a hand.

"Go home, Jazz. Before I forget why I'm supposed to stay away from you."

I took his hand, letting him pull me to my feet. My legs were shaky, but I stood.

"Thank you," I said.

"Don't thank me," he said grimly, turning toward the darker woods. "You just signed up for hell. I'm going to push you until you break, so that the Dravens can't break you."

He disappeared into the shadows without looking back.

I stood alone in the clearing, wearing his shirt and shivering in the cold. But I wasn't afraid anymore. The pain was just a faint memory. Inside, the white wolf in me settled down and slept, content.

We had a schedule.

# CHAPTER 15
# DAMIEN

The woods at midnight were usually my sanctuary. For years, the silence of the Ashen Ones' territory was the only place where the noise in my head would finally quiet down. The pack's demands, my father's expectations, and the constant pressure of the throne, all of it dissipated into nothingness.

But tonight, the silence was screaming.

I stood by the blackened ruins of the old mill, my back pressed to the rough stone of a collapsed wall. The stream roared nearby, churning white water over dark rocks, but even that couldn't drown out the sound of my heart pounding in my chest.

I checked my watch. **11:58 PM.**

I shouldn't be here. Every logical thought, every lesson from the Codex, every instinct that made me a contender for the Wolf Throne, told me to turn around, shift, and run back to the compound. Meeting Jazz Snow, my fated mate, a new shifter from a rival pack and the biggest threat to my claim, wasn't just reckless. It was treason.

If Elford found out I was training her, he wouldn't just kill her. He would use it to strip me of my Alpha status before the Challenge even began. He would paint me as a compromised leader, a slave to his instincts, unfit to rule the five clans.

And he would be right.

Because the moment I caught her scent on the wind, a mix of night-blooming jasmine, ozone, and the clean smell of snow, all thoughts of the Throne disappeared.

She emerged from the tree line exactly at midnight.

She wore black leggings and a tight, long-sleeved tactical shirt, probably bought online because she thought it made her look like a warrior. A duffel bag hung from one shoulder, and her dark hair was pulled back in a strict braid. She looked determined, beautiful, and completely out of her depth.

My wolf paced inside me, restless and eager to close the distance, to mark her as ours, to claim what we had been denied. I forced the beast down, holding it back with cold, iron control.

"You're here," I said, my voice rougher than I intended.

Jazz stopped ten feet away, dropping the duffel bag

to the forest floor with a heavy thud. Her blue eyes—so bright even in the shadows—locked onto mine. "You said Monday, Wednesday, Friday. I'm not the one who ghosts people, Damien."

The barb landed, but I didn't flinch. I deserved it. "Good. Punctuality is the first rule of survival. If you're late in a fight, you're dead."

I pushed off the wall and walked toward her. I saw her breath catch and her pupils widen as I stepped closer. The air between us felt heavy, charged with the energy of our bond. It pressed against my skin, demanding contact.

"Strip," I ordered.

Her eyes widened, and her cheeks flushed a dark, lovely pink. "Excuse me?"

"You brought a change of clothes this time, right?" I nodded at the bag. "If you don't want to ruin that outfit like last time, you need to undress before you shift. Clothes get in the way and make it hurt more. You already have enough pain to handle."

She hesitated, her gaze flickering to the dark woods around us. "It's freezing."

"The cold is just a distraction," I said, lowering my voice. "Use it. Focus on it. Let it help you concentrate."

She set her jaw, the stubbornness I was coming to adore flashing in her eyes. Without breaking eye contact, she reached for the hem of her shirt. She pulled it over her head, revealing a simple sports bra and pale, smooth skin that seemed to glow in the moonlight. She shivered, gooseflesh rising on her arms, but she didn't complain. She pushed down the leggings, stepping out of them with quick, efficient movements.

I made myself watch her as a trainer, not a lover. I studied her muscle tension, her balance, and her breathing. But my wolf noticed every curve and every bit of skin that was ours. It took all my willpower to keep my hands at my sides.

When she was standing in just her undergarments, shivering violently, she looked small. Fragile. But her chin was lifted in defiance.

"Okay," she chattered. "I'm naked. Now what?"

"Now," I said, stepping behind her, "we fix your entry."

I placed my hands on her bare shoulders. Her skin was ice cold, but the moment I touched her, a jolt of heat arced between us, hot enough to burn. She gasped, leaning back slightly into my chest before catching herself.

"Your last shift was a car crash," I murmured, my mouth close to her ear. "You tried to force the wolf out through a door that was locked. You broke your own bones because you were fighting the expansion."

I slid my hands down her arms, feeling the tension in her triceps. "Relax. You're holding yourself like a human. Rigid. Upright. Wolves are fluid."

"It's hard to relax when I know it's going to feel

like being put through a wood chipper," she whispered.

"It only feels like that because you're resisting," I corrected. "Close your eyes."

She obeyed.

"Find the heat," I instructed. "The center of the wolf. Where is it?"

"My chest," she breathed. "It feels heavy."

"Good. Now, don't pull it out. *Sink into it.*" I moved one hand to her stomach, flattening my palm against her diaphragm. "Breathe into my hand. Deep. When you shift, you don't push the wolf out. You let the human fall back. It's a surrender, Jazz. Not a conquest."

I felt her breathing hitch, then deepen, syncing with the pressure of my hand. The scent of her—aroused, afraid, and trusting—was filling my lungs, intoxicating me.

"Surrender," I whispered, the word heavy with double meaning.

She exhaled a long, shuddering breath. "Okay."

"Now. Let go."

I stepped back, giving her space.

This time, she didn't scream. She groaned, a low, rough sound, as her body arched. I watched, both fascinated and afraid, as the magic took over. Her spine stretched with a wet pop that made her flinch, but she didn't resist. She dropped to her hands and knees, her skin rippling as fur appeared. The sound of her bones changing shape was still gruesome—the jaw cracking, the ribs snapping—but it was faster and cleaner.

In ten seconds, the woman was gone. In her place stood the *White Wolf.*

She was magnificent. Smaller than me, sleek and built for speed, with a coat that shimmered like starlight. She shook herself, sending a spray of loose fur into the air, and looked up at me with those intelligent, human-blue eyes trapped in a predator's face.

*Better,* I projected the thought to her, tapping into the pack's mind-link. It was weak, just a thread, but she heard me.

She chuffed, wagging her tail tentatively. She took a step, stumbling slightly on paws that still felt too large.

*Run,* I commanded. *Feel the ground. Learn your center of gravity.*

She took off. It wasn't graceful; she skidded on wet leaves, bumped into a sapling, and tripped over her own feet, but she kept moving. She ran a lap around the clearing, picking up speed as she felt the strength in her hind legs. I watched her, pride swelling in my chest. A Snow wolf is running. It was a sight that hadn't been seen in these woods for a generation.

When she came back, panting, her tongue lolling, she looked up at me expectantly. *Did I do well?*

"Adequate," I said aloud, keeping my tone strict.

"But you're loud. You run like a puppy with oversized feet. You need to be silent."

I pulled my t-shirt over my head. "Stay there."

I skipped the warm-up and let the Alpha take over. The shift hit me hard and fast, but I was used to it. I didn't fight the pain; I let it happen. In three seconds, I was on four paws, towering over her.

My wolf form was massive, a creature of shadow and muscle, scarred from a dozen challenges. I saw Jazz shrink back slightly, her ears flattening. The size difference was intimidating.

I lowered my head, bumping my nose against her neck in a reassuring gesture. *Follow.*

I took off into the deeper woods. I didn't run at full speed, but I didn't slow down to a crawl either. I forced her to keep up. We wove through the ancient pines, jumped over fallen logs, and navigated the treacherous, rocky terrain of the stream bank.

For an hour, we were only wolves. There was no throne, no Codex, no betrayal. Just the sound of paws on the ground, the scent of pine and prey, and my mate running beside me. It was the most free I had felt since my father died.

We circled back to the mill ruins as the moon began to dip. I shifted first, the return to human form smooth and practiced. I quickly pulled on my pants, turning my back to give her privacy as she shifted.

The sounds of her return were softer this time, just whimpers of discomfort instead of screams of pain, sitting on the log, wrapped in a towel she'd pulled from her bag, shivering. Her hair was damp with sweat, plastering to her neck. She looked exhausted, battered, and utterly exhilarated.

"That was..." she started, her eyes shining. "That was incredible. The smells. The speed. I felt like I could run forever."

"The adrenaline will fade," I warned, walking over and handing her a bottle of water from my bag. "Then you'll feel exhausted. You'll sleep for twelve hours if your parents let you."

She took the water, her fingers brushing mine. The spark was still there, hot as ever. "They won't. I have a shift at the library at nine."

"Call in sick," I said. "Your muscles need to rebuild."

"I can't. I have to maintain the cover, remember?" She took a long drink, then looked up at me. "So, I can shift. Now what?"

"Now," I said, "we fight."

"Like wolves?"

"No. Like humans." I took the empty bottle from her and set it down. "Elford won't always wait for you to shift. If he catches you in the library or the parking lot, you can't rely on the wolf. You need to know how to defend this body."

I pulled her up from the log. The towel slipped a little, revealing the curve of her shoulder, but she tightened it.

"Stand with your feet apart," I instructed, nudging her right foot back with my boot. "Knees bent. Center of gravity low."

She adjusted her stance. "Like this?"

"Better. Now, throw a punch. Aim for my chest."

She hesitated. "I don't want to hurt you."

I snorted. "You couldn't hurt me if you had a baseball bat, Jazz. Hit me."

She threw a tentative jab. I caught her fist easily in my open palm, wrapping my fingers around it.

"Pathetic," I said. "You're pushing, not striking. And you're making it obvious. I could see that coming from Tallow."

"I'm a librarian!" she protested, trying to yank her hand back. I held on.

"You're a target," I snapped, pulling her closer until our chests were inches apart. "Elford will snap this wrist before you can blink. Again. Harder. Use your hips."

I released her. She scowled, reset her feet, and threw another punch. This one had more weight behind it. I blocked it with my forearm, the impact jarring but solid.

"Good," I said. "Again."

For the next twenty minutes, I drilled her. Jabs, hooks, blocks. I forced her to move, to sweat, to get angry. I wanted her exhausted. I wanted her to stop thinking and start reacting.

"Again!" I barked.

She swung wild, a sloppy hook aimed at my head. I ducked under it, stepped into her guard, and swept her legs.

She gasped as the world turned upside down. She landed on the soft forest floor with a *thump*, and the towel slipped off her body.

Before she could scramble away, I was on top of her.

I pinned her wrists above her head with one hand, my legs bracketing hers, my weight pressing her into the leaves. It was a classic dominance move, a way to show her how vulnerable she was on the ground.

But the lesson died the moment our skin touched.

She was naked and panting, her chest rising and falling against mine. Sweat gleamed across her moonlit skin. Her scent, a mix of arousal, effort, and wolf, hit me hard. I was blown wide, black holes swallowing the blue. Her lips were parted, swollen from biting them in concentration. She wasn't fighting me. She was looking up at me with a raw, naked hunger that mirrored my own.

"Damien," she whispered, her voice wrecking me.

My control fractured.

I lowered my head, burying my face in the crook of her neck. I inhaled deeply, groaning as her scent filled my head. My hips pressed instinctively against hers, and I felt her buck up to meet me, a desperate, seeking friction.

"You have no idea," I rasped against her skin, "how dangerous this is."

"I don't care," she breathed. She twisted her wrists, not to escape, but to grab my hand. Her fingers interlaced with mine, squeezing tight.

My wolf roared, demanding I claim her. *Right here. Now. Mark her. Make the other packs smell us on her for a century.*

I kissed a path up her throat, feeling her pulse flutter wildly under my lips. I reached her jaw, her cheek, and finally, her mouth.

The kiss was explosive. It was frustration, fear, and desire all at once. I tasted blood; she must have bitten her lip during the shift, and it drove me wild. I let go of her wrists and tangled my hands in her hair, tilting her head to deepen the kiss.

She wrapped her legs around my waist, pulling me closer, erasing the space between us. Her hands roamed over my back, her nails digging in, leaving trails of fire.

For a moment, I forgot the throne. I forgot Elford. I forgot that this woman was the match that could burn my entire kingdom to the ground. There was only Jazz. Only the mate.

But then, a sound cut through the haze.

A twig snapping.

It was distant, maybe a hundred yards away, but my Alpha senses caught it right away.

I froze.

Jazz felt the change in me. "What?" she whispered, breathless.

I pulled back, my breathing ragged, my heart pounding like a war drum. I scanned the perimeter, my eyes shifting to gold.

"Someone's close," I hissed. "A scout. Maybe a deer. But I can't take the risk."

I rolled off her, the loss of her warmth a physical pain. I stood up, offering her a hand, keeping my body angled between her and the sound.

"Get dressed," I ordered, my voice harsh with the effort of restraint. "Now."

She scrambled up, snatching her clothes from the ground. She dressed with frantic speed, her hands shaking.

I watched the woods, every muscle coiled. The sound didn't repeat. Whatever it was, it had stopped or moved on.

When she was dressed, she looked at me, her face flushed and confused. "Damien..."

"Go," I said, not looking at her. I couldn't. If I looked at her now, messy and flushed, staring at me like I was her whole world, I wouldn't let her leave. "Take the creek bed back. It hides your scent. Don't stop until you're inside."

"But—"

"Go!" I roared, the Alpha command cracking like a whip.

She flinched, hurt flashing in her eyes, but she

nodded. She grabbed her bag and turned, running toward the creek, disappearing into the darkness.

I stood there until the sound of her footsteps faded completely.

I was alone again. My body ached with unspent adrenaline and blue-balled fury. My wolf was pacing, furious at the interruption, furious at me for stopping.

I turned to the tree where the sound had come from.

"Come out," I said to the empty air. "I know you're there."

A squirrel darted out from behind the trunk and scurried up the bark.

Just a squirrel.

I let out a long, shaky breath and leaned my forehead against the rough stone of the mill.

I was losing my mind. The paranoia was setting in. But the paranoia was the only thing keeping her alive.

I looked down at my hands. They were still trembling.

Monday, Wednesday, Friday.

Today was Monday.

God help me, I just had to make it to Wednesday.

# CHAPTER 16
# JAZZ

By Friday, my body was covered in bruises, each one a lesson I learned the hard way at night.

The midnight training sessions were tough. Damien didn't treat me like his girlfriend, his mate, or even as a woman. He treated me like a recruit who showed up late to a war. He was relentless, demanding, and pushed me hard.

And I loved every second of it.

The old mill ruins felt like our own world. The sound of the stream, the smell of wet earth and pine, and the cold Maine night all faded until only the space between us mattered.

"Again," Damien barked, circling me.

I wiped sweat from my forehead with the back of my hand, my breath coming in ragged gasps. "I'm... tired, Damien."

"Elford doesn't care if you're tired," he countered,

lashing out with a leg sweep that I barely managed to jump over. "The Shadowfangs don't care if you have a cramp. Move, Jazz. Stop thinking and move."

I growled, a low sound that rumbled in my chest, and lunged at him.

We weren't in wolf form tonight. This time, it was about learning human combat, which mostly meant Damien kept throwing me into the dirt until I figured out how to stop him.

I threw a jab at his jaw, which he blocked effortlessly, but I used the momentum to spin, driving my elbow toward his ribs. He caught it, his grip like iron, and twisted me around, pinning my back against his chest. His arm locked across my throat, not cutting off the air, but threatening to.

"Dead," he whispered in my ear. "You overextended. You left your flank exposed."

His body pressed tightly against mine, warm and solid. I felt his heart pounding against my back, matching my own wild heartbeat. His scent—musk, sweat, and that deep Alpha smell—filled my senses, making me forget this was only training.

For three sessions, we circled around this. We touched, grappled, and shared the same air, but we hadn't crossed the line again. We hadn't kissed since Monday. The tension between us grew stronger with every accidental touch.

"Let go," I panted, clawing at his arm.

"Break the hold," he challenged, tightening his grip slightly. "Don't ask. Take."

Something inside me snapped. It wasn't anger; it was pure need. The wolf, the woman, the mate in me all rose together in defiance.

I didn't try to pry his arm away. Instead, I dropped my weight, stomping hard on his instep. He grunted, his grip loosening for a fraction of a second. I used that instant to throw my head back, slamming it into his nose.

It was a dirty move. It was desperate.

He cursed, stumbling back, his hands flying to his face. "Christ, Jazz!"

I spun around, but I didn't retreat to a defensive stance. I launched myself at him.

I hit him with the full force of my body, driving him back until his shoulders hit the rough stone of the ruined mill wall. I grabbed the front of his shirt, yanking him down to my level, and smashed my lips against his.

It wasn't really a kiss. It was more like a collision.

For a heartbeat, he froze, his hands hovering in the air, caught between pushing me away and pulling me closer.

Then, the dam broke.

He groaned, a raw, animal sound, and pulled me close. The kiss deepened right away, turning wild. His tongue slid into my mouth, tasting of blood from the headbutt and desire.

"Jazz," he rasped, breaking the kiss to bury his face in my neck, his teeth grazing the sensitive skin over my pulse. "We can't... we're supposed to be training."

"Shut up," I whispered, pressing closer to him, my hips moving against his. "I don't want to train. I want you."

"I could hurt you," he warned, his hands sliding down to grip my hips, his fingers digging in hard enough to bruise. "My wolf is... he's close to the surface, Jazz. He wants to claim."

"Then let him," I whispered. "I'm not afraid of him. I'm not afraid of you."

He pulled back and looked down at me. His eyes glowed gold in the dark, the pupils narrow. He looked both terrifying and beautiful.

"You should be," he growled.

He didn't wait for permission. He swept me up, lifting me off the ground as if I weighed nothing. I wrapped my legs around his waist, burying my hands in his dark hair, pulling him back to me.

He carried me away from the wall, toward the softer ground beneath the shelter of a massive, over-hanging pine. He dropped to his knees, taking me with him, laying me back on the bed of pine needles and discarded clothes.

The cold air stung my skin as he ripped my shirt open, buttons scattering into the brush. I didn't care. The heat from his body was like a furnace.

"Mine," he snarled, his voice distorted, layering with the growl of the wolf.

"Yours," I answered, the word feeling like a vow.

He stripped the rest of my clothes off with frantic, trembling hands. I helped him with his, fumbling with his belt buckle, desperate to feel skin against skin. When we were finally bare, pressed together in the dirt and the dark, the relief was agonizing.

It wasn't gentle. It couldn't be. We had denied the bond for too long, holding it back because of politics, fear, and lies. Now that it was free, it wanted everything.

He kissed me everywhere—my throat, my breasts, my stomach—leaving his scent, the scratch of his stubble, and the heat of his mouth on my skin. I moved beneath him, grabbing his shoulders, my own wolf howling in my mind, pushing him on.

*Mate. Mate. Mate.*

When he finally positioned himself between my legs, looking down at me with that intense, possessive stare, the world narrowed down to a single point of focus.

"Look at me," he commanded, his voice thick. "I want you to see who you belong to."

I looked at him and saw the Alpha, the killer, and the man who disappeared to save me. I loved him so fiercely it scared me.

He entered me in one smooth, powerful thrust,

filling the empty ache that had been hollowing me out since the day we met.

I cried out, arching my back and digging my nails into his arms. It was overwhelming and perfect at the same time.

We moved together in a rhythm as old as the forest. This wasn't gentle lovemaking; it was primal. It was teeth, claws, sweat, and the desperate need to become one.

I felt the bond settle into place, tight and real. It was like a golden thread pulling our hearts together. I felt his pleasure, his possessiveness, and his relief. I knew he felt mine, too.

"Damien," I sobbed, the pleasure building, tightening, winding me up until I felt like I was going to shatter.

"I've got you," he gritted out, his forehead resting against mine, his sweat dripping onto my face. "Let go, Jazz. I've got you."

The climax hit me like a lightning strike. My vision went white. I screamed his name, my body convulsing around him, every muscle seizing in ecstasy.

He followed me seconds later, throwing his head back with a roar that echoed through the trees, his body shuddering violently as he poured himself into me.

We collapsed together, tangled up and breathing hard. The cold air slowly returned as our heat faded.

For a long time, there was only the sound of our

ragged breath and the rushing stream. He lay heavy on top of me, his face buried in the crook of my neck, his arms wrapping me in a protective cocoon.

I lay there, looking up at the pine branches and watching the stars through the needles. My body felt heavy, satisfied, and relaxed. The wolf inside me was calm and content.

But as my heartbeat slowed and the adrenaline faded, my human thoughts returned.

And with those thoughts came guilt.

I was lying in the dirt, naked, with the Alpha of the Ashen Ones. The rival Alpha. The man who was currently at war—cold or otherwise—with my own pack.

My parents' faces flashed in my mind. My father's terrified, angry eyes. My mother's pleading voice. *We are neutral. We survive by being invisible.*

I had just betrayed them. Not just by sneaking out, not just by training, but by cementing a bond that could get us all killed. By sleeping with the enemy.

I shivered, and it wasn't only because of the cold.

Damien felt it immediately. He lifted his head, his gold eyes searching my face. The glow had faded, leaving them a warm, melted honey color.

"You're cold," he said softly, moving to pull his flannel shirt over us like a blanket. It wasn't enough, but the gesture was gentle.

"It's not that," I whispered, looking away.

"Then what?" He brushed a pine needle from my hair, his touch gentle. "Regret?"

"No," I said quickly. "Not regret. Never that. But... Damien, what did we just do?"

"We accepted the inevitable," he said simply, resting his chin on my chest, looking up at me. "We stopped fighting nature."

"Nature doesn't care about the Codex," I said, my voice shaking. "Or my parents. Or your pack. Damien, if anyone finds out about us, it proves everything Elford says. It makes me a traitor to my pack, and you a traitor to yours."

He stiffened slightly, the softness leaving his expression. "You are not a traitor, Jazz. You are following the oldest law there is. The law of the mate bond supersedes the Codex. It supersedes packs."

"Try telling that to my father," I said bitterly. "Or to your council. You said it yourself: if you claim me, you lose the Throne."

"I haven't claimed you publicly," he argued. "This... us... this is ours. No one has to know."

"We're lying to everyone we love," I said, tears stinging my eyes. "I lie to my parents every time I leave. They think I'm asleep. They think I'm safe. If they knew I was here with you, it would break them."

He pushed himself up, sitting back on his heels, pulling me up with him so we were sitting face to face, huddled under the shirt.

"Jazz, look at me."

I met his gaze.

"Your parents are good people," he said, picking his words carefully. "But they're living in a fantasy. They think being neutral keeps them safe, but it just makes them a target. Elford was coming for the Snows no matter what. He wants the coast and the territory. You being my mate makes things harder, but it also gives you a chance to fight back."

"How?" I asked. "By making me a bigger target?"

"By giving you an Alpha who would do anything to keep you safe," he said fiercely.

He reached out and cupped my face. "I don't care about politics right now. I don't care what things look like. When I'm with you, when I'm close to you, everything else fades away. The fear disappears. Do you feel that?"

I nodded slowly. "Yes."

"Then hold onto that," he said. "Guilt is just a weapon the enemy uses to make you weak. Don't let them. You belong to me, Jazz, and I belong to you. That's the only truth that matters."

"But what happens when the sun comes up?" I asked softly. "When you have to go back to being the Alpha who rejected me, and I have to go back to being the invisible librarian?"

"Then we act," he said, stroking my cheek with his thumb. "We play our parts. We lie. We fight. But we know that in the dark, in the woods, we're real."

He kissed me again, soft and lingering. It tasted of promise and defiance.

"I can't promise you it will be easy," he whispered against my lips. "I can't promise you we won't get hurt. But I promise you this: I will never reject you again. Not in here." He tapped his chest, over his heart. "And not in here." He tapped his temple.

"Okay," I whispered, feeling my anxiety ease a little. The fear for my family was still there, heavy in my stomach, but Damien was right. The bond was the only thing that felt real in a world that kept shifting beneath me.

He pulled back and looked at the sky. The eastern horizon was starting to turn a deep purple.

"We have an hour before dawn," he said, his voice shifting back to the pragmatic trainer. "We should work on your defensive grappling. If you're going to be my mate, you need to know how to throw a three-hundred-pound wolf off you."

I stared at him, incredulous. "You want to train? Now? After... that?"

He smirked, flashing that bad boy grin. "Best time to train. Your endorphins are high, your pain threshold is up, and..." He leaned in and nipped my earlobe. "...it gives me an excuse to tackle you again."

I laughed, a startled, genuine sound that echoed in the quiet woods. I shoved his chest, but there was no heat in it.

"You're a tyrant," I accused, reaching for my scattered clothes.

"I'm an Alpha," he corrected, standing up and stretching, unashamed of his nakedness in the biting cold. "Come on, Snow. Let's see if you can sweep my leg when I'm actually expecting it."

I pulled on my leggings and watched him. The worry was still there, buzzing in my mind like a trapped fly. I was scared of what would happen when the truth came out. I was scared for my parents.

But as I stood up and faced him, my body humming with power and his scent clinging to my skin, I knew one thing for certain.

I would lie. I would sneak. I would fight.

Because he was worth it.

"Ready," I said, dropping into a defensive stance.

Damien smiled, his eyes glowing gold.

And in the shadow of the ruined mill, we went back to war.

# CHAPTER 17
# DAMIEN

The mist in the Tallow woods was thicker than usual tonight, a heavy grey blanket that muffled sound and hid everything from view. For a human, it would be blinding. For a wolf, it was just more to notice: the dampness, the pressure in the air, the scent of rain on the way.

I sat on the high stone wall of the ruined mill, my legs dangling over the edge, watching the clearing below.

Down there, a white blur was moving with lethal precision.

Jazz wasn't the clumsy, newborn pup who crashed into trees two weeks ago. Now she moved smoothly and quickly, running through the obstacle course I'd set up with fallen logs and jagged rocks. Watching her, I felt both proud and deeply uneasy.

She didn't just run, she moved like water. She used

the land, pushing off tree trunks and leaping over ravines, her white coat shining in the moonlight like a ghost.

*Turn,* I projected the command, keeping the mental link tight.

She didn't pause. She dug her claws into the ground, turned sharply, and sprang at the target dummy I'd made from old tires and canvas. She hit it in mid-air, her jaws closing on the 'throat' with a crunch of rubber and wood. She shook it hard, twice, then let go and landed in a crouch, growling low.

It was perfect. It was terrifying.

She shifted back before I could even tell her to. Changing forms was getting easier for her. One moment she was a predator, the next she was a woman standing in the mist, breathing hard, her skin shining with sweat and adrenaline.

She didn't rush to cover herself anymore. She stood there, looking up at me on the wall, a challenge in her eyes. "Time?" she rasped, her voice still rough from the growl.

I checked the stopwatch I held in my hand, though I didn't need to. "Forty-two seconds."

A grin broke across her face, fierce and wild. "That's a personal best. That's faster than the perimeter run you did on Tuesday."

"I was pacing myself on Tuesday," I lied, jumping down from the wall. I walked over to her clothes, picked up her oversized flannel shirt—my shirt, really, since she'd claimed it—and held it out to her.

"Admit it, Ashford," she said, snatching the shirt and slipping her arms into it. "I'm getting fast."

"You're getting fast," I conceded, watching her button the flannel. "For a Snow."

"For anyone," she corrected, stepping into her sweatpants. "I feel... heavy. But light at the same time. Does that make sense? Like my bones are made of lead, but my muscles are made of helium."

"It's the density," I said, leaning against a tree and crossing my arms to keep from reaching for her. I always wanted to touch her. The bond was a constant ache, always pulling me closer. "Shifter muscle is three times denser than human muscle. Your center of gravity has changed. You're getting used to the strength."

She walked over to me, stopping just inside my personal space. She smelled of exertion, pine needles, and the sweet, ozone scent of the shift. It was intoxicating.

"I'm ready," she said quietly.

"Ready for what?"

"For the fight. For Elford."

The confidence in her voice chilled me. It was the unearned confidence of someone who had learned to box but had never been in a street brawl. She knew how to run, how to bite, how to shift. But she didn't know *war*.

"No," I said harshly. "You're not. You're fit, Jazz. You're controlled. But you're not a killer. And Elford... Elford is a butcher."

I turned away and walked toward the stream. The worry I'd felt for weeks grew stronger. Every night we trained like this, it felt like taking a risk. We were borrowing time, and sooner or later, we'd have to pay for it.

"You need to understand who we are up against," I said, looking back at her. "You know the names... Dravens, Shadowfangs, Grimvales. But they aren't just names on a map. They are cultures. They are ideologies bred over centuries."

She followed me, sitting on a large, flat rock near the water's edge, wrapping her arms around her knees. "Then teach me. You taught me how to shift. Teach me how to survive them."

I sighed, running a hand through my hair. I sat down opposite her, grabbing a stick and clearing a patch of dirt between us.

"The Five Clans," I began, drawing a rough circle in the dirt. I divided it into five uneven slices. "It's a balance of power. Or it was, when my father was alive."

I stabbed the stick into the largest slice on the west side. "The Grimvales."

"The brutal ones," Jazz supplied, remembering the brief description I'd given her before.

"Brutal is an understatement," I said. "They

occupy the deep mountain territory to the west. It's hard land—rock, ice, scarce prey. It breeds wolves who are massive, scarred, and angry. Their Alpha is a monster named Kane. He doesn't believe in strategy. He believes in overwhelming force. If you fight a Grimvale, you don't grapple. You don't try to submit them. They fight to the death every time. Their initiation rite involves surviving a week in a bear den. If Kane comes for the Throne, he will try to turn the Challenge into a slaughterhouse."

Jazz shuddered slightly. "Okay. Avoid the mountains. Got it."

I moved the stick to the slice bordering the Grimvales. "The Shadowfangs."

"The cunning ones."

"The spies," I corrected. "They hold the valley territory, the land that connects all the others. They control the information. Their Alpha is a female named Selene. She's... complicated."

"Complicated how?"

"She's brilliant," I admitted, a grudging respect in my voice. "And she's a viper. The Shadowfangs aren't the strongest fighters physically. They rely on ambush, poison, and psychological warfare. They find your weakness—your family, your secrets, your fears—and they exploit it. Selene doesn't want to win a physical fight; she wants to maneuver you into a position where you have to surrender."

I looked at Jazz pointedly. "If Selene finds out

about us... about you... she won't attack you. She'll kidnap your parents. Or she'll leak the information to Elford and watch us tear each other apart while she walks to the Throne unscathed."

Jazz's face paled. "My parents..."

"Are safe for now," I assured her quickly. "The Snow territory is neutral. But Selene is the reason we have to be invisible."

I stabbed the stick into the jagged slice that bordered my own territory. "The Dravens."

My voice dropped an octave. The anger was automatic.

"Elford's pack," Jazz whispered.

"The Dravens are the scavengers," I spat. "They hold the marshlands and the old logging territories. It's a place of rot and decay. They attract the exiles, the criminals, the wolves who were kicked out of other packs for being too violent or too unstable. They have no honor. They don't follow the Codex unless forced to. They fight dirty...sand in the eyes, biting the genitals, ganging up five-on-one. They are a mob, Jazz. And Elford is the ringleader who promises them that if they follow him, they can take whatever they want."

I looked at her, making sure she understood. "Elford wants the Throne not to rule, but to dominate. He wants to turn the Five Clans into a reflection of his own chaotic, violent pack. If he wins, Tallow burns. The Snows will be enslaved or wiped out."

She stared at the map in the dirt, her eyes wide. "And the Ashen Ones?" she asked softly. "Your pack?"

I looked down at the slice that represented my home. "We are the guardians," I said, the weight of the title settling on my shoulders. "We hold the central forests. We have always held the Throne because we balance the others. We have the strength to fight the Grimvales, the discipline to outwit the Shadowfangs, and the order to suppress the Dravens. We are the shield."

"And the Snows?" she asked, pointing to the small, coastal sliver.

"The Snows are the soul," I said, surprising myself with the words. "You keep the history. You maintain the connection to the human world. You remind us that we aren't just monsters."

I tossed the stick into the stream. "That's why the Codex forbids mixing. Each pack has a function. If you mix the Brutality of a Grimvale with the Cunning of a Shadowfang, you get a tyrant. If you mix the Order of an Ashen One with the... gentleness of a Snow..."

"You get a weakness?" Jazz finished, bitterness coating her voice.

"You get a target," I corrected. "Because you represent a unity that terrifies them. If the Shield and the Soul unite... we don't just rule. We change the game."

Jazz stayed quiet for a while, watching the water move over the dark rocks. She picked at a loose thread on the flannel shirt—my shirt.

"Has it ever happened?" she asked suddenly.

"Has what happened?"

"Unity," she said, looking up at me with a desperate, hopeful intensity. "Has an Alpha ever claimed a mate from a different pack and... made it work? Has there ever been a time when the packs united because of a marriage, instead of a war?"

Her question lingered in the damp air. I looked at her and saw hope in her eyes, and I hated that I had to take it away. I wanted to say yes. I wanted to tell her a story with a happy ending.

But she needed the truth to survive.

"No," I said flatly.

Her face fell.

"There was an attempt," I continued, my voice grim. "Sixty years ago. An Alpha from the Shadowfangs fell in love with a Grimvale warrior. They tried to hide it. They tried to run."

"What happened?"

"The packs didn't see it as love," I told her. "They saw it as a political alliance that threatened the balance. The other three packs—including the Ashen Ones, my grandfather—united against them. They hunted them down. It started a civil war that lasted three years. Half the wolf population in Maine was wiped out."

I leaned forward, locking eyes with her. "They died, Jazz. Both of them. Executed by their own families to stop the bleeding. That's why the Codex is so strict now. That's why the 'purity' of the pack lines is law. It's written in blood."

Jazz wrapped her arms tighter around herself, shrinking slightly. "So we're doomed. That's what you're telling me. History says we end up dead."

"History is a guide, not a shackle," I said fiercely. "They died because they ran. They died because they were weak. We aren't running."

"We're hiding," she countered.

"We are biding our time," I corrected. "I am going to win that Throne, Jazz. I am going to beat Kane into the dirt. I am going to outsmart Selene. I am going to kill Elford for what he did to my father. And when I sit on that Throne, when I am the King and my word is absolute law... then I will change the Codex."

I reached out, taking her hand. Her fingers were cold, but her grip was strong.

"I will rewrite the laws," I vowed. "I will make it so that a Snow and an Ashen One can stand together without starting a war. But I have to win first."

She looked at our joined hands, her thumb tracing the scarred knuckles of my right hand. "You really believe that? That you can change centuries of hate just by sitting in a chair?"

"I believe in us," I said. And it was the truest thing I had ever spoken. "The bond... It's not just biology, Jazz. It's power. When I'm with you, I feel stronger. Clearer. My father didn't have a mate. He ruled alone. Maybe that's why he fell. Maybe the

King needs the Queen to see the knives coming from the shadows."

She looked up, a ghost of a smile touching her lips. "So I'm your secret weapon?"

"You're my heart," I said, the admission raw and terrifying. "And you don't bring your heart into a knife fight until you're ready to kill everyone in the room."

A twig snapped.

We both froze. The tender moment shattered instantly, replaced by the razor-sharp tension of predators.

I was on my feet in a microsecond, pulling Jazz up behind me. My eyes shifted to gold, scanning the dense tree line. The mist swirled, obscuring shapes.

"Damien?" Jazz whispered, her voice barely audible.

"Hush."

I extended my senses, smelling past her scent, past the stream.

Damp earth. Rotting leaves. And... *sulfur*.

Elford.

No, not Elford. Too faint. But definitely Draven. A scout. A long-range patrol.

"We have to go," I hissed. "Now."

"Did they see us?"

"I don't know," I lied. I was ninety percent sure we were hidden by the ruins and the mist, but ninety percent wasn't enough when her life was on the line.

"Shift. Take the creek bed. Go deep. Don't go home for at least an hour. Circle back."

"What about you?"

"I'll draw them off," I said, stripping off my shirt and tossing it to the ground. "If they catch my scent, they'll just think the Ashen Alpha is patrolling his borders. It's not a crime for me to be here."

I looked at her one last time. She looked terrified, but she looked ready.

"Go, Jazz. Run."

She didn't argue. She dropped the flannel shirt and shifted mid-stride, a seamless transition into the white wolf. She vanished into the mist like smoke.

I waited five seconds, giving her a head start. Then I let my own wolf loose.

The Black Wolf burst from my skin, a massive, snarling beast. I didn't run away from the scent of sulfur. I ran toward it.

I let out a roar that shook the trees, a challenge to any Draven stupid enough to be this close to my territory.

*I am here,* the roar said. *Come and get me.*

As I ran into the darkness, sending my mate the other way, I knew our time was up. They were getting too close. Our secrets were slipping out.

The space between enemies was closing in, and soon, we'd have nowhere left to hide.

# CHAPTER 18

# DAMIEN

The scent of sulfur and rot was a lie.

I tore through the underbrush in my black wolf form, my paws digging into the damp earth as I chased the Draven scout I had sensed just moments before. The trail was obvious, almost suspiciously so. A strong, pungent scent led straight from the mill ruins into the dangerous ravines at the edge of Ashen Ones' territory.

At first, all I wanted was to catch the intruder, kill him, and drag his body back to the border as a warning. But when I crossed the second ridge, the trail suddenly disappeared.

The scent didn't fade away. It just stopped, as if the wolf had vanished into the mist.

I slid to a stop, my claws digging deep into the soil. I stood there, panting in the quiet, ears turning as I listened for any sound—a twig snapping or leaves rustling.

There was nothing. Only the wind and the silent, empty forest.

*A decoy.*

The truth hit me hard, making my blood run cold. The Draven scout wasn't patrolling—he was bait. He had led the Alpha away from what mattered.

*Jazz.*

I turned and ran back the way I came, not caring about the pain in my shoulders. Panic, cold and sharp, took over. I had left her alone. I told her to take the creek bed, thinking I was protecting her. Instead, I had made it easier for them.

I ran faster than ever before. The trees blurred into a tunnel of gray and black. My heart pounded in my chest, beating out a desperate rhythm: *No, no, no.*

As I neared the mill ruins, the scents hit me. Not one pack. Not just the rotting sulfur of the Dravens.

I caught the dry, dusty smell of old parchment: Shadowfangs. I also smelled the heavy, iron scent of dried blood: Grimvales.

They weren't just trespassing. They were coming together. This wasn't a fight—it was a tribunal.

I burst into the clearing by the creek bed, shifting forms as I leaped. The pain of changing tore through me, bones snapping and healing in seconds, but I kept moving. I landed on my human feet, stumbled, and reached for the knife strapped to my ankle.

"Get away from her!" I roared, the sound tearing from my throat raw and primal.

What I saw stopped me cold.

Jazz stood with her back to the rock wall of the ravine. She wasn't shifting—she knew she couldn't overpower them—but she refused to back down. She crouched in the defensive stance I'd taught her, her face pale but her eyes fierce. She gripped a jagged stone from the riverbed in her hand.

Twelve wolves surrounded her, forming a tight, unbreakable semi-circle.

They didn't attack. They waited.

Four huge, scarred Grimvale wolves stood on the left, baring their yellow teeth. On the right, four sleek, gray Shadowfangs paced quietly, their eyes sharp and searching for weakness.

And in the center, flanked by his personal guard, stood Elford.

He wasn't in wolf form. He stood there as a man, dressed in dark tactical gear, looking every bit the warlord he wanted to be. His arms were crossed, and a smug, victorious smile twisted his scarred lips.

"You're late, Ashford," Elford sneered, his voice echoing off the canyon walls. "We were just getting acquainted with your little... pet."

I stepped forward, putting myself between the pack and Jazz. I was naked, shivering from the shift and the cold mist, with only a knife and my anger. But I didn't feel any of it. All I felt was the sharp clarity of someone who knows he's walking to his own execution.

"This is Ashen territory," I snarled, my voice vibrating with Alpha power. "You are trespassing. By the laws of the Codex, I have the right to slaughter every single one of you."

"The Codex?" Elford laughed, a harsh, barking sound. He gestured to the wolves around him. "We aren't here to break the Codex, Damien. We're here to enforce it."

From the shadows of the Grimvale line, a man stepped forward. It wasn't Kane, their Alpha, but his Second—a giant of a man named Brone, known for his absolute loyalty and absolute cruelty.

"We received a tip," Brone rumbled, his voice like grinding stones. "An anonymous tip that the Ashen Alpha was harboring a fugitive. That he was consorting with the enemy."

From the Shadowfang line, a woman emerged. She was lithe, sharp-featured, her eyes like polished flint. Vesper, Selene's Second. The spy.

"We didn't believe it, of course," Vesper said, her voice silky and dangerous. "Damien Ashford, the grieving son, the dutiful Alpha? Surely he wouldn't risk the Throne for a roll in the hay with a pacifist."

She took a step closer, inhaling deeply, her nose wrinkling in distaste. "But the nose doesn't lie, does it? The scent is... overwhelming."

I stiffened. I knew what they smelled.

They didn't just smell Jazz. They smelled *us*.

We had made love in the pine needles less than an hour ago. My scent covered her skin—possession, claiming, lust. Her scent was on me, too. It wasn't just two people standing close; it was the scent of a bond that had been fully formed.

"She is a Snow," I said, my voice steady despite the adrenaline crashing through my system. "I found her trespassing. I was interrogating her."

"Interrogating her?" Elford mocked, taking a step toward me. "Is that what we call it now? Is that why she smells like your come and your sweat? Is that why you're standing here naked, protecting her like a she-wolf guarding her pup?"

He turned to the other wolves, spreading his arms wide. "Look at him! The righteous Damien Ashford! The man who claims he is fit to be King! He breaks the most sacred law of the Challenge before the first battle is even fought!"

"I have broken nothing!" I roared, tightening my grip on the knife. "She is a rogue element! I was handling it!"

"You were mating with it!" Brone shouted, spitting on the ground. "A Snow! A weakling! You pollute the bloodline of the Alphas!"

"It's treason," Vesper added quietly, the word landing heavier than the shout. "To the Challenge. To the Alliance. To your own father's memory."

I glanced back at Jazz. She hadn't moved. She was

staring at me, her eyes wide with horror—not for herself, I realized, but for me. She knew what this meant. She knew that by existing, by letting me love her, she had just handed my enemies the weapon they needed to destroy me.

"Damien," she whispered, her voice barely audible over the rushing stream. "Run."

"No," I said, locking my gaze on Elford. "I don't run."

"Then you die," Elford said simply.

He nodded to his wolves. "Kill the girl. Leave the traitor for the Council."

The four Draven wolves lunged.

**"NO!"**

I didn't think. I reacted.

I didn't shift—there wasn't time. I threw myself backward, tackling Jazz, twisting my body in mid-air to shield her with my own. We hit the hard ground, my back taking the brunt of the impact.

A set of jaws snapped shut inches from my ear. I drove my knife upward blindly, feeling it sink into fur and muscle. A yelp of pain, and the weight lifted.

But they were on us instantly. A Grimvale wolf bit deep into my calf, tearing muscle. I roared, kicking out with my free leg, connecting with a snout.

"Get up!" I screamed at Jazz, shoving her toward the ravine wall. "Get behind me!"

She scrambled up, grabbing the rock she had

dropped. A Shadowfang lunged for her, aiming for her throat.

She didn't freeze. She pivoted, swinging the rock with a guttural cry. It connected with the wolf's skull with a sickening crack. The wolf went down, stunned.

"Flank left!" I shouted, instinctively falling into the rhythm of our training.

She moved right away, sliding to my left to cover my blind side. We stood back-to-back in the clearing: a naked man bleeding from the leg and a woman in torn clothes holding a bloody rock, surrounded by monsters.

For a second, the attackers paused, surprised by the coordination. Surprised that the "weak" Snow female had just dropped a Shadowfang warrior.

Elford's face twisted in fury. "She fights," he snarled. "You trained her. You trained the enemy!"

"She is not the enemy!" I bellowed, blood dripping down my leg. "She is my MATE!"

The confession hung in the air, absolute and irrevocable.

I hadn't meant to say it. It was the death knell of my political ambition. But in the face of their violence, the truth tore its way out. I couldn't deny her. I wouldn't.

The silence that followed was heavy, broken only by the whimpering of the stunned wolf.

Vesper looked at me, her expression unreadable. "You admitted it. A Fated Bond with a rival pack."

"It changes nothing," I panted, shifting my stance to keep my weight off the injured leg. "The Challenge is for the strongest. If I am the strongest, who I mate with is my business."

"The Codex disagrees," Brone rumbled. "It calls for disqualification. And execution of the distraction."

"Try it," I challenged, raising the bloody knife. "Come and take her. But know this: I will kill the first three of you who step forward. And I will haunt the rest of you from the grave."

My eyes glowed gold as Alpha power surged through me, filling the clearing with a force that made the lesser wolves whine and back away. Even Brone hesitated. An Alpha protecting his mate is the most dangerous creature alive. We don't fight just to win—we fight to destroy.

Elford saw the hesitation. He knew he was losing the momentum of the mob.

"Cowards!" he screamed. "He is one man! He is bleeding! Finish it!"

He shifted.

Elford's wolf form was hideous—a mottled, scarring brown-and-black beast, lopsided from old injuries but massive and radiating malice. He launched himself at me, aiming not for my throat, but for my chest, intending to crush me with his weight.

I braced myself, ready to die, taking him with me.

But before Elford could connect, a sound pierced the night.

It wasn't a howl. It was a siren.

Loud, wailing, and distinctly human.

Blue and red lights flashed through the trees from the access road above the ravine.

"Police!" a voice boomed over a megaphone. "This is the Tallow Sheriff's Department! We have reports of a disturbance! Come out with your hands up!"

The wolves froze.

The supernatural world stayed hidden in the shadows. Being seen by humans, especially the police, was the one thing the Codex feared more than forbidden love.

Elford skidded to a halt, snarling in frustration. He looked at the lights, then back at me.

"This isn't over, Ashford," he hissed, his human voice warring with the wolf's vocal cords. "You saved her for tonight. But you lost the Throne. The Council knows. The packs know. You are a dead man walking."

He barked a sharp command. The Dravens turned and vanished into the darkness.

Brone looked at me with disgust. "You have shamed your blood, Ashford." The Grimvales followed the Dravens.

Vesper lingered for a second longer. She looked at Jazz, then at me. "Run," she mouthed silently. Then the Shadowfangs melted away like smoke.

I stood there, panting, the adrenaline crashing. My leg gave out, and I dropped to one knee.

"Damien!" Jazz was beside me instantly, her hands

pressing against the wound on my calf. "Oh my god, you're bleeding. It's deep."

"We have to go," I gritted out, trying to stand. "The police... they'll find us."

"Let them find us," she argued, tears streaming down her face mixed with dirt and blood. "You need a hospital!"

"No hospitals," I groaned. "Wolf blood... heals too fast. They'll ask questions. We have to get to the compound."

"The compound?" she asked, helping me up, her shoulder wedged under my arm to support my weight. "But the Council... they'll know."

"They already know, they already know," I said, leaning on her. The pain was intense, but what had just happened was even worse. "Elford will make sure of it. The secret is out, Jazz. We can't go back to the library. We can't go back to Tallow."

"Where do we go?" she asked, her voice trembling.

"We go to war," I whispered, looking at the dark woods. They weren't my sanctuary anymore—they were my battlefield. "I just declared it. I claimed you. I challenged them all."

I looked down at her. She was battered, terrified, and supporting a man twice her size. She hadn't run. She hadn't flinched.

"I'm sorry," I said, the guilt crushing me. "I ruined everything."

"You saved me," she corrected fiercely, tightening

her grip on my waist. "Now shut up and walk, Alpha. We have a war to win."

We vanished into the mist, leaving the ruins behind. The ambush hadn't killed us, but it had done something even more dangerous.

It had stripped us of our masks.

There were no more mechanics. No more librarians.

There was only the King, the Queen, and the army coming to take our heads.

# CHAPTER 19

# DAMIEN

The woods had stopped being a safe place. Now, they felt like an obstacle course.

My left leg dragged behind me, heavy and burning with the sharp pain of a Grimvale bite. I could feel the muscle trying to heal, hot and itchy under my torn jeans, but the wound was deep. Each step sent pain up my back, reminding me of the ambush that had just taken away all the political protection I had worked for my whole life.

Jazz was tucked under my arm, her small body holding up more of my weight than seemed possible. She didn't complain or cry. She just kept moving, quiet and determined, which made my chest hurt. She smelled like dirt, sweat, and my blood, but beneath it all was that steady, snowy scent that reminded me of home.

We moved away from the flashing blue police lights, away from the ruined mill, heading for the only place left: the Ashen Ones' compound.

"You're getting slower," Jazz whispered, her voice tight. "We need to stop. Let me look at the leg."

"No stopping," I gritted out, forcing my boot to find purchase on a mossy root. "If we stop, the adrenaline crashes. And if the adrenaline crashes, I'm not walking out of these woods."

"Damien, the Council..."

"The Council is the least of my worries," I lied. The Council was exactly my worry. "Elford didn't kill me back there because he wants me to suffer the humiliation of a formal trial. He wants the Ashen Ones to eat their own. He wants my pack to strip me of my title before he moves in for the kill."

"They won't," Jazz said fiercely. "You're their Alpha."

"I'm an Alpha who just confessed to bedding the enemy in front of witnesses," I corrected her grimly. "In their eyes, I'm already dead."

We walked on in silence for another mile. The ground got steeper as we climbed the ridge that guarded the center of my territory. The mist faded, and the forest looked bare and cold in the moonlight.

When we finally reached the edge of the compound, the welcome was just as I expected—quiet, unfriendly, and armed.

The perimeter guards, wolves I had trained and

men I had grown up with, stepped out of the shadows. They didn't bow or salute. They stood with their rifles lowered but ready, watching how I leaned on the Snow woman.

"Open the gate," I ordered. My voice was rough, but I injected every ounce of Alpha command I had left into it.

The guard on the left, a young Beta named Thorne, hesitated. "We were told... There were reports, Alpha. Of treason."

"Do I look like a traitor, Thorne?" I snarled, letting my eyes flare gold. "Or do I look like an Alpha who just fought off a Shadowfang ambush to protect our borders? Open the damn gate."

Thorne flinched at the display of dominance. The instinct to obey the Alpha was hardwired, even amidst doubt. He signaled to the tower. The heavy timber gates groaned open.

I didn't wait. I led us through, ignoring the stares from the pack members gathered in the courtyard. News spread quickly among wolves. They could smell the blood and the Snow woman at my side. The whispers had already started, a low buzz of judgment and fear.

I didn't stop at the infirmary or my cabin. I went straight to the Council Hall.

"Damien," Jazz hissed, trying to pull me toward the medical wing. "You need stitches. You need rest."

"I need a throne," I muttered. "And I need it tonight."

I kicked the doors of the Council Hall open.

The three Elders, Kai, Lyra, and Roric, were already there, sitting at the long oak table as if they had been waiting forever. The room felt stifling, thick with the smell of burning sage and disapproval.

They looked up as we entered. Their gazes didn't land on my bloody leg. They landed on Jazz.

"So it's true," Lyra said softly, her voice echoing in the cavernous room. She didn't look angry. She looked resigned. "You brought her here. Into the heart of the sanctuary."

"I brought my Mate here," I said, letting go of Jazz so I could stand by myself. The pain in my leg was sharp without her help, but I forced myself to stay upright. I was the Alpha. I wouldn't show weakness.

"A Snow," Roric spat, slamming a hand on the table. "You have doomed us, boy. Elford has already sent a runner. He claims you violated the Codex. He claims you attacked a peacekeeping force to protect a spy."

"Peacekeeping force?" I laughed, the sound rough. "Twelve wolves, Roric. Grimvales, Shadowfangs, and Dravens all together. Elford led them. That wasn't a peacekeeping force. It was an execution squad."

"And why were they there?" Kai asked, his voice calm and deadly. "Because you were meeting her.

Because you have been meeting her for weeks. Don't bother denying it, Damien. We can smell the bond from here. It reeks."

"It is a Fated Bond," Jazz spoke up. Her voice was shaking, but her chin was high. She stepped forward, out of my shadow. "He didn't choose it. Neither did I. But he saved my life tonight. And he saved your borders from being overrun by Elford's coalition."

"Silence, girl," Roric growled. "You have no voice here."

"She has my voice," I roared, the sound causing the lantern flames to flicker. "And as long as I am Alpha, that is the only voice that matters!"

"But you are not Alpha," Lyra said quietly.

The silence that followed was complete.

"What did you say?" I asked, my voice dropping to a dangerous whisper.

"You have broken the fundamental law of the Challenge," Lyra continued, standing up. She looked old, tired, but unyielding. "The Codex states that during the interregnum, the contenders must remain pure of compromised alliances. By taking a mate from a rival pack—especially one as strategically vital as the Snows—you have compromised the Ashen Ones. You are a liability."

She reached for a scroll on the table. "We have drafted the order. We are stripping you of command, Damien. We will surrender the female to Elford as a peace offering to prevent a war. And we will nominate a new champion for the Challenge."

Jazz gasped, stepping back toward me. I felt her terror spike, sharp and acrid.

Surrender her to Elford. They were going to feed her to the wolves to save their own skins.

A cold, dark understanding came over me. This was the moment I had dreaded since I first saw her in the garage. Duty and love were about to collide.

I could accept their judgment. I could let them strip me of my title, run with Jazz into the wilds, and live as a rogue until Elford hunted us down.

Or I could destroy the whole system.

I looked at the scroll in Lyra's hand. I looked at Roric's hand hovering near his knife. I looked at Kai's calculating eyes.

"You're right," I said.

Jazz looked at me, betrayal flashing in her eyes. "Damien?"

"You're right," I repeated, limping toward the table. "The Codex does forbid a contender from forming compromised alliances. It forbids pack-mixing without the sanction of the King."

I reached the table and placed my bloody hands on the wood, leaning in close to Lyra.

"But here is the problem, Elders. There is no King."

I let the words linger.

"The Throne is empty," I continued, my voice gaining strength. "The King is dead. Murdered, as we established, by the very wolf you now want to appease. And because there is no King, there is no final arbiter of the Codex."

"The Council interprets the Codex in the King's absence," Kai argued, though he looked unsure.

"Interpretations are for peacetime," I snapped. "This is war. And in war, the only law is power."

I stood up straighter, ignoring the pain in my leg. I reached into my belt and pulled out my ceremonial dagger, the one my father gave me. I slammed it into the table, right through the middle of the scroll Lyra was holding.

"You want to cite the law? Let's cite the law." I pointed to the dagger. "Article 4, Section 7 of the Throne Laws. *'In the event of a dispute regarding the eligibility of a contender, the accused has the right to bypass the Council and appeal directly to the Throne.'*"

"There is no Throne to appeal to!" Roric shouted.

"Exactly," I said, showing a cold, wild grin. "Which means the only way to settle this is to fill the Throne."

I looked at Jazz. She was watching me, her eyes wide, understanding beginning to dawn.

"I am issuing the *Alpha's Gambit,*" I declared.

The Elders froze. The color drained from Lyra's face.

"You can't," she whispered. "That hasn't been invoked in three hundred years. It's suicide."

"It's the only way," I said. "The Gambit states that if a contender's legitimacy is questioned, he can demand an immediate, total resolution. No more delays. No more political maneuvering. No more waiting for the moon cycles."

I turned to the open doors of the hall, speaking to the night, the pack, and the enemies out in the woods.

"I am claiming that only the King has the right to judge my bond with Jazz Snow. Therefore, until there is a King, no judgment can be passed. And to ensure there is a King..."

I turned back to the Council, my eyes full of fierce conviction.

"...I am moving the timeline up. I challenge them all. Not one by one. Not in a month. Now."

"You want to fight Elford, Kane, and Selene simultaneously?" Kai asked, horrified.

"No," I said. "I want to fight them consecutively. A gauntlet. I am sending the formal declaration tonight. I challenge every Alpha to the Stone Circle in three days. I will fight them until I am the last one standing, or until I am dead."

I took Jazz's hand and pulled her close. "And when I win, when I am King, my first act will be to approve this bond. I'll rewrite the Codex. I'll make her my Queen, and anyone who questions it will answer to the Throne."

I looked at Roric. "So, you have a choice, Elder. You can strip me of my command, hand me over to Elford, and watch as he enslaves this pack. Or you can back your Alpha, send the challenge, and bet everything on me."

The room stayed quiet for a long, tense moment. The only sounds were the torches crackling and my rough breathing.

Finally, Roric took his hand off his knife. He looked at the dagger embedded in the table. He looked at the blood dripping from my hands.

"He's crazy," Roric muttered. "Completely crazy."

"He's his father's son," Lyra said quietly. She looked at me with a hint of respect in her eyes. "The Gambit is accepted. If you die, Damien, the Ashen Ones die too."

"If I lose, we were dead anyway," I said.

Kai stood up. "I will send the runners. The challenge will be issued to the Dravens, the Grimvales, and the Shadowfangs. The Stone Circle. Three days."

He paused, looking at Jazz. "And the Snows?"

"The Snows are exempt," I said quickly. "They are neutral."

"Not anymore," Kai said, gesturing to Jazz. "She is here. She is a Snow. If you win, you unite the packs. If you lose... the Snows will be the first casualty."

I squeezed Jazz's hand. "Then I won't lose."

"Get him to the infirmary," Lyra ordered, waving a hand. "Patch him up. If he's going to fight three Alphas in three days, he needs more than adrenaline holding him together."

I pulled the dagger from the table, sheathed it, and

turned to leave. Jazz walked beside me, her shoulder once again taking my weight.

We left the Council Hall and stepped into the cold night. The pack was still watching, but something had changed. They didn't see a traitor now. They saw someone who had just risked everything on a fight he might not win.

"You're insane," Jazz whispered as we moved toward the medical cabin. "You challenged all of them? Elford? That giant Grimvale guy?"

"It was the only move," I said, feeling the pain start to break through the adrenaline. "It gives us time. Elford can't touch us for three days. The Codex doesn't allow violence against a challenger after the Gambit is called. We're safe until the fight."

"And then?" she asked, her voice trembling.

"And then I kill them," I said simply. "Or they kill me."

We reached the infirmary door. I stopped, leaning heavily against the frame, and turned to face her. I brushed a smudge of dirt from her cheek.

"I told you," I said quietly. "I'd do anything to keep you safe. I just started the fire."

She looked at me, her blue eyes filled with fear and a fierce, devastating love. "Then let it burn," she whispered.

She opened the door, and we went inside, leaving the politics behind for the clean smell of antiseptic and the reality of the war I had just started.

The Alpha's Gambit had begun. Time was running out.

Three days.

I had three days to heal, three days to get ready, and three days to say goodbye to the woman I was risking my life to save.

## CHAPTER 20
# DAMIEN

The sky above the Ashen Ones' compound shifted from a bruised, ugly purple to the usual, unyielding gray of a Maine morning. I sat on the edge of my narrow cot in the infirmary, staring at the wall. My leg throbbed with a deep, steady ache that matched the pounding in my head. The Grimvale bite was healing fast, thanks to my wolf blood, but the muscle underneath was stiff and sore, protesting every move.

Jazz slept in the chair beside me, curled up under a rough wool blanket. Her hand dangled off the armrest, fingers almost touching the floor. Even asleep, worry tightened her face. She looked too small for the fight I had brought to our door.

*Three days.*

The words echoed in my head, mocking me. I had challenged three Alphas to a gauntlet. Kane, the mountain of muscle who snapped spines for sport. Selene, the shadow who killed with poison and whispers. And Elford, the butcher who had murdered my father.

It was madness. It was suicide. And it was the only reason Jazz was still breathing in that chair instead of being dragged to the Draven marshlands.

I stood up, testing the leg. It held, though a sharp bolt of pain shot up my hip. I gritted my teeth and walked to the window.

The compound was waking up, but not with the usual morning routines of training and patrols. Instead, there was a quiet, urgent energy, like a siege. Wolves sharpened weapons. Guards doubled their shifts. The air smelled of ozone and fear. Everyone knew what was coming. They knew I had risked their lives on a gamble.

A commotion at the main gate drew my attention.

The heavy timber doors, usually barred tight, were groaning open. A runner—one of my perimeter scouts—sprinted into the courtyard, shifting mid-stride from a grey wolf to a stumbling, panting human boy.

"Alpha!" he screamed, his voice cracking. "They're here! At the line!"

I didn't need to ask who. The sudden shift in the wind told me. The clean pine scent of my territory was suddenly overpowered by the stench of sulfur, rot, and arrogant power.

*Elford.*

He hadn't waited for a messenger. He had come himself.

I grabbed my shirt from the back of the chair, pulling it on with a hiss of pain. Jazz stirred, her eyes fluttering open.

"Damien?" she murmured, groggy, confused. "What's happening?"

"Stay here," I ordered, my voice leaving no room for argument. I grabbed my ceremonial dagger from the bedside table and strapped it to my belt. "Don't come out, Jazz. No matter what you hear."

"It's him, isn't it?" she asked, sitting up, the blanket falling away. Her eyes were wide, the blue iris rimmed with gold. The wolf in her knew.

"It's a parley," I said grimly. "Under the banner of the Challenge. He can't attack. But he can talk. And I need to hear what he has to say."

I walked out before she could argue, closing the infirmary door with a heavy click.

I limped across the courtyard. The pack parted for me, their eyes wide, fearful, desperate for reassurance. I didn't look at them. I kept my chin high, my face a mask of cold, unyielding stone. I was the Alpha. If I looked afraid, they would break.

I reached the open gates.

Elford stood ten yards past the gate, surrounded by his personal guards—four huge, scarred men who looked more like bears than wolves. He carried no weapons and wore no armor. Instead, he wore a simple, expensive black suit that looked out of place against the muddy forest edge.

He looked relaxed. He looked victorious.

"Ashford," he called out, his voice smooth and oily, carrying easily over the distance. "You look terrible. That leg give you trouble? Brone has a nasty bite. I'm surprised you haven't succumbed to the infection yet."

I walked out to meet him, stopping five yards away. The neutral ground.

"The leg is fine," I lied, keeping my weight evenly distributed. "It'll be strong enough to stomp your skull into the dirt in three days."

Elford laughed. It wasn't an evil cackle, just a real, amused chuckle. He shook his head and glanced at his guards, as if sharing a private joke.

"Three days," he repeated, turning back to me. "The Alpha's Gambit. I have to admit, Damien, I didn't think you had the stones. Stupid? Yes. Suicidal? Absolutely. But bold. Your father would have been... well, he probably would have been disappointed in your lack of strategy, but impressed by the theatrics."

The mention of my father sent a surge of red-hot rage through my veins. My wolf snarled in my head, demanding I rip out Elford's throat. *Murderer. Coward.*

"Keep his name out of your mouth," I growled. "You're here to accept the terms, Elford. So accept them and get off my land."

"Oh, I accept," Elford said, spreading his hands wide. "We all accept. Kane is sharpening his axe as we speak. Selene is brewing something nasty. And me? I'm just looking forward to the show."

He took a step closer, violating the unwritten rule of personal space. His eyes, usually a dull mud-brown, flashed with a sickly yellow light.

"You realize what you've done, don't you?" he lowered his voice to a conspiratorial whisper. "You didn't just challenge us. You united us. Kane hated me last week. Selene wouldn't return my calls. But now? Now we have a common cause. We have a rabid dog that needs to be put down before it infects the rest of the pack."

"I'm not the infection," I said coldly. "I'm the cure. You're the rot, Elford. You've been poisoning the clans for years. You killed the King because you knew you couldn't beat him in a fair fight. And you're terrified because you know you can't beat me either."

Elford's smile faded. For a moment, I saw the raw, hateful envy underneath.

"You think you're special," he hissed. "Because you have the bloodline? Because you sit in your high tower and preach about honor? You're nothing, Damien. You're a boy playing at war. And your Gambit? It's a joke."

He gestured to the woods behind him. "Do you think Kane is going to fight fair? Do you think Selene is going to announce her attacks? You challenged three Alphas to consecutive combat. By the time you get to me—if you even get to me—you will be a piece of meat. You will be bleeding, broken, and exhausted. And I..."

He smiled again cruelly, baring teeth. "...I will be fresh. I will be waiting. And I will take my time."

"Then why come here?" I asked, refusing to let his psychological warfare land. "If my death is so certain, why are you standing at my gate at dawn? Why aren't you preparing?"

"Because I wanted to see the look on your face," Elford admitted. "I wanted to see the realization set in. The moment you understand that you haven't saved anyone. You've just delayed the inevitable."

He glanced past me, toward the infirmary building. He took a deep breath, inhaling the scent of the compound.

"She's in there, isn't she?" he asked softly. "The Snow girl. Jazz."

My hand twitched toward my knife. "She is none of your concern."

"She smells delicious," Elford murmured, his tongue darting out to wet his lips. "Like vanilla and fear. And power. A newly turned Snow... that's rare, Damien. That's a trophy."

"If you touch her," I said, my voice dropping to a subsonic rumble that shook the gravel between us, "I won't kill you in the Circle. I will drag you into the woods, and I will peel the skin from your body while you are still breathing. I will make you beg for the release of death, and I will deny it."

Elford stared at me. For a second, just a split second, I saw fear in his eyes. He saw the monster I was holding back. He saw the depths I was willing to sink to.

Then he laughed it off, stepping back.

"Big words for a dead man," he scoffed. "But here is my promise to you, Ashford. Listen closely, because I want this to be the last thing you think about before I rip your heart out in the Stone Circle."

He raised his voice, pitching it so that every guard on the wall, every wolf in the courtyard, could hear him.

"When you fall in the Circle, the Gambit ends. The immunity ends. And the moment your heart stops beating, my pack will overrun this compound. We will burn your hall. We will enslave your wolves."

He pointed a finger at the infirmary.

"And her? I won't kill her. Not immediately. I'm going to take her. I'm going to bond with her. I'm going to make her watch as I dismantle everything you ever loved, and then, when she has nothing left but despair, I will mount her head on the spikes of my gate right next to yours."

A heavy silence followed. The birds in the trees stopped singing. Even the wind seemed to pause.

It was a declaration of war. It was a promise of cruelty.

My vision went red. The urge to lunge, to break the

truce, to silence that foul mouth was overwhelming. My muscles coiled, ready to spring.

But that was what he wanted. He wanted me to attack him under the banner of parley. He wanted me to forfeit the Challenge so his guards could gun me down right here, right now.

I forced myself to breathe. In. Out. I forced the wolf down.

"Get off my land," I said. My voice was quiet. Deadly calm.

Elford smirked, adjusting his cuffs. "See you in three days, Damien. Try to get some sleep. You look like you need it."

He turned and walked away, his guards falling in step behind him. They didn't run. They sauntered. They walked away with the arrogance of men who had already won.

I stood there until they disappeared into the tree line, until the stench of sulfur began to fade, replaced by the crisp morning air.

Then, I turned back to my pack.

They were staring at me. I saw the fear in their eyes. I saw the doubt. They had heard the threat. They had heard the promise of slavery and ruin. They were looking at my injured leg, at the exhaustion in my face, and they were doing the math. One against three.

I couldn't let the fear take root.

"You heard him!" I shouted, my voice booming across the courtyard. "You heard the threat! He thinks we are already dead! He thinks the Ashen Ones are sheep waiting for the slaughter!"

I limped forward, sweeping my gaze across the ramparts.

"He is wrong! Elford relies on fear because he has no honor! He relies on numbers because he has no strength! He came here this morning not to gloat, but because he is *terrified*!"

I pointed to the gate.

"He is terrified because for the first time in history, an Alpha had the guts to call his bluff! He knows that in three days, he has to stand alone in the Circle against *me*. And he knows that when he stands alone, he falls!"

A few wolves nodded. A murmur of agreement started.

"Let him have his threats!" I roared. "Let him have his alliances! We have the truth! We are the Ashen Ones! We are the shield of the forest! And in three days, I will bring you his head!"

The pack erupted. It started as a low growl and built into a howl, a collective, defiant scream against the coming dark. It wasn't a howl of victory, but of unity. They were scared, yes. But they were angry. And anger was better than despair.

I held the moment for as long as I could, letting the energy wash over me, feeding my own depleted reserves. Then, I turned and walked back toward the infirmary.

Out of sight in the shadow of the porch, I sagged against the wall. My leg was on fire. My hands were shaking.

The speech had been good. The bravado was needed.

But Elford was right about one thing.

By the time I get to him, after fighting Kane and Selene, I would be broken. I would be running on fumes.

I pushed the door to the infirmary open.

Jazz was standing in the middle of the room. She was fully dressed in the spare clothes I had given her. She was pale, her hands clenched into fists at her sides.

She'd heard it all.

"He's going to kill you," she whispered. The reality of it was in her eyes—the sheer, mathematical impossibility of the Gambit.

"He's going to try," I said, closing the door and locking it.

"He said..." Her voice cracked. "He said he would take me. That he would... bond with me."

I crossed the room in two strides, ignoring the pain, and pulled her into my arms. I buried my face in her hair, holding her so tight it must have hurt, but she clung back just as fiercely.

"He won't touch you," I vowed into her hair. "I swear it, Jazz. He will never put a hand on you."

"You can't fight three Alphas, Damien," she

sobbed, burying her face in my chest. "It's not possible. Kane is a giant. Selene is a witch. And Elford... he's evil."

"I don't have to be stronger than them," I said, pulling back to look at her. I cupped her face, wiping away the tears with my thumbs. "I just have to be more desperate."

"That's not a strategy!" she yelled, pulling away. She paced the small room, her wolf energy spiking. "That's a suicide note! You're injured! You're exhausted! And you just provoked him into promising a massacre!"

"I provoked him into fear," I corrected. "Elford is arrogant. That's his weakness. He thinks I'm foolish, so he'll underestimate me. He thinks I'll be dead before I reach him, so he won't prepare for a real fight."

"And Kane?" she asked, stopping to look at me. "Is he going to underestimate you?"

"No," I admitted. "Kane is going to try to break me in half in the first ten seconds. Which is why I need to be ready."

I walked over to the supply cabinet and started pulling out bandages and salves. "I need you to help me, Jazz."

"Help you what? Pack? Run?"

"Train," I said. "I have three days. I can't heal the leg fully, but I can reinforce it. I can study their fighting styles. I need you to be my sparring partner. I need you to be my second."

"I'm a librarian!" she cried, throwing her hands up. "I've been a wolf for two weeks! How can I help you beat three Alphas?"

"Because you know something they don't," I said, looking at her with total seriousness. "You know what it's like to fight when you're terrified. You know what it's like to be the underdog. All these Alphas... they're used to being the biggest thing in the room. They've forgotten what it's like to survive."

I walked over to her, taking her hands.

"You survived the woods. You survived the shift. You survived the ambush. You have a grit that they don't have, Jazz. I need that. I need you to remind me that survival isn't about being the biggest. It's about refusing to stay down."

She looked at me, searching my face. The fear was still there, vast and consuming. But underneath it, I saw the steel. The Snow backbone that my father had always underestimated.

"Three days," she whispered.

"Three days," I confirmed.

"And if you die?"

"Then you run," I said. "You run to the coast. You take a boat. You disappear. You don't look back."

She shook her head slowly. "No. If you die... I'm not running."

Her eyes flared with that familiar, pale blue fire.

"If you die, Damien, I'm going to kill Elford myself."

It was a ridiculous statement. She wouldn't last five seconds against Elford. But the ferocity of it, the absolute loyalty in her voice, mended something in my chest I hadn't realized was broken.

"Deal," I said, leaning down to kiss her forehead.

The threat outside was real. The promise of death hung over the compound like a shroud. The pack was on high alert, jumpy and terrified.

But here, with the woman willing to fight monsters for me, I felt unstoppable.

Let them come. Let Kane bring his axe. Let Selene bring her poisons. Let Elford bring his hate.

I was the Alpha of the Ashen Ones. I was the son of the King. And I was fighting for my Mate.

They were going to need more than threats to stop me.

## CHAPTER 21
# DAMIEN

The neutral ground wasn't peaceful. Violence just waited there, held back by old laws and a thin layer of mistrust.

The clans called the meeting place Blackwood Lodge. It stood on a rocky point above the rough Atlantic, close to Snow territory but never truly owned. Built from heavy timber and stone three centuries ago, it smelled of salt, cedar, moss, and trunks.

I limped up the stone path, my leg throbbing with each step. Roric, my Second for this mess, walked beside me in his formal leathers, collar high and silver hair pulled back tight. He looked like a true elder of the Ashen Ones, but I could sense his anxiety. He didn't think we could win. To him, this felt like a funeral—mine.

"We are walking into a den of vipers," Roric

murmured, his voice low enough to be lost to the wind.

"It is better than waiting for them to strike in the dark," I replied, keeping my eyes on the heavy oak doors of the lodge. "Besides, vipers don't strike when you're looking them in the eye. They wait until you blink."

"I don't plan on blinking."

Two huge, silent wolves stood guard at the doors. They were lone shifters, arbiters who had left their packs to serve the Codex. Dangerous and loyal only to the Challenge, they nodded as we approached and opened the doors.

Inside, the lodge was one large room with a huge round table made from a single piece of ancient redwood. The air was hot from the fire and heavy with the clashing scents of four Alpha wolves.

They were already there.

To the west sat Kane, the Alpha of the Grimvales. He was a mountain of a man, even seated. His skin was a map of scar tissue, pale and puckered, a testament to the brutal initiation rites of his mountain clan. He wore no shirt, only a fur vest, displaying the thick cords of muscle that made him the most physically feared wolf in the alliance. His Second, Brone—the man who had bitten me—stood behind him like a stone sentinel. Kane didn't look at me. He was sharpening a massive combat axe with a whetstone, the rhythmic shhh-shhh-shhh sound filling the silence.

Selene of the Shadowfangs sat to the east. Where Kane was solid, she was sharp. She was slim and elegant, dressed in dark silk that probably hid many blades. Her hair was a mass of black curls, and her violet eyes were cold and curious. She watched me like a scientist studying something doomed. Behind her stood Vesper, the spy who once let us escape. Vesper glanced at my leg, then looked away.

And to the south, lounging in his chair with his feet up on the sacred table, was Elford.

The Draven Alpha grinned as I entered, a flash of white teeth in a face that was handsome in a cruel, jagged way. He was still wearing the suit from this morning, though he had loosened the tie. Behind him stood a brute I didn't recognize, a new bodyguard to replace the ones I had threatened.

"Well, look who finally dragged himself in," Elford drawled, swinging his legs down. "I was beginning to think the infection had set in early."

I ignored him, limping to the northern chair—the seat of the Ashen Ones. Roric took his place behind me. I placed my hands on the table, leaning forward to take the weight off my injured leg.

"I am here," I said, my voice flat. "Let us begin."

From the shadows near the hearth stepped the High Arbiter. His name was Silas, a wolf so old his fur had turned completely white decades ago. He was the Codex's living memory, the keeper of its lore.

Silas shuffled to the head of the table, placing a heavy, iron-bound book on the wood.

"The terms of the Gambit are ancient," Silas continued. "It bypasses the Council and the waiting period. It is a demand for immediate judgment by combat."

"The Defenders fight to protect their claim to the Throne."

He looked around the table. "Do all parties understand the gravity of this meeting?"

"We understand that Ashford has a death wish," Kane rumbled. His voice sounded like boulders grinding together deep underground. He finally stopped sharpening his axe, slamming it onto the table with a sound that made the wood groan. "I just want to know how long I have to wait to kill him."

"You will wait your turn, mountain dog," Selene said softly, her violet eyes narrowing. "The Gambit requires order. We are not savages."

"Speak for yourself," Elford chuckled. "I'm feeling pretty savage today."

I looked at Silas. "Define the terms, Arbiter. I have limited time."

Silas opened the book, the parchment crackling. "The rules are as follows. The Challenger, Damien Ashford, must defeat all three rival Alphas in the Stone Circle. The fights will be consecutive."

"Consecutive?" Roric interrupted, his hand gripping the back of my chair. "No rest period? That is a slaughter. Even the strongest Alpha needs time to heal between shifts."

"The Throne does not rest," Silas said simply. "The King must be able to hold the line against all enemies, at all times. If the Challenger cannot endure three battles, he is not fit to wear the Crown."

I silenced Roric with a gesture. "I accept the term. Consecutive."

Silas nodded. "There will be a ten-minute window between bouts. Enough to clear the dead, but not enough to sleep. The Challenger may receive medical attention from his Second during this window, but no magical healing or adrenal stimulants are permitted."

"Medical attention," Elford mocked. "You'd better bring a mop, Roric. You're going to need it to clean up what's left of him."

Silas ignored the interruption. "The fights will be to the death, or until the opponent is incapacitated and unable to rise for a count of ten. However, given the nature of the Gambit, death is the expected outcome."

I looked at the three Alphas. I had no intention of just knocking them out. Elford wanted to enslave my pack. Kane was a killer. Selene used poison. If I let them live, I wouldn't survive.

"I accept," I repeated.

"Now," Silas said, peering over his spectacles. "The order of combat."

This was the key moment. If I fought Kane first, I'd

be worn out. If I fought Selene first, I might get poisoned or crippled early. Elford had to be last—not just for the story, but because he was the one behind it all.

"I want the Draven last," I said, pointing a finger at Elford. "He is the architect of this treason. He dies at the end."

"I have no objection to watching my colleagues soften you up," Elford grinned, spreading his hands. "Put me at the end of the line, Silas. I like a grand finale."

"That leaves the Grimvale and the Shadowfang," Silas noted. "By ancient tradition, the order is determined by the drawing of lots."

He produced a leather pouch from his robes. Inside were three stones, each carved with the sigil of a clan.

"Draw, Challenger."

I reached into the bag. My fingers brushed the cold, smooth stones. I pulled one out and slapped it onto the table.

A stylized eye. The Shadowfang.

Selene smiled, a thin, chilling expression. "Ladies first. How chivalrous."

I reached in again. A mountain peak.

Kane.

And finally, the claw mark of Draven.

"So," Silas declared. "The order is set. First, Selene of the Shadowfangs. Second, Kane of the Grimvales. Third, Elford of the Dravens."

I worked it out quickly. Facing Selene first meant I'd need speed and sharp thinking. I'd have to avoid her poisons. If I made it past her, I'd be tired and then face Kane, who fought with brute strength. If I survived that, I'd have to fight Elford with nothing left.

They had set this up to kill me.

"Weapons?" Kane grunted, tapping his axe.

"The Stone Circle is a place of primal law," Silas recited. "No firearms. No modern technology. Alphas may fight in human form with traditional cold steel, or in wolf form with tooth and claw. Shifting is permitted at will during combat."

"I assume poison is considered 'traditional'?" I asked, looking at Selene.

"It is the heritage of my people," Selene shrugged. "Just as brute strength is the heritage of the Grimvales. Would you ask a wolf to dull its claws?"

"If the poison is biological or applied to traditional blades, it is permitted," Silas ruled.

Roric stiffened behind me. "Damien, if she cuts you with nightshade or wolfsbane, you won't make it to the second round. Your healing factor will be consumed fighting the toxin."

"Then I don't get cut," I said, keeping my voice steady despite the cold knot forming in my gut.

"One final matter," Elford interjected, leaning forward. His eyes gleamed with malice. "The stakes."

"The stakes are the Throne," Silas said.

"No," the Draven corrected. "Those are the stakes

for him. If he wins, he becomes King. We bow, we scrape, we pledge fealty. But what if he loses?"

"If the Challenger falls," Silas said, "his claim is nullified. The remaining Alphas will resume the standard Challenge cycle after a period of mourning."

"Boring," Elford yawned. He looked at me, his gaze predatory. "The boy raised the stakes when he brought his pet into the mix. He invoked the Gambit to protect a forbidden bond."

He turned to the Arbiter. "I propose an amendment. If Damien Ashford falls, the Ashen Ones are not just leaderless. They are forfeit. Their territory is divided among the victors. And the Snow female... the 'Mate'... becomes the property of the victor of the final round."

Roric exploded. "You cannot wager a living soul, Elford! That is slavery! It violates the fundamental rights of the Codex!"

"The Codex protects pack members," Elford countered smoothly. "The Snow girl is a rogue element. She is an unclaimed wolf from a neutral pack involved in an illegal union. She has no rights under the Challenge unless they are granted."

He looked at me. "You want to save her, don't you, Damien? That's why we're here. You want to validate your little romance. So put her on the table. If you win, she's Queen. If you lose... she's mine."

The room went silent. Kane stopped tapping his axe. Selene watched me with renewed interest.

I stared at Elford and saw what he was doing. He wanted to shake me, make me angry, make me doubt myself. But he was also giving me the only real way to keep Jazz safe. If I refused and died, they'd hunt her down. If I agreed and won, she'd be protected by my victory.

It was a terrible risk. But I'd already gone all in.

"I accept," I said, my voice ice cold.

"Damien!" Roric hissed.

"If I fall," I said, raising my voice to drown out my Second, "the Ashen Ones submit to the victors. And the Snow female... is forfeit."

I leaned across the table, locking eyes with Elford. "But listen. If I win, I'm taking more than the Crown. I'm taking your heads. Not just your lives—your heads. I'll mount them on my wall as a warning to anyone who threatens my mate again." Silas looked between us, his old face etched with sorrow. He knew he was presiding over a massacre.

"The terms are set," the Arbiter announced. "The Alpha's Gambit will commence at dawn on the third day from today. The location is the Stone Circle in the neutral valley. Until then, the Truce of the Gambit is in effect. No pack may attack another. No scouts across borders. Any violation results in immediate forfeiture."

He closed the heavy book with a thud, like a coffin lid shutting.

"This meeting is adjourned."

Kane stood up first, sheathing his massive axe across his back. He looked at me, his eyes dark pits under a heavy brow. "You bleed easily, Ashford," he rumbled. "Try to stitch yourself up. I want a fight, not a mercy killing."

He walked out, the floorboards groaning under his weight.

Selene rose with fluid grace. She paused as she passed my chair, leaning down to whisper, a scent of orchids and arsenic trailing her. "Speed kills, Damien. But hesitation kills faster. Don't hesitate with me. I certainly won't with you."

She followed Kane.

Elford was the last to rise. He buttoned his suit jacket, checking his reflection in a polished shield on the wall.

"Say goodbye to her, Damien," he said casually. "Make it a good one. Because after Wednesday, she's going to be screaming my name, not yours."

I didn't respond. I didn't rise to the bait. I simply watched him walk out, his laughter echoing in the hall.

When the doors closed, and only Roric, the Arbiters, and I remained, the silence felt heavy.

I slumped in my chair, exhaustion hitting me hard. My leg throbbed in time with my heartbeat.

"You have doomed us," Roric whispered, sinking into the chair beside me. "You bet the pack. You bet the girl. You bet everything on three fights you cannot possibly win."

"I didn't bet, Roric," I said, looking at Elford's empty chair. "I invested."

I stood up, wincing as my leg protested. "We have work to do. I need to know everything about Selene's fighting style. I need to know what poisons she favors. I need to know Kane's reach."

"It won't matter," Roric said, shaking his head. "You are injured. You are emotional. You are fighting for a woman, not for the pack. That makes you weak."

I turned to him, grabbing the lapels of his ceremonial jacket. I pulled him close, ignoring the shock in his eyes.

"That's where you're wrong, old friend," I said quietly. "Fighting for the pack is duty, and duty is heavy. It slows you down. But fighting for her? That's desperation. That's hunger."

I released him, smoothing his jacket.

"And hunger is the only thing that can beat power."

I turned and headed for the door. "Come on. I have to meet with a librarian. I need to show her how to be a Second before I can teach her to be a Queen." Out there, Jazz was waiting. She was the only thing in this world that made sense. And I had just placed her soul on the altar of war.

I hoped she'd forgive me.

I hoped I'd live long enough to ask her.

# CHAPTER 22
# DAMIEN

The Truce of the Gambit was meant to be unbreakable. It was a sacred break from violence to respect the Challenge. But as I sat in the Ashen Ones' war room, looking at the map of Tallow, I realized honor had lost its value long ago.

Twenty-four hours had passed since I issued the challenge. My leg was stiff, healing more slowly as my body saved energy for what was ahead. I was surviving on coffee, adrenaline, and sheer stubbornness.

Jazz sat across from me at the heavy oak table, reading the files Roric had gathered on Selene, the Shadowfang Alpha I would face first. She looked exhausted, with dark circles under her eyes, still wearing my oversized flannel with the sleeves rolled up. She didn't fit in among the axes and maps, but she was the only thing keeping me steady.

"Selene favors neurotoxins," Jazz murmured,

tracing a line of text with her finger. "It says here she coats her claws in a blend of paralytics derived from pufferfish and... wolfsbane?"

"Small doses," I explained, leaning back in my chair. "Not enough to kill instantly, but enough to slow your heart rate until you pass out. Then she opens your throat."

Jazz looked up, her face pale. "How do you fight that?"

"You don't get scratched," I said simply.

"And if you do?"

"Then I have about three minutes to kill her before my lungs stop working."

A heavy silence filled the room until the door banged open.

Roric walked in, looking grim. He didn't salute or say sorry for interrupting. He looked like he'd seen a ghost.

"Report," I barked, standing up. The sudden movement sent a jolt of pain through my hip, but I ignored it.

"We have a situation in sector four," Roric said. "The old lumber yard on the eastern perimeter."

Sector four was on the edge of our territory. It stored spare parts, fuel, and winter supplies. It wasn't a key military target, so it was vulnerable.

"Dravens?" I asked, my hand automatically going to the knife at my belt.

"No," Roric said, shaking his head. "Shadowfangs."

I froze. "The Truce," I whispered. "They broke it."

"Technically, no," Roric said, his voice full of disgust. "They didn't attack the compound or a patrol. They hit the supply line. And they didn't use teeth."

"What did they use?"

"Fire," Roric said. "And panic."

I didn't wait for the rest. I grabbed my leather jacket from the back of the chair. "Get the truck."

"I'm coming with you," Jazz said, standing up.

"No," I ordered, turning on her. "You stay here. If the Shadowfangs are active, the compound is the only safe place."

"I am your Second, remember?" she challenged, her chin lifting in that stubborn way that drove me crazy. "You said you needed me to help you prepare. Seeing how they fight is preparation."

I looked at her. I saw the fear in her eyes, but I also saw the resolve. She wasn't asking permission. She was stating a fact.

"Fine," I growled. "But you stay in the truck. If I tell you to run, you run. No arguments."

"Deal."

We drove to the lumber yard in silence. The black pickup sped down the logging roads, the suspension groaning as we hit potholes at sixty. The sun was setting, throwing long red shadows through the trees.

As we neared sector four, I smelled it.

Smoke. Not the clean smell of wood burning, but the harsh, chemical stink of rubber and diesel on fire.

I slammed the truck to a halt outside the chain-link fence. The gate was open, swinging lazily in the wind.

"Stay here," I told Jazz.

I climbed out, drawing my knife. Roric pulled up in the second vehicle behind me, three of my best enforcers jumping out with rifles.

We moved into the yard.

The place was wrecked. Fuel tanks had been split open and set on fire. The spare trucks were just blackened shells. The warehouse roof had caved in.

But the silence was what unsettled me. Four guards were supposed to be here.

"Check the perimeter!" I shouted to the enforcers. "Find them!"

I moved toward the main office, a small portable building near the center of the yard. The door was unlocked.

I pushed it open and stepped inside.

The smell of almonds and rot hit me instantly.

Three of my men were inside. They weren't dead. They were sitting at the table, playing cards. Their eyes were open, staring blankly at the wall. Their chests were rising and falling in a slow, shallow rhythm.

I walked over to the nearest one—a young wolf named Miller. I waved my hand in front of his face. He didn't blink. I checked his pulse. It was thready, barely there.

"They've been dosed," Roric said from the doorway. He was holding a small, empty vial he had found on the floor. "Nightshade and poppy. It's a waking coma."

"They didn't fight?" I asked, looking around the room. There was no sign of struggle. No overturned chairs. No blood.

"They didn't even know they were under attack," Roric said grimly. "The Shadowfangs must have slipped it into the coffee or the water supply. They neutralized the post without throwing a single punch."

I went back outside, anger burning in my gut. This wasn't just an attack—it was a message. Selene was showing me she could get to me anywhere. She wanted me to know my strength meant nothing if I couldn't see the threat coming.

A shout from the perimeter drew my attention.

"Alpha! Over here!"

I ran toward the fence line, my bad leg protesting every step. One of the enforcers was pointing toward the town.

There, just beyond the tree line, where the forest met the backyards of Tallow, smoke was rising.

Not from a lumber yard. From a house.

"They're moving into the town," the enforcer said, his voice shaking. "They aren't stopping at the perimeter."

A chill ran through me. The Truce protected the

packs, but it didn't mention the humans. It didn't protect the people of Tallow.

Selene was raising the stakes by pulling innocent people into the fight. She knew if humans started dying, the police, state troopers, and maybe even the National Guard would flood the area. The clans would have to go underground. The Gambit would be over.

Or I'd have to spread my people so thin protecting the town that I'd be left defenseless in the Circle.

"Get back in the trucks!" I roared. "We move to the town!"

I sprinted back to my pickup. Jazz was waiting, her face pressed against the glass. I ripped the door open and jumped in.

"What is it?" she asked as I peeled out of the lot, gravel spraying.

"Diversion," I spat, gripping the steering wheel so hard the leather creaked. "They hit the depot to draw us out, but the real target is the town. They're starting fires."

"Why?" Jazz asked, horrified.

"To distract me," I said. "To make me choose. Do I protect my pack, or do I protect the humans?"

We sped toward Tallow. The sun was gone, and the fires glowed against the night sky. It wasn't a huge blaze yet, but it was getting bigger.

As we hit the main road, my phone buzzed. It was a text from an unknown number.

The Shield cannot hold everything, Damien. Some things must burn.

Selene.

I threw the phone onto the dashboard.

We reached the edge of the neighborhood. A small rental house near the woods was on fire. Neighbors were out in the street, shouting and pointing. I could hear the fire truck sirens in the distance.

But I saw something else.

I saw shadows moving between the houses. Wolves—not in wolf form, but people moving with a predator's grace. They were Shadowfangs, causing chaos, cutting phone lines, and slashing tires.

"Stop!" Jazz screamed.

I slammed on the brakes.

"That's Mrs. Gable's house!" she cried, pointing to the burning structure. "She's eighty years old! She can't get out!"

I looked at the house. The front porch was an inferno. I didn't hesitate. I threw the truck into park and jumped out.

"Stay here!" I ordered Jazz again. I ran toward the house. Roric and the enforcers were right behind me.

"Handle the shadows!" I shouted to them. "Clear the streets! I'm getting the civilian!"

I kicked the front door in. The heat was a physical wall, singeing the hair on my arms. I coughed, pulling my shirt up over my nose.

"Mrs. Gable!" I roared.

A weak cough answered me from the back hallway. I stayed low, crawling under the smoke. The fire was eating the wallpaper, curling the paint. I found her in the kitchen, huddled on the floor, clutching a cat carrier. I picked her up—she was light, as fragile as a bird—and grabbed the carrier. I turned and ran back down the hallway. A beam crashed down in front of me, blocking the way.

I didn't have time to think. I used the wolf's strength, kicked the burning wood aside, and broke through the front door just as the windows exploded. I carried her to the lawn, setting her down gently as the paramedics arrived. I backed away, fading into the darkness before anyone could ask questions. I found Roric behind a hedge. He was wiping blood from a knife.

"We got two of them," he panted. "The rest scattered."

I looked around. The street was chaos. People were screaming. The fire was spreading to the next house.

"This isn't a skirmish," I said, my voice hollow. "It's a siege."

I walked back to the truck. Jazz was waiting. She had opened the door and was watching the fire, tears streaming down her face.

"They did this," she whispered. "They burned an old woman's house just to get to you?"

"Yes," I said.

We drove back to the compound in silence.

Saving Mrs. Gable felt hollow. We'd saved one person, but how many more would suffer before Wednesday?

Back in the war room, I slammed my fist onto the map. "We can't do this alone," I said. The truth made me sick.

"What?" Roric asked.

"We don't have enough people," I said, looking at the map. "The Ashen Ones are strong, but we're built for open fights. We can't police a town of five thousand against an enemy that moves like smoke. We can't fight the Grimvales in the mountains and the Shadowfangs in the streets at the same time."

I looked at Jazz.

"We need allies."

"Who?" Roric asked, exasperated. "The lone shifters are neutral. The other packs are trying to kill us."

"Not all of them," I said softly. Roric followed my gaze to Jazz.

"You cannot be serious," he said. "The Snows? They are pacifists! They don't fight!"

"They defended their territory against the Dravens," I reminded him. "They came when Jazz howled."

"That was instinct!" Roric argued. "That wasn't a military operation!"

"It was unity," I said. "And right now, that's the only thing we haven't tried."

I walked over to Jazz. She looked up at me, her eyes red-rimmed but clear.

"I need you to do something for me," I said.

"Anything."

"I need you to call your father."

She stiffened. "He won't talk to you, Damien. He thinks you're the devil."

"I know," I said. "That's why I'm not asking him to talk to me. I'm asking him to talk to you."

I grabbed a marker and circled the Snow territory on the map.

"The Shadowfangs are attacking the periphery. They are hitting the soft targets. Tallow is a soft target. But the Snows... they live in Tallow. They work there. Their children go to school there."

I looked at Jazz intensely.

"If Selene burns Tallow, the Snows burn too. Your father thinks being neutral keeps him safe. You need to tell him that fire doesn't care about neutrality."

Jazz stared at the map. She saw the logic. She saw the burning house in her mind.

"You want the Snows to police the town," she said. "While you fight the Gambit."

"Exactly," I said. "I need the Ashen Ones to guard the edges and get ready for what comes after the Challenge. I can't spare wolves to watch every street in Tallow. But the Snows are already there. They're the doctors, teachers, and neighbors. They see everything in that town."

"If they act as a watch network," I went on, "if they report Shadowfang movements and protect civilians, my pack can focus on the war."

"And if they refuse?" Jazz asked.

"Then Tallow burns," I said. "And we all lose."

Jazz took a deep breath. She reached for her phone, which was sitting on the table.

"He's going to scream at me," she warned.

"Let him scream," I said. "Just make him listen."

She dialed the number. She put it on speaker.

The phone rang once. Twice.

"Jasmine?" Her father's voice was tight, anxious. "Where are you? We've been worried sick!"

"Dad, listen to me," Jazz said, her voice steady. "I'm safe. But Tallow isn't."

"What are you talking about?"

"The Shadowfangs just firebombed Mrs. Gable's house," Jazz said.

There was a silence on the line. A heavy, stunned silence.

"That was a gas leak," her father said weakly. "The news said—"

"It wasn't a gas leak, Dad!" Jazz shouted. "I was there! Damien pulled her out!"

"Damien?" Her father's voice turned cold. "You are with him?"

"Yes, I am. And he's the only reason Mrs. Gable is alive."

"Jasmine, come home immediately."

"I can't, Dad. We are at war. And you are in the middle of it."

"I am not in a war! I am a history teacher!"

"You are a wolf!" Jazz roared, sounding so much like an Alpha that Roric raised an eyebrow. "And your territory is burning! Selene doesn't care about your neutrality! She cares about chaos!"

She took a breath, lowering her voice.

"Dad... Damien needs help."

"I will never help an Ashford."

"You're not helping an Ashford," Jazz said. "You're helping me. You're helping Mom. You're helping Mrs. Gable."

She looked at me, signaling for me to speak.

I leaned over the phone.

"Elias," I said. "This is Damien."

Silence.

"I'm not asking you to fight in the Circle," I said. "I'm not asking you to bleed for my Throne. I'm asking you to protect your home. The Shadow-fangs are moving in the shadows. My pack is too large, too noticeable, to hunt them in the streets without causing a panic. But your pack... You are invisible."

I paused.

"If you watch the town... if you keep the humans safe... I can focus on killing the ones who started this fire."

There was a long pause. I could hear Elias breathing. I could hear the murmur of Eleanor in the background.

Finally, Elias spoke.

"We do not kill."

"I don't need you to kill," I said. "I need you to witness. I need you to guard. If you see a Shadowfang, you call it in. My enforcers will handle the wet work."

Another pause.

"If we do this... it is not an alliance. It is neighborhood watch."

"Call it whatever you want," I said. "Just don't let Tallow burn."

"Fine," Elias said, the word heavy with reluctance. "We will watch. But Jasmine... if you get hurt... if he lets you get hurt..."

"I won't let her get hurt," I vowed.

"You better not."

The line clicked dead.

Jazz slumped back in her chair, exhaling a long breath.

"He agreed," she said, sounding surprised.

"He's a father," I said. "He wants to protect his family."

I looked at Roric.

"Coordinate with the Snows. Give them a direct line to our tactical team. If a Snow calls in a sighting, I want a strike team there in five minutes."

Roric nodded slowly. "It is unorthodox. But... it might work."

"It has to work," I said.

I walked to the window, looking out at the dark forest. The fire in the distance had dimmed, but the smoke still stained the sky.

We'd bought ourselves a little time. We had an ally now, even if he wasn't eager.

But when I looked at my reflection in the glass, haggard and bloody, eyes burning with exhaustion, I knew the truth.

The Shadowfangs had struck the first blow. The war had officially begun.

And I was already bleeding.

# CHAPTER 23

# JAZZ

The truce line was invisible, but tonight, it felt like a tripwire strung across the throat of my hometown.

It had been twenty-four hours since the fire at Mrs. Gable's house, and everything in Tallow felt different. The town had gone from quiet and unaware to tense and suspicious. The humans didn't know what was going on. They whispered about arsonists, gas leaks, and wild summer teens. But the animals knew. The neighborhood dogs paced their fences. The birds were silent.

I walked down Maple Street, my boots crunching on the gravel. My father, Elias, walked beside me. He wasn't in his usual tweed jacket and glasses. Instead, he wore a dark windbreaker and heavy work boots, carrying a big flashlight that looked almost like a baton.

We were the Snow pack patrol. My father liked to call it the Community Safety Watch.

"Keep your pace steady, Jasmine," he murmured, scanning the shadows between the houses. "We are observing. We are not hunting."

"Tell that to them," I whispered back, nodding toward a rustle in the hedges of the darkened park across the street.

"Squirrels," he dismissed, though his grip on the flashlight tightened.

"Squirrels don't smell like sulfur and rotting meat," I countered, my nose twitching. The scent was faint, carried on the wind coming off the marshlands, but it was there. The scent of the Dravens.

My father stiffened. He smelled it too. "They are testing the boundaries. Elford knows we agreed to watch. He wants to see if we will bite."

"And will we?" I asked, stopping under a streetlight that flickered ominously. "If they cross the street? If they break a window? At what point does 'observing' become 'cowardice'?"

"It is not cowardice to value life," he said sharply, turning to face me. "We have survived for generations by being the water, not the rock. The rock breaks. The water flows around."

"Damien says the rock is about to smash the water into vapor," I said.

"Damien Ashford is a hammer looking for a nail," my father spat. "He has corrupted you with his warmongering. Look at this. You are vibrating with aggression."

He was right. I was. My skin felt too tight, and my senses were painfully sharp. The wolf inside me, the White Wolf, was restless. I was annoyed by the slow walk and the lectures. It remembered running free at the mill. It remembered the power of shifting.

"I'm vibrating with survival," I said. "There's a difference."

We kept walking in tense silence. We passed two other pairs of Snow wolves: my cousin Sarah and her husband, and old Mr. Henderson from the bakery. They looked scared, holding their flashlights tightly. They nodded at us and hurried by, eyes wide.

We reached the edge of the neighborhood, where the neat lawns ended, and the woods of the nature preserve began. This was the most vulnerable part of Tallow. There were no streetlights and no fences.

The smell of sulfur spiked.

I stopped dead. "Dad."

"I smell it," he whispered. "Go back. We call it into Roric. We let the Ashen Ones handle it."

"Roric is ten minutes away," I said, my voice dropping to a low growl. "They are ten feet away."

From the shadows of the preserve, shapes emerged.

They weren't hiding. They weren't slinking like the Shadowfangs. They sauntered out onto the pavement, their boots heavy, their laughter crude.

Five men. They were human in form, but their eyes reflected the moonlight with a dull, yellow shine. They were big, dirty, and reeked of the marsh. Dravens.

I recognized the leader. He wasn't Elford—Elford wouldn't dirty his hands with a perimeter probe. It was a lieutenant I had seen at the ambush, a man with a jagged scar running through his eyebrow.

"Well, well," the scar-faced man drawled, stopping in the middle of the street. He held a baseball bat loosely in one hand, tapping it against his thigh. "If it isn't the History Teacher. And the... what are you? The librarian?"

My father stepped in front of me, holding up his flashlight. "This is a private neighborhood. You are trespassing. Go back to the marsh."

The Dravens laughed. It was a wet, ugly sound.

"Trespassing?" Scar-face sneered. "There are no lines anymore, old man. Didn't you hear? The Truce is for the Alphas. The rest of us? We're just... taking a walk."

He took a step forward. His men fanned out, blocking the street.

"We heard the Snows were watching the town," Scar-face continued. "Elford wanted to know what you'd do if we decided to... redecorate."

He swung the bat, smashing the mailbox of the nearest house. The metal clang echoed like a gunshot in the quiet street.

"Go home," my father warned, his voice shaking slightly. "We do not want violence."

"That's your problem," Scar-face grinned, baring yellow teeth. "We love violence."

He signaled to his men. "Grab the girl. Elford said she's property of the Gambit. Might as well take her into custody early."

My father froze. He was torn between his pacifist beliefs and his instinct to protect me. He stood his ground, but he didn't shift or attack. He waited, hoping they would stop.

But predators don't stop because you ask them nicely.

Two of the Dravens lunged.

My father raised his flashlight, a pathetic defense against wolves who could snap bones with their jaws. One of the men shoulder-checked him, sending him flying into the ditch. He hit the ground with a grunt of pain.

"Dad!" I screamed.

The other Draven grabbed my arm, his grip bruising. "Come here, little—"

I stood my ground instead of thinking or hesitating.

I twisted my arm, using the move Damien had drilled into me a hundred times. Rotate against the thumb. Drop the weight.

I broke his grip and drove my knee into his groin.

The Draven doubled over with a wheeze. I didn't

stop. I grabbed the back of his head and slammed his face into my rising knee. There was a satisfying crunch of cartilage. He dropped to the pavement, unconscious.

Silence fell over the street.

The other three Dravens stared at me. Scar-face lowered his bat, his expression shifting from amusement to confusion.

"She fights," he muttered. "The bitch fights."

"Yeah," I panted, falling into a defensive crouch, my hands raised. "She does."

"Get her!" Scar-face roared. "Shift! Tear her apart!"

The air shimmered as the three remaining men shed their human skins. Bones cracked, clothes tore, and three massive, marsh-brown wolves stood snarling on the asphalt.

My father was scrambling out of the ditch. "Jasmine! Run!"

"No!" I shouted back.

I couldn't fight three wolves in human form. I knew that. Damien had taught me the odds.

So I let go.

I reached for the heat in my chest, the molten core of the White Wolf, and I pulled it to the surface. I didn't fight the pain this time. I welcomed it. It was armor.

I shifted

It was fast. Violent. My clothes shredded, falling away as the white fur burst through. My vision sharpened into grayscale clarity. The smell of the Dravens went from unpleasant to enraging.

I roared—a high, clear sound that was pure Snow challenge—and launched myself at the nearest wolf.

We collided in mid-air. He was bigger, heavier, smelling of rot. But I was faster. I twisted, sinking my teeth into his shoulder, tasting the hot, copper tang of blood. He yelped, snapping at my neck, but I was already moving, using his own weight to throw him off balance.

We hit the ground, rolling. I scrambled free, claws scrabbling on the pavement for traction.

The second wolf lunged. I ducked, feeling his jaws snap inches from my ear. I raked my claws across his flank, leaving deep, red furrows.

Pain. That was good.

I was getting lost in the fight. The fear was gone, replaced by a cold, focused anger. This wasn't pacifism. This was defending our home.

Scar-face, now a massive, scarred wolf, circled me. He was the Alpha of this little hunting party. He looked at his bleeding packmates, then at me. He growled low, a sound that vibrated in my chest.

He charged.

I braced myself. I was going to take the hit. I was going to let him tackle me, and then I was going to rip his throat out.

But before he reached me, a grey blur slammed into him from the side.

My father.

He had shifted.

The History Teacher was gone. In his place was a sleek, grey wolf, smaller than the Draven but fighting with a desperate, parental ferocity. He hit Scar-face with enough force to knock the breath out of him, snapping at his legs, hampering his movement.

Then, from the shadows of the houses, more shapes emerged.

Mrs. Henderson's poodle started barking, but it was drowned out by the sound of shifting bones. The baker. My cousin Sarah. The quiet accountant from down the street.

The Snows were coming out of their houses.

They weren't warriors. They were clumsy, terrified, and hesitant. But they were packed.

They flooded the street, a dozen grey and white wolves forming a wall between the Dravens and me. They yipped and snarled, a cacophony of amateur aggression that was overwhelming in its sheer volume.

Scar-face scrambled to his feet, bleeding from a bite on his leg. He looked at the wall of angry neighbors. He looked at me, the White Wolf, standing bloody and triumphant in the center.

He realized he had made a mistake. He came expecting to scare weaklings, but instead found a pack of wolves who remembered their strength.

He barked a retreat order.

The Dravens turned and ran, fleeing back toward the marshlands, tails tucked between their legs.

The street went silent, save for the heavy panting of the Snow pack.

We stood there for a long moment, looking at each other. My father, in wolf form, limped over to me. He nudged my shoulder with his nose, checking for injuries. I had a long gash on my flank, and my lip was split, but I was standing.

I nudged him back. You fought.

He chuffed, a sound that sounded suspiciously like a sigh.

We shifted back.

It was chaos as bruised people hurried to grab robes and blankets from nearby porches. Usually, Snows felt embarrassed after shifting, but tonight there was no shame—just adrenaline.

I sat on the curb, pulling the remnants of my windbreaker over my chest. My side was burning. Blood was trickling down my ribs.


"Jasmine," my father said, limping over. He had wrapped a towel around his waist. He looked old, tired, and terrified. But there was something new in his eyes. Respect.

"You shifted," he said. "In the middle of the street."

"They were going to take me," I said, wincing as I touched my side. "And they were going to hurt you."

He looked at the broken mailbox. He looked at the blood on the asphalt.

"We fought," he whispered, as if he couldn't believe it. "The Snows fought."

"We had to," I said. "Neutrality doesn't stop a baseball bat, Dad."

He sat down beside me, putting his head in his hands. "Elford will retaliate. This... this is an act of war."

"We were already at war," I told him. "Now we're just admitting it."

A roar of an engine cut through the night.

Headlights swept over us, blindingly bright. A black pickup truck screeched to a halt right in the middle of the street, ignoring the lane markers.

The door flew open.

Damien was out of the truck before it stopped rocking.

He wasn't limping tonight. He was running on pure panic. He scanned the scene—the blood, the gathered Snows, the destruction. His eyes locked onto me sitting on the curb.

"Jazz!"

He covered the distance in three strides, dropping to his knees in the dirt beside me. He didn't care that my father was there. He didn't care that half the Snow pack was watching.

"Where are you hurt?" he demanded, his hands hovering over me, terrified to touch and cause more pain. His eyes were gold, blazing with Alpha fury. "I felt it. I felt the shift. I felt the fear."

"I'm okay," I said, though my voice shook. "Just a scratch on the flank. And I think I pulled a muscle kicking a guy in the balls."

He didn't smile. He gently peeled back the ruined windbreaker to inspect the gash on my side. It was deep, oozing red, but already starting to clot thanks to the wolf blood.

He swore viciously, a string of curses that would have made a sailor blush.

"Dravens?" he asked, his voice low and deadly.

"Scouts," I said. "Five of them. Led by the scar-faced one."

"They trespassed," Damien snarled. "During the Truce. I will kill them. I will hunt them down tonight and—"

"They're gone," I said, putting a hand on his chest. His heart was hammering against my palm like a trapped bird. "We drove them off."

He froze. He looked around at the gathered Snows, who were watching him with a mixture of fear and awe. He looked at my father, who was sitting silently in his towel.

"You fought?" Damien asked, looking back at me.

"We all did," I said.

Damien looked at Elias. "You broke the peace."

"They broke my mailbox," Elias said, his voice strangely flat. "And they touched my daughter."

Damien nodded slowly. It was a warrior's nod. An acknowledgment.

He turned back to me, his expression softening into pure, agonizing relief. He reached into his pocket and pulled out a small jar of salve—the same stuff he used on his own wounds.

"This is going to sting," he warned.

He applied the salve with gentle, calloused fingers. I hissed at the contact, gripping his knee. He murmured soft words of comfort—nonsense words, Alpha words—as he worked.

"You were brilliant," he whispered, his forehead touching mine. "I felt you. You didn't panic. You controlled the shift."

"I was angry," I admitted.

"Good," he said. "Anger keeps you alive."

He took off his leather jacket and put it over my shoulders. It was heavy, warm, and smelled like him. It felt like a claim.

"You can't stay here," he said, standing up and pulling me with him. "They know you're active now. They know the Snows are fighting back. They'll come back with more numbers."

"I can't leave my family," I argued.

"Your family is coming too," Damien said. He turned to the group.

"Listen to me!" his voice boomed, the Alpha command rolling over them. "The Truce is broken in spirit, if not in law. The Dravens have marked this street. You are no longer safe in your homes."

The Snows looked at each other, murmuring.

"Go to the community center," Damien ordered. "It's brick. Defensible. Roric has a squad of enforcers two streets over. I'm calling them in to guard you."

He looked at my father. "Elias. Get them moving."

My father stood up. He looked at his house, then at Damien. The hatred was still there, but it was buried under necessity.

"Sarah, Mr. Henderson," Elias called out, taking charge. "Gather everyone. Ten minutes. We move to the center."

Damien turned back to me. "I'm taking you to the compound."

"No," I said. "I stay with my pack."

"Jazz," he growled, "I need you where I can see you. I have two days before the Gambit. I can't focus if I'm terrified you're bleeding out in a gymnasium."

"You need me to be your Second," I reminded him. "But tonight, I'm a Snow. If I leave them now, after we just fought together... I lose them. They need to see that fighting works. They need to see that I'm not just your mate, but their blood."

He stared at me, frustration warring with pride. He ran a hand down his face.

"You are the most stubborn creature I have ever met."

"I learned from the best."

He sighed, defeated. "Fine. But I'm staying with you."

"You can't," I said. "The Gambit. You need to rest. You need to heal."

"I'll rest in the damn gym," he said. "Roric can bring my gear. I am not leaving you in an unsecured location with a gash in your side."

He wrapped an arm around my waist, taking my weight. "Don't argue with me, Jazz. I just watched you bleed. Let me have this."

I looked up at him. The fear in his eyes was raw. He wasn't the Alpha right now. He was just a man who had almost lost everything.

"Okay," I whispered. "You can stay."

He kissed the top of my head, holding me tight against his side.

"Let's go," he said.

We walked down the street together, surrounded by our pack. The others were still learning how to stand up for themselves.

The pacifists had fought. The line had been crossed.

As we left behind the broken glass and blood, I knew things had changed for good. Tallow was no longer just a town.

It was a fortress. And we were the garrison.

CHAPTER 24

# DAMIEN

The Tallow Community Center smelled like floor wax, stale popcorn, and the sharp, lingering scent of wolf fear. I knew that smell well. It was the scent of a pack cornered, forced to face the monster hiding in the dark.

I sat on a folding metal chair near the gym doors, my injured leg stretched out. Roric had shown up twenty minutes ago with a squad of Ashen enforcers. They were securing the perimeter, boarding up windows, and setting up patrols that matched the local police routes. Hiding a war in plain sight was tricky, but Roric knew how to do it.

Inside the gym, the Snow pack huddled together in a mess of blankets and quiet voices. There were about forty of them, mostly families. The baker. The accountant. The mechanic from the rival shop. They looked like refugees from a disaster. In a way, they were. The disaster was me.

I watched Jazz move among them. She still wore my leather jacket, the heavy black material too big for her, and she walked with a new stiffness, favoring her injured side. She talked to her cousin, handed out water bottles, and calmed a crying child. She looked exhausted and battered, but still magnificent.

Every time she winced, I felt a phantom pain in my own ribs. When her heart raced, mine did too.

The Bond.

It wasn't just a connection anymore; it was a live wire. Since the fight in the street, since she had shifted and drawn blood, the barrier between us had dissolved completely. I could feel her exhaustion like a lead weight in my own bones. I could feel her worry for her parents like a knot in my own gut.

"She is your weakness," a voice rumbled beside me.

I didn't look up. I recognized the footsteps. Elias Snow stood over me, holding two Styrofoam cups of coffee. He looked like he had aged ten years in just two hours. His windbreaker was torn, and a purple bruise marked his jaw where Draven had hit him.

"She is my strength," I corrected, accepting the coffee. It was lukewarm and tasted like mud, but the caffeine was necessary.

Elias sat in the chair next to me. It creaked under his weight. We didn't speak for a long time. We just watched the gym, two men from different worlds stuck in the same lifeboat.

"I hated your father," Elias said suddenly.

I took a sip of the coffee. "I know. He thought you were a coward. You thought he was a tyrant."

"He was a tyrant," Elias said, staring into his cup. "But he kept the Dravens in the marsh. He kept the peace in his own brutal way. I respected the result, if not the method."

He turned to look at me. His grey eyes were sharp and, right now, full of reluctant acceptance.

"You are not your father, Damien."

"Is that a compliment?"

"It is an observation," Elias said. "My father would have let the Dravens burn this gym to the ground before he asked an Ashford for help. And your father would have let them burn it just to prove a point about weakness."

He gestured to the room, to the Ashen enforcers standing by the bleachers, watching over the Snow families.

"You sent your wolves to protect us. You are sitting in a drafty gym with a leg that I know is screaming in pain, just to make sure my daughter sleeps."

"She's not sleeping," I noted, watching Jazz argue with a stubborn elderly woman about blankets.

"She never sleeps when there is work to do," Elias said, a ghost of a smile touching his lips. "She gets that from her mother."

The smile faded. Elias leaned forward, resting his elbows on his knees.

"We cannot go back to the houses," he stated. "Not tonight. Maybe not tomorrow. The Dravens marked the street. They know who we are now."

"No," I agreed. "You are active combatants. Neutrality is dead."

"So what is the proposal?" Elias asked. "You talked about an alliance on the phone. About us watching the town. Is that still the offer?"

"It has to be," I said, turning to face him. "I have three days, Elias. Three days to get ready for a fight everyone says I'll lose. If I have to worry about the Shadowfangs burning Tallow while I'm trying to figure out how to stop Kane's axe, I will lose. And if I lose..."

"We die," Elias finished. "Elford made that clear."

"Yes."

Elias took a deep breath. He looked at his pack, the civilian wolves who had found their teeth tonight. "We got lucky. But if Elford sends a real war party... we will be slaughtered."

"I don't need you to be soldiers," I said. "I already have soldiers. Roric has three squads of enforcers. What I need is coverage. You know this town. You know which alleys the delivery trucks use. You know which neighbors stay up late. You know when something feels off."

I leaned in. "I am formally requesting an alliance.

The Snow pack becomes an auxiliary unit of the Ashen Ones for the duration of the Gambit. You provide intelligence, surveillance, and early warning. In exchange, the Ashen Ones provide heavy defense. We will station guards at this center. We will patrol your streets. An attack on a Snow is an attack on an Ashford."

Elias looked at me. It was a heavy offer. It meant submitting his pack's autonomy to my command. It meant officially picking a side in a war that had destroyed his ancestors.

"And Jasmine?" he asked quietly.

"Jasmine is... complicated."

"She is not complicated," Elias said sharply. "She is Bonded. Do not insult me by pretending otherwise. I saw you with her in the street. I see you looking at her now."

He pointed a finger at my chest. "If you lose this Gambit, she is forfeit. Elford said it. You wagered her life."

"I wagered her life to save it!" I snapped, my control slipping. "If I hadn't agreed to the terms, they would have killed her in the ravine tonight. This way, she has a chance."

"A chance that depends entirely on you staying alive," Elias said. "Which brings me to my point. She cannot stay here."

I blinked, surprised. "What?"

"Look at her," Elias said, nodding toward Jazz. She had finally sat down on some gym mats, leaning against the wall, her eyes closing. "She's terrified. Not for herself, but for you. And you... You're distracted. I can smell your anxiety, Damien. It comes from her."

He lowered his voice. "The Bond works both ways, doesn't it? If she is hurt, you feel it. If she is afraid, you feel it."

"Yes," I admitted. The pain in my leg was a dull roar compared to the constant, low-level static of Jazz's distress in my mind.

"Then she is a liability if she is separated from you," Elias said, his logic ruthless. "If Elford is smart —and he is a snake, so he is smart—he won't attack you directly before the Gambit. He will attack her. He will try to terrorize her, to hurt her, just to rattle you. If she is here, in this gym, she is a target. And if she gets hurt five minutes before you step into the Circle..."

"I will fall," I whispered.

"You will shatter," Elias corrected. "So, as much as I hate it... as much as I despise the idea of my daughter in the middle of a war camp... she has to go with you."

I stared at him. This was the man who had forbidden her from seeing me. The man who had hidden her nature for twenty-four years.

"You're giving her to me?"

"I am securing the asset," Elias said, his voice hard. "She is the strongest link you have to this world, Damien. But she is also the wire they will use to choke you. Keep her close. Keep her safe. Because if you die in that Circle, I will not be able to save her from what comes next."

He stood up, crushing the empty coffee cup in his hand.

"The Snows accept the alliance," he announced formally. "We will watch the town. You watch my daughter."

He walked away before I could respond, moving to comfort his wife.

I sat there for a moment, processing. The pacifist had just given me a war lesson. The pacifist had just taught me something about war. He was right. Jazz wasn't just my motivation; she was a tactical weakness. The bond was a two-way radio I couldn't turn off. She opened her eyes as I approached. "Is everything okay? I saw you talking to my dad. Was he yelling?"

"Surprisingly, no," I said, holding out a hand. "Come on. We're leaving."

She frowned, not taking my hand. "Leaving? I told you, I'm staying with the pack. They need me."

"Your father just ordered you to go with me," I said.

Her jaw dropped. "He what?"

"He did the math," I said. "You're a target here. And if you're a target, I'm distracted. We need to consolidate our assets."

"I am not an asset," she grumbled, but she took my

hand. I pulled her up, and she swayed slightly, exhaustion hitting her. I wrapped an arm around her waist, pulling her into my side. The contact was an immediate relief, like balm on a burn. The static in my head quieted.

"You're my asset," I murmured into her hair. "Let's go home, Jazz."

We walked out of the gym, past the Ashen guards who nodded in respect. We climbed into my truck, the silence of the cab wrapping around us.

As we drove back to the compound, the reality of the next forty-eight hours hit me. I had the alliance. I had Jazz. But I still had three Alphas to face.

Roric was waiting for us in the war room when we arrived. He looked like he hadn't slept in a week. The map of Tallow was covered in new markers: red for Shadowfang sightings, blue for Snow patrol routes. "Secured?" Roric asked without looking up.

"Secured," I said, helping Jazz into a chair. She curled her legs under her, looking small in the over-sized leather chair. "Elias agreed to the alliance. The Snows are officially our eyes and ears in Tallow."

Roric nodded, marking the gym with a blue star. "Good. That frees up two squads. We'll need them for the perimeter. We've had probes from the Grimvales in the western hills."

"Probes?" I asked.

"Noise," Roric said. "Howling. Tree-knocking. Psychological warfare. Kane wants to keep you awake."

"It's working," I muttered.

Roric looked at Jazz, then at me. His expression softened slightly, but the tension remained.

"We need to talk about the Gambit, Damien. Specifically, the prep."

"I know," I said. "I need to spar."

"You can't spar," Roric said, pointing at my leg. "You tear those stitches, you lose mobility. We need to work on the strategy. Mental conditioning."

He tossed a thick file onto the table. "Selene. I pulled everything we have. Her fighting style is defensive. She waits for you to overcommit. She uses her size, or lack of it, to frustrate you. She wants you angry."

"I am angry," I said.

"That's the problem," Jazz spoke up. Her voice was quiet, but it cut through the room.

We both looked at her.

"Selene relies on you being the aggressor," Jazz said, sitting up. "She knows you're bigger. She knows you're stronger. She expects you to try to crush her like a bug. So she'll dance. She'll make you chase her until you're tired, then she'll nick you with the poison."

"So what's the counter?" I asked.

"Don't chase her," Jazz said. "Make her come to you."

Roric snorted. "Selene won't engage if you stand still. The fight could last for hours. The Gambit has time limits on inactivity."

"Not if you give her a reason to attack," Jazz said. She looked at me, her blue eyes sharp. "What does Selene hate more than anything?"

"Disrespect," I said immediately. "She's obsessed with the elegance of her lineage."

"Exactly," Jazz said. "So you don't fight her like a warrior. You fight her like she's boring you. You insult her. You stand in the center of the Circle, and you laugh at her poison."

"Taunt the Viper," Roric mused. "Risky."

"It's only risky if he gets hit," Jazz said. "But Damien... I felt you in the woods. When you're protecting something, you're immovable. When you're attacking, you're reckless."

She stood up and walked over to the map, placing her hand on the Stone Circle marker.

"Don't try to beat Selene at her own game," she said. "Make her play yours. You're the Shield, right? The Ashen Ones are the Shield. So be a wall. Let her break herself against you."

I looked at Roric. He was nodding slowly.

"She has a point," Roric admitted. "Selene has a fragile ego. If you treat her like a nuisance rather than a threat, she'll get sloppy. She'll try to prove she can hurt you."

"And when she steps in to strike," I finished, "I crush her."

"Exactly," Jazz said.

I looked at her with new respect. She had only been a wolf for two weeks, but she was already breaking down Alpha strategies like a veteran. Elias was right. She wasn't a liability. She was a weapon I hadn't learned to use yet.

"Okay," I said. "We work on defense. Static holding. Counter-strikes."

"And Kane?" Roric asked.

"Kane is different," I said. "Kane, I have to break."

I walked over to Jazz and rested my hand on her shoulder. The bond hummed, a warm, steady note of reassurance.

"You should sleep," I told her. "Real sleep. Not a nap in a chair."

"I'm not sleeping until you do," she said.

"I have to review the files on Kane."

"Then read them out loud," she said, sitting back down. "I learn fast."

Roric watched us, a strange expression on his face. "You two are terrifying," he muttered. "You're feeding off each other."

"Is that a problem?" I asked.

"Normally? Yes," Roric said. "Emotional entanglement is a distraction. But this..." He gestured between us. "It's like a feedback loop. Her survival instinct is redlining your aggression. And your aggression is sharpening her tactical mind."

He gathered his papers. "Fine. Read the files. I'm going to check the perimeter. If I see a Grimvale, I'll shoot him."

"Roric," I called out as he reached the door. "Thank you."

"Don't thank me yet," he said grimly. "Win the damn fight. Then you can thank me."

He left.

I was alone with Jazz in the war room. The silence was heavy, but it wasn't uncomfortable. It was the silence of the bunker.

"Your leg is hurting," Jazz said, not looking up from the file she had opened.

"It's fine."

"I can feel it, Damien. It feels like a hot poker."

"Sorry," I muttered. "I'll try to block it."

"Don't," she said. She stood up and walked over to me, pushing me gently until I sat in the chair. She knelt in front of me, placing her hands on my thigh, just above the bandage.

"What are you doing?"

"Dad told me something," she whispered. "About the bond. He said it's not just about feeling pain. It's about sharing the load."

She closed her eyes and took a deep breath.

I felt a strange sensation, like cool water flowing

down my leg. The heat in the wound didn't go away, but it spread out and faded into a dull, manageable hum. I saw Jazz wince slightly.

"Stop," I said, grabbing her wrists. "You're taking the pain."

"Just a little," she said, opening her eyes. "You have to fight in two days. You need to heal. If I take the edge off, your body can focus on knitting the muscle instead of fighting the inflammation."

"I won't let you take pain in my stead," I said fiercely.

"You took a knife for me," she countered. "You took a bite for me. Let me take a headache for you."

She leaned forward, resting her forehead against my knee. "We're in this together, remember? The King and the Queen."

I looked down at her. The devotion in her eyes scared me. She was willing to bleed for me. She was willing to take my pain as her own.

Elias was right. If they hurt her, I would shatter.

But he was wrong about one thing.

If they tried to hurt her, I wouldn't just shatter. I would explode.

"Together," I agreed, my voice rough.

I pulled her up into my lap, careful of the leg. She curled against me, her head on my shoulder, her hand resting over my heart.

We stayed like that for a long time, the file on Kane forgotten on the table. We sat in the center of the fortress, surrounded by enemies, held together by the impossible, forbidden magic between us.

The strong link.

It was the most dangerous thing in the world. But it was also the only thing that could save us.

# CHAPTER 25

# JAZZ

The War Room of the Ashen Ones was a place where silence felt heavy, like a woolen blanket soaked in ice water.

It was three in the morning. My body buzzed with a strange, mixed exhaustion. My human muscles screamed for sleep, but the wolf blood in my veins was wide awake, fueled by caffeine and leftover adrenaline from the night's chaos.

I sat at the massive oak table, surrounded by stacks of manila folders Roric had left earlier. Damien paced. He always did that when he was thinking, moving with a restless, predatory stride that crossed the room in three steps, turning sharply so his boots squeaked on the floorboards.

His leg was bothering him. I could feel it through the bond—a dull, throbbing echo in my own left thigh—but he was doing an admirable job of ignoring it.

"Selene," Damien muttered, stopping in front of the map of Tallow for the tenth time. "She's the wild-card. Kane is physics—mass times acceleration. I know how to calculate that. But Selene is chemistry. She's volatile."

I looked down at the file open in front of me. It was a dossier on the Shadowfang operations over the last five years. It was thin. Painfully thin.

"There's almost nothing here," I said, rubbing my eyes. "Just rumors and ghost stories. 'Suspected involvement in the Portland Docks fire.' 'Possible link to the disappearance of the rogue Alpha in Vermont.' It's all hearsay."

"That's how she operates," Damien said, turning to face me. "The Shadowfangs don't leave fingerprints. They don't claim credit. If a building burns down, it's the faulty wiring. If a wolf dies, it's a heart attack."

He walked over to the table, leaning his hands on the wood, his face illuminated by the harsh overhead light. He looked tired, the lines around his eyes deepening, but the gold in his irises was bright, burning with that relentless Alpha drive.

"They rely on the supernatural," he continued. "Stealth. Glamour. Poisons that mimic natural causes. They fight a war of whispers."

"Maybe," I said slowly, flipping a page. "But they still have to eat. They still have to move. They still have to buy the gasoline to burn down Mrs. Gable's house."

I pulled a second folder toward me, the one with

public records I'd asked Roric to get from the town council archives. It was dry, boring stuff: property tax records, business permits, zoning applications. Most wolves would find it dull, but it made a librarian's brain light up.

"Damien, look at this."

He moved around the table to stand behind me, looking over my shoulder. His heat radiated against my back, a comforting, solid presence that made the wolf inside me settle.

"What am I looking at?" he asked. "Tax codes?"

"Look at the ownership transfer for the old lumber yard," I said, pointing to a document dated six months ago. "The one they attacked tonight to draw us out. It was bought by a shell company called 'Apex Logistics.' Now look at this."

I pulled up a business permit for a courier service that had opened a distribution hub in the Shadowfang Valley territory two years ago.

"Apex Logistics," Damien read. "So? They own a delivery company. Wolves need supplies."

"Wolves need meat and ammo," I corrected. "Apex Logistics has a fleet of twenty vans. But look at their routes." I traced a line on a map I had sketched out on a notepad. "They don't deliver to residential addresses. They deliver to commercial lots. Empty commercial lots."

I tapped the map where Mrs. Gable's house stood. "And three days ago, a permit was pulled for a 'utility upgrade' on that street. By a subcontractor hired by Apex."

Damien stiffened. "They were digging lines?"

"They were digging access," I said, my mind racing, connecting the dots that had nothing to do with claws and everything to do with bureaucracy. "They weren't just sneaking around in the bushes, Damien. They were prepping the ground. They used a utility permit to cut the gas line to Mrs. Gable's house, then capped it so it would look normal until they were ready to blow it."

I looked up at him. "Selene isn't just using magic and stealth. She's using infrastructure. She's using the human world's own systems against us. While you guys are patrolling the woods for scents, she's moving hazardous materials through town in delivery vans with valid permits."

Damien stared at the papers, his expression shifting from confusion to a dawning, horrified realization.

"We've been looking for wolves," he murmured. "We should have been looking for contractors."

"Exactly," I said. "Roric said the Shadowfangs are weak fighters. So they don't fight. They engineer disasters. If I'm right, Apex Logistics probably has 'utility work' scheduled all over Tallow for the next three days."

Damien swore softly. He grabbed the map of

Tallow, his eyes scanning the streets with a new perspective.

"Here," he pointed to the bridge that connected the Snow territory to the mainland. "And here, the power substation behind the high school."

"Both have active work permits," I confirmed, checking the list.

"She's rigging the board," Damien growled. "She's not planning to fight me in the Circle. She's planning to hold the town hostage. If I start winning, she blows the substation. Or drops the bridge."

"And blames it on infrastructure failure," I finished. "Chaos. Distraction. Just like tonight."

Damien straightened up, his fists clenching. "Roric needs to know this. We need to shut down every Apex van in the county. We need to inspect every work site."

"My dad can do that," I said. "The Snows... we're the ones who work those jobs. Mr. Henderson is on the zoning board. Sarah's husband works for the power company. We can audit the permits. We can find the traps without alerting Selene that we know."

Damien looked at me, a mixture of awe and intensity in his gaze that made my breath hitch.

"You found in ten minutes what my intelligence network missed in six months," he said softly.

"Your intelligence network is looking for threats with teeth," I said, feeling a flush rise in my cheeks. "I'm looking for threats with paperwork. It's... what I do. I organize information."

"You are a weapon," Damien said, his voice low and fervent. He reached out, his hand cupping my cheek, his thumb brushing my lower lip. "A librarian weapon. Who knew?"

The touch sent a jolt of electricity straight to my core. I leaned into his hand, closing my eyes for a second. The bond hummed with a note of pure, resonant pride from him.

"We have a chance," he whispered. "If we can neutralize her traps before Wednesday... I just have to fight her. And I can beat her in a fight."

"You have to beat three of them," I reminded him, opening my eyes. "Consecutively."

The light in his eyes dimmed slightly, replaced by the grim reality of the Gambit.

"Yeah. About that."

He pulled his hand away, the loss of contact leaving my skin cold. He walked over to a metal cabinet in the corner of the room and pulled out two pairs of heavy, padded gloves.

"Get up," he said.

"What? Why?"

"Because you're right," he said, tossing a pair of gloves onto the table in front of me. "Selene fights dirty. Elford fights dirty. And if they realize we're dismantling their infrastructure traps, they're going to come for the people doing the dismantling."

He looked at me, his expression hard and unyielding. "They're going to come for you, Jazz. And

I won't always be there to jump in front of the bullet."

I looked at the gloves. "I know how to punch. You taught me."

"I taught you how to spar," he corrected. "I taught you form. Discipline. The kind of fighting you use in a ring."

He walked over to the open space in the center of the room, shoving the table aside with a screech of wood on wood.

"Tonight, I'm going to teach you how to survive."

I stood up, pulling the flannel shirt tighter around me. "Okay. What's the lesson?"

"The lesson is unfairness," he said. "Put the gloves on."

I slipped my hands into the thick padding. They felt clumsy, heavy.

"Shift," he ordered.

"What?"

"Shift into the wolf. Now."

I hesitated. "Here? In the War Room?"

"Do it."

I closed my eyes, finding the heat. It came faster now, a familiar pathway worn into my neural map. The bone-snap was a dull ache rather than agony. I dropped to all fours, the white fur bristling, my senses exploding into the sharp clarity of the wolf.

I looked up at him, panting slightly.

Ready, I projected.

"Good," Damien said. "Now, attack me."

I paused. Attack you?

"Yes. You're a Draven scout. I'm the target. Take me down."

I circled him, looking for an opening. He was standing relaxed, his arms loose at his sides. He looked vulnerable.

I lunged.

I aimed for his thigh, intending to trip him.

Before I even made contact, he moved. Fast. Too fast. He stepped inside my guard, grabbed the scruff of my neck with one hand and my flank with the other, and used my own momentum to slam me into the floor mats.

The impact knocked the wind out of me. I yelped, scrambling to get my paws under me, but he was already on top of me, his knee pressing into my ribs—not hard enough to break, but hard enough to pin.

"Dead," he said calmly. "You telegraphed the lunge. You dropped your shoulder."

He released me and stood up. "Again."

I scrambled up, shaking myself off. The wolf was annoyed. It snarled, baring teeth.

*You're cheating*, I thought at him.

"I'm winning," he countered. "Again."

We went for an hour. He tossed me. He pinned me. He sidestepped me and let me crash into the wall. Every time, he pointed out the flaw. Too wide. Too slow. You're exposing your throat. You're hesitating.

. . .

I was panting, bruised, and frustrated. The wolf wanted to bite him for real. Just a little nip. Just to wipe that calm look off his face.

"Shift back," he ordered finally.

I shifted, the return to human form leaving me gasping on the mats, sweat soaking my clothes.

"That sucked," I wheezed, staring up at the ceiling.

"It sucked because you're fighting like a wolf who thinks she's a tank," Damien said, standing over me. "You're not a tank, Jazz. You're a Ferrari. You need to use speed, not mass."

He reached down and hauled me to my feet.

"Now," he said. "Human form. Gloves up."

I raised my hands, my shoulders burning.

"I'm going to grab you," he said. "From behind. Like an abduction. Like Elford tried in the ravine."

He stepped behind me. "Ready?"

"Rea—"

He wrapped his arm around my throat, pulling me back against his chest, locking my movement. It was terrifyingly effective. I clawed at his arm, but it was like clawing at a steel bar.

"Don't pull the arm," he whispered in my ear. "You're not strong enough. Use the environment. Use your body."

He tightened the grip. "I'm choking you out. You have three seconds. Go."

I panicked. I tried to stomp on his foot, but he moved it. I tried to elbow him, but he was too close. The edges of my vision started to dim.

"Panic kills," he hissed. "Think."

Think.

I stopped fighting the arm. I went limp.

He instinctively adjusted his grip to support my dead weight.

In that split second of adjustment, I dropped completely, sliding through the circle of his arm. I twisted as I fell, driving my shoulder into his groin and grabbing his leg.

I didn't have the strength to throw him. But I had the leverage.

I drove forward, taking his knee out. He stumbled, losing his balance, and crashed to the mat. I scrambled on top of him, pinning his wrist with my knee and raising a gloved fist to strike.

"Dead," I panted, looking down at him.

He looked up at me. He wasn't angry. He was grinning. A wild, proud, bloody grin.

"Alive," he corrected. "That was ugly. It was clumsy. And it worked."

He lay there for a moment, catching his breath. I was straddling him, my hair wild, my chest heaving. The adrenaline of the fight was slowly turning into something else, something hotter and darker.

The bond flared.

"You went limp," he said, his eyes tracing my face.

"That takes guts. To surrender control to gain leverage."

"I remembered what you said about the shift," I whispered. "Surrender to win."

He reached up, his hand tangling in the back of my hair, pulling my face down to his.

"You learn fast," he murmured.

He kissed me hard, our teeth clashing in a rush of passion that tasted of sweat and violence. I kissed him back, letting all my fear and frustration pour into it.

For a moment, we weren't preparing for war. We were just two people desperate to feel alive in the face of death.

But Damien broke the kiss, gently pushing me up.

"Not yet," he said, his voice ragged. "We're not done."

"I'm tired, Damien."

"I know," he said, sitting up and moving me to the side. "But there's one more thing. The most important thing."

He stood up and walked to his jacket, pulling something out of the pocket.

He came back and pressed it into my hand.

It was a knife. Small, curved, with a handle wrapped in black leather. It looked like a claw made of steel.

"This is a Karambit," he said. "It's a close-quarters weapon. It's designed for someone smaller fighting someone bigger."

. . .

I LOOKED AT THE BLADE. It was sharp enough to shave with.

"You want me to carry a knife?"

"I want you to carry this knife," he said. "It's iron. Cold-forged. It burns shifters. It stops regeneration."

He closed my fingers around the handle.

"If Elford gets his hands on you," Damien said, his voice dropping to a whisper that terrified me more than any shout. "If I fall in the Circle. If the alliance fails. If you are cornered and you can't shift and you can't run..."

He looked me in the eye.

"...you use this. You don't threaten with it. You don't wave it around. You wait until he's close. Until he thinks he's won. And you put this in his throat."

I stared at the weapon. It felt heavy. It felt real.

"I don't know if I can kill someone," I said softly.

"You won't be killing a person," Damien said grimly. "You'll be killing a monster."

He covered my hand with his own.

"Promise me, Jazz. If it comes down to it... if it's you or him... You choose you."

I looked at the blade, then up at the man who was willing to die three times over to keep me safe. I saw the desperation in his eyes. He needed to know that even if he failed, I had a chance.

I tightened my grip on the handle.

"I promise," I said.

He nodded, letting out a breath he seemed to have been holding for days.

"Good."

He stepped back, wiping sweat from his forehead.

"Now," he said, picking up the dossier on Apex Logistics. "Let's figure out which transformer Selene is planning to blow up first."

We went back to the table. We went back to the maps, the permits, and the strategy.

The knife lay on the table between us, gleaming under the harsh lights. It was a silent third partner in our alliance.

I had ditched the garb of a librarian, of the defenseless, cowering woman who knew not what was better for her and what was dangerous. Not anymore. I was a soldier. And I was armed.

# DAMIEN

The waiting was always worse than the bleeding.

We were thirty-six hours away from the Alpha's Gambit. The compound felt frozen, like everyone was holding their breath before a scream. The Snows patrolled Tallow, sending hourly updates about quiet streets and anxious people. The Shadow-fangs had disappeared, probably getting ready for whatever Selene had planned.

But the Grimvales didn't know how to be quiet.

I stood on the Ashen Ones' wall, looking west at the trees. It was midday, but the sun barely made it through the thick coastal fog. My leg was stiff, like iron in my muscle, but the sharp pain had faded to something I could handle.

Jazz stood next to me, wearing a tactical vest over

my flannel shirt and her hair pulled back tight. Every hour, she looked less like a librarian and more like a soldier. She scanned the woods with binoculars.

"They're loud," she noted, lowering the glass. "I can hear them breaking branches a mile out."

"They want to be heard," I said, leaning my hands on the rough timber of the wall. "Kane is sending a message. He's bored. He wants to see if I'm still limping."

"Are you?"

I looked at her. "Does it matter?"

"It matters if you fall over," she said dryly.

A howl cut through the air, deep and aggressive. It wasn't an attack signal. It was a formal greeting.

"Open the gate," I called down to the courtyard.

Roric looked up from where he was inspecting a rifle. "Damien, this could be a trap. A pre-Gambit assassination."

"They invoked the Hail," I said. "If they attack under a formal greeting, they forfeit their honor. Even Grimvales care about that, in their own twisted way. Open it."

The gates groaned open.

Three wolves emerged from the tree line. They were massive, their coats thick and matted with the mud of the western mountains. They didn't shift until they were ten yards from the gate.

· · ·

THE LEADER WAS a man I knew: Tor. He was a top lieutenant in Kane's guard, known for two things—never feeling pain and being strong enough to flip a car. He was almost seven feet tall, with a chest covered in hair and scars.

He was flanked by two younger enforcers, but Tor was the main event.

I walked out to meet him, keeping my stride even, suppressing the limp through sheer force of will. Jazz walked a step behind me on my left—the traditional position of the Second. Roric flanked my right.

"Tor," I said, stopping five paces away. "You're a long way from the rocks."

Tor grinned, showing teeth filed to points. Grimvales did this to look scary, but it just seemed desperate.

"The Mountain sends its regards, Ashford," Tor rumbled. His voice sounded like gravel in a blender. "Kane heard a rumor. He heard the Ashen Alpha needs a girl to hold him up."

He flicked his eyes toward Jazz. He sniffed the air, a loud, wet sound. "She smells like milk. And fear."

Jazz didn't flinch. She stared right back at him, her hand resting casually near the hilt of the Karambit tucked in her belt. "And you smell like you haven't bathed since winter," she said calmly.

Tor's grin faltered. His eyes narrowed.

"Watch your tongue, bitch. Or I'll rip it out."

"State your business, Tor," I interjected, stepping into his line of sight. "Or get off my land. I have a war to prepare for."

"That's the business," Tor said, puffing out his chest. "Kane is worried. He thinks the Gambit is sacred and shouldn't be insulted by someone who's injured."

He pointed a thick, dirty finger at my leg.

"We demand a Proof of Vitality."

I tensed. A Proof of Vitality was an old, rarely used rule in the Challenge codes. It let a rival pack demand a spar to make sure the challenger wasn't hiding a serious injury. Usually, it was only used for Alphas who were old or sick.

For Kane to demand it now, just two days before the fight, was a clear insult. He was saying I was already finished.

"You want proof?" I asked, my voice dropping to a dangerous low.

"I challenge you," Tor announced, spreading his arms. "Here. Now. First blood or submission. If you can't beat me, you aren't fit to step into the Circle with Kane."

Roric stepped forward. "This is ridiculous. He saves his strength for the Alphas. Fight me, Tor. I'll show you vitality."

"No," Tor sneered. "I want the cripple."

I looked at Tor. He was huge and slow. He was the perfect test for my leg before I faced Kane. Kane was quicker and smarter, but just as strong. I didn't handle Tor; I had no business fighting Kane.

"I accept," I said.

"Damien," Jazz hissed. "Your leg."

"My leg needs a test drive," I murmured to her. "Better to blow a tire here than in the Circle."

I unzipped my leather jacket and handed it to Jazz. I unbuttoned my shirt and handed it to her as well. The cold air hit my skin, tightening the scars on my chest.

"Circle up!" Roric shouted to the perimeter guards.

The Ashen Ones flooded out of the gate, forming a wide ring around us. They were silent, tense. They needed to see this, too. They needed to know their Alpha wasn't broken.

Tor stripped off his vest. He cracked his neck, the sound like a pistol shot.

"Human form or wolf?" I asked.

"Let's start like men," Tor grunted. "I want to hear your bones snap."

He didn't wait for a signal. He charged.

He charged like a freight train, all speed and weight. I saw his attack coming from far away—a wide, swinging punch aimed at my head. I didn't block it. I stepped inside the arc. Jazz's voice echoed in my head: Don't be a tank. Be a Ferrari. I bent my injured knee and dropped lower. Pain shot through me, sharp and hot, but the joint held. I drove my shoulder into Tor's stomach, using his momentum against him.

It was like hitting a brick wall. He grunted, stumbling back a step, but he didn't fall. He grabbed my shoulders, his fingers digging into my trapezius muscles, and tried to headbutt me. I twisted, breaking his grip, and circled to his left.

Tor roared and swung again. I blocked it, my forearm slamming into his. The hit rattled my teeth. He was strong—almost unnaturally so.

He followed up with a kick to my bad leg.

He knew exactly where to aim.

I blocked the kick, lifting my leg so his shin hit my bone instead of the muscle. It hurt, but it hurt him too. He winced.

"Is that all?" I taunted, dancing back. "I thought Grimvales hit hard."

Tor snarled and rushed me again. This time, he didn't swing. He tackled. He wrapped his massive arms around my waist, lifting me off the ground, intending to slam me into the packed earth.

It was a bear hug. If he completed the slam, he could crack my ribs or dislocate my spine.

I didn't panic. I went limp.

Just like Jazz had done in the war room.

Tor, expecting resistance, overbalanced. I drove my elbows down into the junction of his neck and shoulder—once, twice. Hard.

He dropped me. I landed on my feet, rolling backward to create distance.

My leg screamed. I ignored it. "You're slow, Tor," I

said, panting slightly. "Kane is going to be embarrassed."

Tor's face turned purple. "I'll kill you!"

He shifted.

Shifting broke the rules of a 'men' start, but Grimvales ignored the rules when they were losing. In seconds, he turned into a huge, grey-brown wolf.

The crowd gasped. An Alpha fighting a shifted warrior in human form was suicide.

"Damien!" Jazz shouted.

I didn't shift. Not yet. I wanted to see if I could hold him.

The wolf lunged, jaws snapping for my throat.

I sidestepped, grabbing the thick fur of his neck ruff as he flew past. I swung myself up, mounting his back like a rodeo rider. It was a dominant move. It was the ultimate insult.

Tor thrashed, bucking wild, trying to throw me. I wrapped my arms around his neck, applying a chokehold. My legs clamped around his ribs.

He slammed himself sideways, trying to crush me against the ground. I released the hold at the last second, rolling clear, and sprang to my feet.


HE WAS ON ME INSTANTLY, swiping with a paw the size of a dinner plate. Claws tore through the skin of my chest, leaving four hot, bleeding lines.

First blood.

The crowd went silent. Tor paused, panting, looking at the blood on my chest. By rights, the challenge was over. He had drawn first blood.

But he didn't stop. He licked his chops and crouched for another spring. He wanted to finish it.

Fine.

I closed my eyes and let the Alpha out.

The shift took one second. The Black Wolf emerged, driven by pain and anger. I roared, and the sound shook the leaves from the trees. I met him head-on.

We collided with a sound like thunder. Teeth met fur. Claws met flesh. We rolled in the dirt, a ball of snarling fury.

He went for my leg again. He clamped his jaws onto my injured calf, grinding down.

The pain was blinding. It was a universe of agony.

But pain is fuel.

I didn't pull away. I drove into it. I used the anchor of his bite to pivot my body, bringing my own jaws down on the back of his neck.

I didn't bite to kill. I bit to dominate.

I bit down on the scruff, right over his spine, and pressed hard. It was enough to bruise the bone and make him freeze with fear.

Then I used my weight. I slammed him into the dirt, pinning him. I growled, a subsonic vibration that went straight into his skull.

*Submit.*

He struggled. I bit harder. I tasted his blood.

*Submit.*

He whined. His tail was tucked. He went limp.

I HELD him there for ten long seconds, letting the pack see. Letting the Grimvale enforcers see.

The Ashen Alpha wasn't broken.

I released him and backed away, shifting back to human form. I stood there, naked, chest bleeding, leg throbbing, breathing hard.

Tor shifted back. He curled into a ball in the dirt, clutching his neck. He was weeping. Not from pain, but from shame.

"Tell Kane," I rasped, spitting blood onto the ground, "that he needs to hit harder than that."

I turned my back on him, the ultimate dismissal, and walked toward the gate.

Roric met me with a towel. "You're bleeding."

"Superficial," I said, wiping my chest. "Get him out of here. If he comes back, shoot him."

I walked over to Jazz. She was pale, her hands gripping my jacket so hard her knuckles were white.

"You let him bite you," she accused quietly.

"I needed to know," I said, leaning on her as we walked back into the compound.

"Know what?"

"If the leg would hold under pressure."

"And?"

"It held," I said. "It hurts like a bitch, but the bone is solid."

She looked at the bloody mess on my calf. "You just undid three days of healing."

"I also just put the fear of God into the Grimvales," I said. "Tor will go back and tell Kane that I mounted him in human form and pinned him in ten seconds. Kane will hesitate. He'll wonder if the limp is a trap."

"Is it?"

"No," I admitted, wincing as we climbed the steps to the infirmary. "It's a liability. But now it's a liability with a psychological edge."

As the adrenaline faded, I started to shake and feel cold. The medic went to work. She cleaned the chest wound—four shallow scratches—and then turned her attention to the leg.

"He tore the stitches," she said, her voice tight. "I have to redo them."

"Do it," I grunted, staring at the ceiling.

She worked quietly for a few minutes. I could feel her anger, sharp and prickling through our bond.

"Say it," I said.

"You enjoyed that," she said, not looking up. "You liked hurting him."

"He insulted my pack. He insulted you."

"You liked the dominance," she pressed, looking me in the eye. "I felt it, Damien. Through the bond. It wasn't just strategy. It was... pleasure. You liked holding his life in your teeth."

I didn't deny it. "I am an Alpha, Jazz. Dominance is my nature. If I didn't enjoy it, I wouldn't be fit to sit on the Throne."

"It scares me," she whispered. "When you're like that... you're not the man who taught me how to breathe. You're a monster."

I reached out, grabbing her hand. I pulled her toward me until she was leaning over the cot.

"I have to be a monster," I said intensely. "For two more days. I have to be the thing that nightmares are afraid of. Because if I'm not... Elford wins. And if Elford wins, you don't get the man who taught you to breathe. You get a head on a spike."

She looked at me, searching my face. She saw it was true. The brutality was my armor.

"Just promise me," she said softly, "that when it's over... You can come back. That you won't get stuck in the monster."

"I have an anchor," I said, bringing her hand to my lips. "You pull me back. That's the deal."

She sighed, her shoulders relaxing. She leaned down and kissed me, soft and gentle, so different from the violence of the last hour.

"I'll pull you back," she promised. "But you have to survive long enough for me to do it."

"I plan to."

Roric knocked on the doorframe.

"Alpha. Report from the Snows."

I sat up, instantly alert. "What is it?"

"Quiet," Roric said. "Too quiet. The Shadowfangs have pulled back completely. No sightings in Tallow. No activity at the lumber yards."

"She's bunkering down," I said. "Or she's preparing the final trap."

"One more thing," Roric said. "We got a message from the lone shifters. The Stone Circle has been prepped. The Gambit starts at dawn on Wednesday."

"Tomorrow," Jazz whispered.

"Tomorrow," I agreed.

"Get some sleep," Roric advised. "You proved your point today. Now you need to heal."

He left. I lay back down. Jazz finished bandaging my leg. She didn't leave. She curled up on the cot beside me, careful of the injuries, resting her head on my good shoulder.

"Damien?"

"Yeah?"

"Tor was big."

"Huge."

"Kane is bigger?"

"About fifty pounds heavier. And meaner."

She was silent for a moment.

"You're going to have to be a very scary monster tomorrow."

"I know."

I closed my eyes, listening to her heartbeat. It was steady. Strong. The test was done. I was battered, bleeding, and tired. But I was ready. I knew my limits. I knew my pain. And I knew exactly how much blood I was willing to spill to keep her safe. All of it.

# CHAPTER 27

# DAMIEN

The night before a battle is never quiet. You hear blades being sharpened, soft prayers, and it almost feels like ghosts are gathering in the corners.

I sat on the edge of the narrow cot in the Alpha's private quarters, a whetstone in my left hand and my father's ceremonial dagger in my right.

*Shhhk. Shhhk. Shhhk.*

The steady scrape of steel on stone was the only thing stopping my mind from spinning out about tomorrow. The sound was rough, matching how raw my nerves felt.

Outside, the compound was locked down. Bright lights cut through the thick Maine fog, like lighthouses warning ships away. Roric had doubled the guard, and I heard enforcers pacing the hallway. We were ready for a siege, but the real fight would be in the neutral valley at dawn.

The Gambit.

Three fights. Three Alphas. One survivor.

I tested the edge of the blade with my thumb. A thin line of red appeared on the callus of my skin. Sharp enough to shave. Sharp enough to kill.

Jazz sat on the rug by the fire, adding logs to the fading flames. She wore my flannel shirt, sleeves rolled up, legs tucked under her. She watched the fire, her face lit by its glow. She hadn't spoken in an hour, but just having her there kept me from getting lost in my thoughts.

"Stop," she said softly, not turning her head.

I paused the whetstone mid-stroke. "Stop what?"

"Stop thinking so loud. You're projecting anxiety like a radio tower. It's making the fire crackle."

I set the knife down on the nightstand next to the lamp. "It's not anxiety. It's preparation. A dull blade is a suicide note."

"It's dread," she corrected, finally turning to face me. Her blue eyes were dark in the low light, stripping away my defenses with a glance. "I can feel it, Damien. The bond is vibrating with it. You aren't just thinking about the fight. You're thinking about the grave."

I sighed, running a hand through my hair. "It's a possibility I have to plan for. If I fall tomorrow, the vacuum of power will be instantaneous. The Grimvales will move to the western border. The Shadow-fangs will liquidate our assets. And Elford..."

"Elford will come for me," she finished for me.

"Yes." The word tasted like bile. "He will come for you."

Jazz stood up and walked to the window, peering out through the crack in the heavy curtains. She looked small against the backdrop of the night, but her spine was straight. She had changed in the weeks she had been with me. The librarian who had hidden in the stacks was gone, replaced by a woman who carried a knife and looked at war without flinching.

"Tell me," she said, her breath fogging the glass slightly. "If we're going into this tomorrow, I need to know. I need to understand why he hates you so much. It's not just about the Throne, is it? It's not just about territory."

"No," I admitted. "It's deeper than that. It's blood."

"Tell me."

I patted the spot beside me on the bed. She hesitated, then walked over and sat down, tucking her legs beneath her. She was close enough that I could smell the rain and vanilla scent of her, close enough that the warmth of her body radiated against my arm.

"It started with our fathers," I began, staring at the dagger. "Marcus Ashford and Vargas Draven. Thirty years ago, the coast was a slaughterhouse. There were no treaties. No neutral zones. Just packs killing each other for scraps of land."

I leaned back against the headboard and closed my eyes, letting memories that weren't really mine, but passed down through stories and nightmares, wash over me.

"Vargas was a brute," I said. "He believed that strength was the only virtue. He hunted humans for sport. He burned villages. He was a monster in every sense of the word. My father... Marcus was different. He believed that we could be more than just animals. He believed in the Codex."

"The laws," Jazz whispered.

"The laws," I agreed. "My father wrote half of them. He spent years trying to unite the packs diplomatically. But Vargas wouldn't listen. He saw diplomacy as weakness. So, inevitably, it came to war."

I opened my eyes and looked at her.

"The final battle wasn't an army against an army. It was a duel. Just like tomorrow. Marcus challenged Vargas to single combat to end the bloodshed. They met on the cliffs overlooking the sea."

"And your father won," Jazz said.

"He did. He was faster. Smarter. He disarmed Vargas. He had him on his knees, with a blade to his throat. The entire coast was watching. The packs were waiting for the kill."

I swallowed hard. This part of the story always caught in my throat.

"But he didn't do it. Marcus looked at Vargas—defeated, humiliated, broken—and he showed mercy.

He sheathed his blade. He told Vargas to go home. He said, 'Live, and learn to be better.'"

Jazz was silent, watching my face.

"It was the noblest thing anyone had ever done," I said bitterly. "And it was the worst mistake of his life."

"Why?"

"Because Vargas didn't learn," I said. "He didn't go home and become a better wolf. He went home and festered. He felt the shame of that mercy every single day. It ate him alive. He became cruel, bitter, and paranoid. And he took it out on his son."

I looked at the fire. I could almost see the young Elford, watching his father crumble.

"Elford grew up watching his father wither," I explained. "Vargas told him every day that the Ashfords had stolen his manhood. That mercy was a poison. He beat it into Elford. He taught him that honor was a lie told by the victors to keep the losers down."

"So Elford hates you because your father spared his," Jazz realized.

"He hates me because my existence proves his father was weak," I said. "Every time he looks at me, he sees the mercy that ruined his family. He wants to kill me, not just to take the throne, but to rewrite history. He wants to prove that Marcus was wrong. That the only truth is the kill."

"And the assassination?" Jazz asked softly. "My

father... he told me rumors. That Marcus didn't die of natural causes."

"He didn't," I rasped. "Elford killed him. Ten years ago. He didn't challenge him to a duel. He didn't declare war. He walked into this very room, under a flag of truce, and he shot him."

I clenched my fists, the leather of the bedspread creaking under my grip.

"My father let him in. He offered him a drink. He thought... he thought the son might be different from the father. He thought Elford had come to make peace."

I looked at Jazz, letting her see the guilt that I carried.

"Elford shot him in the stomach. A slow death. And then he walked out. There was no proof. No witnesses. Just a dead King and a smiling rival. That is why I became the Warlord, Jazz. That is why I built the walls and trained the army. I swore I would never be caught with my hand open again."

Silence stretched between us, heavy and thick. The fire popped, a log settling into the ash.

"And now," I whispered, "I am walking into the same trap. The Circle. The Challenge. Elford accepted because he thinks I am my father. He thinks I am bound by honor. He thinks I will hesitate."

"Will you?" Jazz asked.

I looked at the dagger. "I don't know. I have tried so hard to be the man Marcus wanted me to be. I have tried to be the King of the Codex. But inside... inside, I want to tear Elford apart. I want to do what my father couldn't. I want to end the line."

"That doesn't make you a monster, Damien," she said. "That makes you a survivor."

"It makes me Vargas," I countered. "If I kill him out of hate... if I abandon the law to get revenge... then the Draven philosophy wins. Mercy dies. And we go back to being animals."

Jazz moved then. She climbed fully onto the bed, kneeling in front of me so that our faces were level. She took my face in her hands, her palms cool against my heated skin.

"Your father was a good man," she said fiercely. "But he was wrong about one thing. Mercy isn't a gift you give to everyone. It's a currency. You spend it on those who deserve it."

She leaned closer, her eyes locking onto mine with an intensity that stole my breath.

"Elford doesn't deserve it. He stole your father. He burned my town. He threatened to take me. That is not a man you spare, Damien. That is a rabid dog you put down."

"You sound like a Grimvale," I managed a weak smile.

"I sound like a woman who wants her husband to come home," she said. "Don't be your father tomorrow. And don't be Vargas. Be Damien. Be the man who fixed my truck. Be the man who taught me to run. Be the King who protects his pack."

She brushed her thumb over my cheekbone.

"You can be brutal," she whispered. "But do it because you love something. Not because you hate something. If you kill him to save me... to save the pack... that isn't hate. That's duty."

I looked at her, thinking of her as my civilian, my conscience, my heart. She had stripped away all the philosophy and left only the truth.

"I promised you I would come back," I said, my voice thick with emotion. "But I'm afraid that to come back, I have to leave the good man behind in that valley."

"No," Jazz said, shaking her head. "You bring him with you. You carry the scars. But you come back."

She reached over and picked up the dagger from the nightstand. She looked at it for a moment, the fire-light dancing on the steel, and then she set it down on the floor, out of reach.

She placed her hands on my chest, over my heart. I could feel it beating against her palms—a heavy, steady rhythm.

"Come to bed," she whispered. "Roric has the watch. The guards are posted. There is nothing more you can do tonight."

"I can't sleep," I admitted. "If I close my eyes, I see the Circle."

"Then don't sleep," she said. "Just be here. With me."

She leaned in and kissed me. It wasn't a hungry kiss, not yet. It was a grounding wire. It was soft, slow, and full of a quiet desperation that mirrored my own.

I wrapped my arms around her, pulling her against me. She felt solid. Real. She was the only thing in the world that made sense.

We lay down together on the narrow cot, fully clothed, tangled in each other's arms. The fire cast long shadows across the ceiling, dancing like the ghosts we were trying to outrun.

I didn't leave. I didn't go to the trucks to check the engines one last time. I didn't go to the armory to count bullets. I stayed right there, breathing in the scent of her hair, listening to the rhythm of her breathing.

I thought about my father, dying on the floor of this room. I thought about Elford, laughing in his marsh.

But mostly, I thought about her.

If I died tomorrow, this would be the last thing I felt. Her warmth. Her weight. Her belief in me.

I tightened my grip on her.

"I won't hesitate," I whispered into the darkness. "I swear to you, Jazz. I won't be Marcus."

She snuggled closer, her head resting on my chest.

"I know," she murmured sleepily. "You're Damien. And that's enough."

The war could wait for the sun. The blood and the iron and the death could wait for the dawn.

Tonight, I belonged to her. And for the first time in thirty years, the ghost of my father wasn't standing in the corner of the room. He was gone, leaving me to face the morning on my own terms.

I closed my eyes, and for a few hours, there was peace.

# CHAPTER 28
# JAZZ

The fire in the hearth had faded to a bed of glowing embers, filling the room with a gentle, red light that seemed to pulse.

I lay on the narrow cot, listening to the wind howl against the stone walls. The sound was lonely and mournful, the kind of wind that strips leaves from trees and warns of a hard winter. But under the heavy wool blankets, I was warm.

Beside me, Damien was quiet.

To anyone else, he would have looked asleep. His breathing was slow and steady, his arm over his eyes, his body still. But I knew better. I was his mate. I was the other half of a soul that had been split and then forced back together.

I could feel him.

The bond in my mind was still active. It buzzed with a low, tense energy, like standing under a power line. He was guarding the room, his mind checking the locks, the windows, the perimeter. Even while trying to rest, the Alpha couldn't stop protecting us.

"You're awake," I whispered into the semi-darkness.

Damien didn't move, but the rhythm of his breathing hitched slightly.

"I'm trying not to be," he murmured, his voice rough with exhaustion. "I'm trying to do what you said. Just be here."

"You're not here," I said, rolling onto my side to face him. I traced the line of his jaw with my finger, feeling the roughness of the stubble that had grown in over the last twelve hours. "You're out there. You're in the valley. You're counting the stones in the Circle."

He turned his head slowly, his arm sliding down to rest on the pillow. In the gloom, his eyes were open, reflecting the dying embers of the fire. They looked dark, haunted, filled with the ghosts he had told me about earlier.

"I can't turn it off, Jazz," he admitted. "Every time I close my eyes, I see Elford. I see Kane. I see the axe coming down."

"Then don't close your eyes," I said.

"If I don't sleep, I'll be slow tomorrow. And if I'm slow..."

"If you're slow, you compensate," I interrupted. "You're not going to lose because you're tired, Damien.

You're going to lose if you go in there believing you're already dead."

I sat up, letting the blanket fall to my waist. The air felt cool on my skin, but I didn't care. I needed him to see me. I had to break the cycle of worry running through his mind.

"I heard you earlier," I said softly. "Before we came to bed. When you were telling me about the exit strategy."

He winced, a flicker of pain crossing his face. "It's a contingency, Jazz. A good soldier always has an extraction plan."

"I don't want an exit strategy," I said fiercely, leaning over him, planting my hands on either side of his shoulders. "I don't want to know which boat to take or which safe house has the most canned goods. I want you to come back."

"I plan to," he said.

"Planning isn't enough!" I snapped, the fear finally breaking through my calm facade. "You have to know it. You have to believe it. If you go into that Circle thinking about how I'm going to survive your death, you've already accepted it."

"I'm scared," he whispered.

His words hung in the air between us, heavy and surprising. Damien Ashford, the Warlord, the Alpha, the man who once faced down a mob in my hometown, was admitting he was afraid.

"I know," I said, my voice softening. "I can feel it. It

tastes like copper in my mouth. You're terrified that you're not strong enough to beat them all."

"There are three of them, Jazz. And I am one man."

"You are not one man," I corrected. "You are a pack. You are a lineage. And you are mine."

I moved, swinging my leg over his hips to straddle him. He grunted at the sudden weight, but his hands quickly steadied me, resting on my waist. His thumbs pressed into the soft fabric of the flannel shirt I wore, his shirt.

"Jazz..." he warned, his voice straining.

"Don't," I hissed. "Don't tell me to go back to sleep. Don't tell me to save my strength. I don't want to save anything tonight."

I leaned down, my hair falling around us like a curtain, shutting out the rest of the room. I was inches from his face. I could see the gold flecks in his irises, swirling with the turmoil of his emotions.

"Fill the space," I commanded him. "Push the fear out. Fill it with this. Fill it with me."

I kissed him.

It wasn't a gentle kiss. It wasn't the soft, comforting press of lips we had shared before. This was a demand, a collision. I poured everything I had into it: my belief in him, my anger at the world, my desperate need to keep him here, alive.

He froze for a second, surprised by the ferocity of it. Then, with a low groan that vibrated in his chest, he surrendered.

He wrapped his arms around me, pulling me close. He kissed me back with a hunger that almost felt wild. His tongue swept into my mouth, tasting and claiming me. The bond came alive, burning away the anxiety.

"Jazz," he gasped, breaking the kiss to bury his face in the crook of my neck. "We need to rest. Tomorrow..."

"Screw rest," I breathed against his ear. "We can rest when we're dead. Tonight, I want to feel alive. I want you to feel alive."

My hands went to the buttons of the flannel shirt. My fingers were shaking, fumbling with the fabric. I ripped the last button open, shrugging the shirt off my shoulders. It fell to the floor with a soft rustle.

I wasn't wearing anything underneath.

Damien's breath hissed in his throat. He looked up at me, his gaze traveling over my bare skin in the fire-light. He looked at my breasts, rising and falling with my ragged breathing. He looked at the curve of my waist, the flare of my hips.

"You are beautiful," he rasped. "God, you are beautiful."

"I'm yours," I told him. "Every inch. Every breath. Prove it, Damien. Claim me."

He reached up, his calloused palms skimming my ribs, his thumbs tracing the underside of my breasts. His touch was electric. It sent shockwaves through my nervous system, grounding me and setting me on fire all at once.

"Mine," he snarled, the Alpha rising to the surface. "You are mine, Jasmine Snow."

He sat up, flipping us over in one fluid motion. Suddenly, I was on my back, pressed into the mattress, and he was looming over me, a dark silhouette against the dying fire.

He tore his own shirt off, popping the buttons, not caring where they landed. His chest was heaving, the muscles corded and tense. He looked like a god of war who had decided to lay down his sword for a moment of worship.

He kissed me again, deeper this time, slower. His hands explored my body, mapping me, memorizing me. He touched the scar on my knee from when I fell as a child. He touched the pulse point at my throat. He touched the soft skin of my inner thigh.

"Show me," I begged, my hips lifting instinctively to meet him. "Don't hold back. I don't want the gentle mechanic tonight. I want the wolf."

"You have him," he promised.

He took off the rest of his clothes with impatient, jerky movements. When our skin finally touched, full and uninterrupted, the air in the room seemed to catch fire. It was a physical relief, like a circuit finally closing.

He didn't rush. Despite the desperation, despite the war waiting outside the door, he took his time. He wanted to make sure I was ready. He wanted to make sure I was with him.

He positioned himself between my legs, his weight heavy and comforting. He looked down at me, his eyes locked on mine.

"I love you," he said. The words were gritty, raw. "If this is the last time..."

"It's not," I interrupted, reaching up to pull him down. "It's the first time. The first time of the rest of our lives. Now come here."

He entered me.

It was a slow, devastating slide. I gasped, arching my back, my fingers digging into his shoulders. He filled me completely, stretching me, grounding me. It felt like coming home.

We moved together in the dark. It wasn't about technique or finesse. It was about connection. Every thrust was a statement. *I am here. I am not leaving. You are not alone.*

The bond roared. It wasn't just physical pleasure; it was a psychic merging. I could feel his heart beating in my chest. I could feel his love, fierce and protective, pouring into me and pushing out the fear.

"Damien," I moaned, wrapping my legs around his waist, pulling him deeper.

"I've got you," he gritted out, sweat slicking his skin. "I've got you, Jazz."

The tension coiled tighter and tighter. It was a spiral of heat and sensation. I forgot about Elford. I forgot about the knives and the guns. There was only this. Only him.

"Let go," he urged me, his voice a growl against my lips. "Give it to me."

I shattered.

The climax hit me like a physical blow. I cried out, my body convulsing, waves of pleasure rolling through me that were so intense they bordered on pain. I felt him shudder above me, heard the guttural roar tear from his throat as he followed me over the edge.

He collapsed on top of me, his weight pressing the air from my lungs in the best way. We lay tangled together, breathing the same air, our hearts pounding in sync.

Finally, Damien rolled to the side, pulling the blanket up over us. He tucked me against his chest, his arm heavy over my waist. He buried his face in my hair, inhaling deeply.

"You shouldn't have done that," he whispered, his voice thick with sleep and satisfaction. "You're going to be exhausted tomorrow."

"I feel more awake than I ever have," I murmured, tracing the damp hair at the nape of his neck. "I feel... solid."

"You are solid," he agreed. "You're the rock, Jazz. I'm just the wave that crashes against you."

"We're the ocean," I corrected. "Can't have one without the other."

He caught my hand, bringing my knuckles to his lips. He kissed each one, a silent reverence.

"When I win," he said, his voice steady with a new,

terrifying resolve. "When I walk out of that Circle... I'm going to claim you. Not just in here. Not just in the dark."

I looked up at him. "What do you mean?"

"Publicly," he said. "I'm going to tell the Council. I'm going to tell the packs. No more hiding in the library. No more pretending you're just an advisor. You will be the Wolf Queen. My equal. My partner."

Tears pricked my eyes. "They won't like it. The Grimvales... the traditionalists..."

"Let them hate it," Damien growled. "Let them try to stop us. Tonight... you reminded me of something."

"What?"

"That I fight better when I have something to defend. And I am going to defend this. Us."

"I want that," I whispered. "More than anything."

"Then we take it," he said.

He kissed me one last time, a soft, lingering seal on the promise. Then he sat up. The air felt cold where his body had been.

He didn't dress immediately. He sat on the edge of the bed, the firelight highlighting the powerful curve of his back, the scars that mapped his history of violence. He looked at his hands, flexing them.

He seemed to come to a decision.

He turned to look at me, his expression shifting. The lover was receding, replaced by the Alpha. The General. But the fear... the fear was gone. It had been burned away.

"Get up, Jazz," he said softly.

"Where are you going?" I asked, sitting up and clutching the blanket to my chest. "Is it time?"

"Not yet," he said. "But there is one more thing. One more piece of the puzzle I need to give you before I go."

"What is it?"

He stood up, moving to the center of the room. He looked dangerous. Lethal. And utterly magnificent.

"If I fall," he said, his voice calm, "I need to know that you can finish it. I need to know that if Elford corners you, you aren't helpless."

He beckoned me.

"Leave the blanket," he ordered. "Come here. I'm going to teach you the one thing my father forbade me to teach anyone."

I looked at him, confused but compelled by the steel in his voice. I slid out of bed, the cold floor biting my feet, and walked to him.

"What are you going to teach me?" I asked.

"I'm going to teach you," Damien said, "how to kill a King."

# CHAPTER 29
# JAZZ

The first light of dawn slipped through the thick velvet curtains, filling the room with shades of gray. The closeness of the last hour still hung in the air: the scent of musk, the warmth of tangled sheets, and the sound of our breathing slowing together.

But Damien's mood had shifted.

The lover was gone, replaced by a strict, disciplined presence. The General was back.

He stood by the bed, completely unashamed of the scars that showed his violent past. His eyes were distant, focused inward. He seemed as still and intimidating as a granite statue.

"Get up," he repeated, his voice devoid of the softness he had used moments before. "And leave the blanket."

I slid out of bed, shivering slightly as the cool

morning air hit my skin. I felt vulnerable, exposed, but I didn't reach for the cover. I walked to where he stood in the center of the room.

"What is it?" I asked, my voice small in the quiet room. "Is something wrong?"

"I'm going to teach you how to kill me," he said.

My breath hitched. The words landed like a physical blow. "What?"

He turned to face me fully. His expression was intense, burning with a fierce, terrifying pragmatism.

"Not me, specifically," he corrected, though his gaze didn't waver. "But someone like me. Someone bigger. Stronger. An Alpha."

He took a step closer, invading my space.

"It's a fail-safe, Jazz. If Elford cheats... if he gets past the walls... if I fall in that Circle and the line breaks... You need this. I cannot die in peace if I think you are defenseless."

He reached out and took my right hand. His grip was firm as he shaped my fingers into a strange, rigid claw: index and pinky extended, middle fingers pressed tightly to my palm.

"It's called the *King's Fang*," he said.

He tapped the hollow of his own throat, right where the collarbones met.

"Alpha physiology is built for high performance," he explained, his voice cool and distant. "We burn hotter, heal faster, move quicker. But that comes at a cost. Our nervous system is very sensitive." I could feel the steady, powerful thud of his heart beneath the muscle.

"If you strike here, at the suprasternal notch, you catch the vagus nerve cluster," he continued. "If you hit it hard enough and with precision, it sends a shock straight to the heart. It interrupts the electrical signal."

I stared at him, horrified. "It stops the heart?"

"It causes instant cardiac arrest," he confirmed. "Or at least, it resets the heart. It gives you three minutes. For those three minutes, an Alpha is paralyzed, gasping for air, unable to move or fight back."

"You want me to stop someone's heart?" I asked, pulling my hand back. "Damien, I can't. I'm a librarian. I fix books, I don't break people."

"You are a survivor," he said fiercely, grabbing my wrist and pulling my hand back to his throat. "And today, survival means violence. If Elford corners you, he won't hesitate. He won't care that you're a librarian. He will see a weakness, and he will exploit it."

He leaned down, his face inches from mine.

"I need you to be dangerous, Jazz. Attack me."

"No."

"Attack me!" he roared, the sudden volume making me jump. "Do it! Strike me!"

"I don't want to hurt you!"

"You can't hurt me unless you mean it!" he shouted. "Do you think Elford will pause? Do you think he'll ask nicely? He will tear you apart! Now hit me!"

He shoved me backward. I stumbled, hitting the wall.

Something inside me broke. The fear, exhaustion, and terror of losing him all came together and turned into anger.

I lunged.

I drove my hand toward his throat, fingers splayed.

He caught my wrist effortlessly, inches from his skin.

"Too slow," he growled. "You're telegraphing. Don't look at the target. Look at my eyes."

He shoved me back again.

"Again."

We practiced for twenty minutes. The room was filled with the sounds of scuffling feet and heavy breathing. He didn't go easy on me. He pinned me against the wall, against the door, forcing me to find the angle, forcing me to find the leverage.

"Drop your weight," he instructed, twisting my arm behind my back. "You're smaller. Use gravity. When you strike, you don't push. You fall into it."

"I'm trying!" I gasped, sweat dripping down my back.

"Try harder. Imagine it's Elford. Imagine he has his hands on me. Imagine he's killing me."

The image seared into my mind. Elford is standing over Damien's broken body. Elford laughing.

I let out a roar, a sound more animal than human, and twisted out of his grip.

I dropped my weight just like he showed me. I didn't push. I drove upward, my fingers rigid as iron.

I struck him.

My hand connected with the hollow of his throat. It wasn't a hard impact, but it was precise. I felt the soft tissue yield. I felt the hook.

Damien's eyes went wide.

He gagged. His knees buckled.

He collapsed onto the rug, gasping for air, clutching his chest. His skin flushed a dark, alarming red.

"Damien!" I screamed, dropping to my knees beside him. "Damien, breathe!"

For ten terrifying seconds, he couldn't. He wheezed, his body seizing up, his heart stuttering in his chest.

Then, he sucked in a massive, ragged breath. He coughed, rolling onto his side, shaking his head.

"It works," he croaked, his voice a broken rasp.

"I hurt you," I whispered, tears streaming down my face. "I'm sorry. I'm so sorry."

He reached out, grabbing my hand. His grip was weak, but steady.

"Good," he rasped, looking up at me with fierce, raw pride. "Be lethal."

He sat up slowly, rubbing his throat. There was a

red mark where I had struck him. A bruise I had put there.

He looked at the window. The sun was up now, a pale yellow circle shining through the fog. The night was over.

He stood up and got dressed. He moved quickly, pulling on tactical pants and a heavy black shirt, covering the skin I had just touched. He laced his boots tightly and strapped the ceremonial dagger to his thigh.

He seemed like a stranger now. He looked like the Warlord again.

But when he turned to me, his eyes were soft.

"Stay here," he ordered gently. "Roric has the perimeter. Do not leave this room until you see my signal flare. If the flare is white, we won. If it's red..."

He didn't finish the sentence. He didn't have to.

"If it's red, I use the Fang," I whispered.

"If it's red, you run," he corrected. "You run to the coast. You find the boat. And you disappear."

He walked to the door. He paused with his hand on the handle.

"Lock it behind me," he said. "And put the chair under the handle."

"I will."

He looked at me one last time, memorizing my face.

"I love you, Jazz."

"Come back," I said. "Just come back."

He opened the door and stepped out. I heard Roric greeting him in the hallway, their voices low and urgent.

The door closed.

I listened to his footsteps fade away down the corridor.

I walked to the door and locked it. Then I dragged the heavy oak chair over and wedged it under the handle.

I slid down to the floor, pressed my back against the door, and pulled my knees to my chest.

I looked at my hand. My fingers were still tingling from the impact. I flexed them into the claw shape.

*The King's Fang.*

I was alone. And the war had begun.

# CHAPTER 30
# JAZZ

The silence after the door clicked shut was absolute.

I sat on the floor with my back against the heavy oak, knees pulled to my chest, listening as Damien's boots echoed down the stone corridor. Outside, Roric's voice murmured something low and reassuring, maybe a change of the guard or a check on the perimeter. Then that sound faded too.

I was alone.

An hour ago, the room had been warm and safe. Now it felt huge and cold. The fire in the hearth was down to grey ash, matching the pale dawn light coming through the velvet curtains. The sheets on the narrow cot were still tangled, proof of the desperate life we clung to before everything changed.

I stood up, my legs shaking a little. The adrenaline

from the lesson on the King's Fang was wearing off, leaving only a cold, empty dread.

*Three minutes,* he had said. *It buys you three minutes.*

I looked at my hand. It looked small, pale, incapable of stopping a heart. But I flexed my fingers into the shape he had taught me: index and pinky extended, rigid as iron. I practiced the motion in the empty air. *Strike. Hook. Drop.*

I paced the room. Four steps to the window. Four steps back to the bed.

I couldn't look out the window. If I did, I would see the convoy leaving. I would see the dust rising as they drove toward the Neutral Valley. I would see him leaving me.

*Trust him,* I told myself. *He is the Warlord. He is the Black Wolf.*

But he was also the man who had looked at me with raw terror in his eyes and taught me how to kill him because he didn't think he was coming back.

Time stretched. Minutes felt like hours. I checked the antique clock on the mantle. 6:15 AM.

The Gambit would begin at 7:00 AM.

Forty-five minutes.

I walked to the heavy oak chair I had wedged under the door handle. It was solid. Roric was outside. The window was three stories up, overlooking a sheer drop to the rocky coastline. I was safe. I was in a vault.

So why did the hair on the back of my neck stand up?

I sat on the edge of the bed, trying to slow my breathing. I closed my eyes and reached for the bond. I could feel it, like a golden thread tying me to him. It was tight, full of focus and a simmering, controlled rage. He was in the truck, on the move. He wasn't thinking about me now; he was pushing me out of his mind so he could do what he had to.

*Good,* I thought. *Forget me. Survive.*

A sound scratched at the edge of my hearing.

It wasn't at the door. It wasn't at the window.

It was a soft, rhythmic *thump... drag... thump* coming from beneath me.

I froze.

The compound stood on old foundations. Damien once said they were smuggler's dens from the prohibition era. There were basements and sub-basements, a maze of concrete and earth that Roric swore had been sealed up years ago.

The sound came again. *Scrape. Click.*

It was coming from directly under the bed.

I stood up slowly, backing away toward the fireplace. My heart hammered against my ribs like a trapped bird.

*Check under the bed.*

The thought flashed through my mind, irrational and terrifying.

The floorboards beneath the heavy rug groaned. Not the groan of settling wood, but the groan of pressure being applied from below.

I grabbed the iron poker from the fireplace. It was heavy and rusted, a rough weapon compared to the precision of the Fang, but at least it gave me some reach.

The rug twitched.

Then, with a screech of tearing wood and rusted metal, the floor beneath the bed exploded upward.

I screamed, backing into the mantle.

The bed flew aside as if it weighed nothing and crashed into the wardrobe. A section of the floor—a hidden trapdoor covered by the rug and years of neglect—was thrown open.

Dark shapes poured out of the hole like smoke.

They weren't shadows. They were men. Men in tactical gear, faces covered by rebreathers and black masks. They moved with the silent, fluid grace of predators.

Shadowfangs.

There were three of them. No, four. They spread into the room, bringing with them the smell of damp earth and ozone.

I didn't freeze. Damien had drilled the freeze out of me.

I swung the poker.

The first man—the point man—didn't expect resistance. He expected a cowering girl. I caught him across the temple with the iron bar. There was a sickening crunch of impact, and he dropped like a stone, sliding back into the hole he had crawled out of.

"Secure her!" a voice hissed from the tunnel.

The other three fanned out. They didn't draw weapons. They had orders. *Alive.*

I scrambled onto the heavy oak desk, putting higher ground between us.

"Roric!" I screamed, hoping the sound would penetrate the heavy door. "Roric! Breach!"

The door handle rattled violently. The chair held.

"Open it!" Roric's voice roared from the hallway. I heard the sound of shoulders slamming against wood.

But the door was solid oak, reinforced with steel bands. It was meant to keep enemies out. Now it was keeping my rescuers out.

The Shadowfangs didn't wait. Two of them lunged for the desk.

I swung the poker again in a wide arc, trying to clear some space. One of them ducked under it with unnatural speed, the speed of a shifter. He grabbed my ankle and pulled.

I fell hard, hitting the edge of the desk with my ribs. The poker clattered away across the floor.

Pain exploded in my side, white-hot and blinding.

I scrambled backwards, kicking out, my heel connecting with a masked face. He grunted but didn't let go. He dragged me off the desk.

I hit the floor.

He was on top of me instantly, his weight pinning my legs. He reached for my arms.

*The Fang.*

I didn't struggle against his weight. I went limp for a fraction of a second, letting him think he had me.

His hand moved to grab my wrist.

I snapped my hand up. I didn't make a fist. I made the claw.

I drove my rigid fingers into the soft hollow of his throat, right above the tactical vest.

I poured every ounce of fear and rage into the strike.

*Strike. Hook. Drop.*

My fingers dug in. I felt the cartilage give. I felt the pulse.

The Shadowfang stiffened. His eyes went wide behind the mask. He made a choking, gurgling sound, his hands flying to his throat. His body convulsed, seizing up as his nervous system misfired.

He collapsed on top of me, a dead weight.

I shoved him off, gasping, scrambling crab-like across the rug.

It worked. God, it worked.

But there were two more.

They paused, looking at their fallen comrade, then at me. The wariness in their posture shifted. They weren't looking at a package anymore. They were looking at a threat.

One of them reached for his belt and pulled out a small, silver pistol.

*No guns in the room.*

He fired.

There was no bang. Just a soft *pfft* of compressed air.

A dart hit me in the thigh.

It burned like a hornet sting. I ripped it out instantly, but the damage was done.

"Grab her," the gunman ordered.

I tried to stand. I tried to run for the window. But the room tilted. The floor seemed to rush up to meet me. My legs turned to water.

*Ketamine blend,* my mind supplied, remembering Damien's warnings about Shadowfang tactics. *Fast acting.*

I fell to my knees.

The remaining two men advanced. The world was blurring, smearing into streaks of grey and black.

"Roric..." I tried to shout, but my tongue felt thick, heavy.

The door behind me splintered. An axe blade punched through the wood. Roric was coming.

"Too late," the gunman whispered. He grabbed me by the hair, hauling me up.

I tried to fight, but my limbs felt like lead. They dragged me toward the hole in the floor.

But then, the bedroom door exploded inward.

The door was shattered off its hinges. Roric charged in. He was already half-shifted, his eyes glowing amber and his teeth bared in a furious snarl. Two Ashen enforcers followed behind him.

The Shadowfangs hesitated. They looked at the

tunnel, then at the enraged wolf charging them. They looked at me, dead weight in their arms.

They made the calculation. They couldn't carry me and fight Roric at the same time.

They dropped me.

I hit the rug hard, the air wooshing out of my lungs.

"Abort!" one of them hissed.

They dove into the hole in the floor, disappearing into the darkness of the sub-basement just as Roric reached them.

Roric didn't follow. He skidded to a halt beside me, dropping to his knees.

"Jazz!" he shouted, tapping my face. "Jazz, stay with me!"

I tried to focus on his face, but he was swimming in and out of view.

"Tunnel..." I slurred. "Elford..."

"They're gone," Roric said, his voice tight with relief and rage. "We have the perimeter locked. You're safe."

He touched the dart in my leg. "Ketamine," he cursed. "Get the medic! Now!"

I felt myself being lifted. Not roughly, like the Shadowfangs, but gently. Securely.

"Damien..." I whispered. "Don't tell him."

"He needs to know," Roric said grimly.

"No," I managed to say, grabbing his shirt with

numb fingers. "If he knows... he comes back. He forfeits. Promise me."

Roric looked at me, torn. He knew I was right. If Damien knew the compound was breached, he would leave the Circle. He would lose the war to save me.

"Promise," I begged, the darkness closing in.

"I promise," Roric whispered. "Sleep now, Luna. We've got you."

The last thing I saw was the shattered door and the hole in the floor where the monsters had come from.

I had failed to stay safe. But I had held them off long enough.

I closed my eyes, and the drugs pulled me under.

# CHAPTER 31
# JAZZ

I woke up to the smell of bleach and iron.

For a long, confusing moment, I didn't know where I was. The ceiling was unfamiliar, with rough timber beams instead of the popcorn plaster in my apartment or the canvas of a tent. My body felt heavy, weighed down by a strange, chemical tiredness, like I was swimming through molasses.

I tried to sit up, but a sharp, biting pain in my side slammed me back down. I groaned, the sound scraping against a throat that felt raw, as if I had been screaming for hours.

"Easy," a voice said. "Don't move yet. The sedative hasn't fully cleared."

I turned my head, fighting the dizziness. A woman stood by the window. She was a healer from the Ashen Ones pack. I recognized her vaguely; she had been in the infirmary when Damien's leg was stitched.

"Where is he?" I croaked.

"Gone," she said gently, wringing out a cloth in a basin of water. "The Alpha left hours ago. The sun is already up."

Gone.

The word hit me harder than the pain in my ribs. Damien was gone. The flare hadn't been fired. The war was happening, and I was... here.

Then the memories crashed back. The scuff of boots. The lock turned. The door exploded inward. Scar-face. The Grimvales.

My hand flew to my waist, seeking the Karambit, but found only the soft cotton of a clean t-shirt.

"Where is it?" I panicked, struggling to sit up despite the healer's hands on my shoulders. "The knife! Where is the knife?"

"It's on the table," she soothed, pushing me back down with surprising strength. "It's clean. You're safe, Jazz. They're dead."

Dead.

I closed my eyes, and the image flashed behind my eyelids in high-definition horror. The way Scar-face had lunged. The way I had dropped my weight, just like Damien taught me. The feel of the curved blade sinking into soft tissue. The blood. So much blood.

I had killed him. I had killed a man.

Technically, I had killed a wolf, but the distinction felt meaningless in the cold light of day. I had taken a life. The librarian from Tallow was gone, washed away in a tide of red violence, replaced by something colder, sharper.

"The others?" I asked, opening my eyes.

"One dead," the healer reported grimly. "The other two fled when the perimeter guard responded to the noise. You held them off long enough for backup."

She looked at me with a mixture of fear and awe. "You gutted a Draven lieutenant in close quarters. Without shifting. The pack... they are talking about it."

"I don't care what they're talking about," I whispered. "I care about Damien. Does he know?"

"No," she said. "Roric gave the order. Total communication blackout. If the Alpha knew the compound had been breached... if he knew you had been attacked... he would leave the Circle. He would forfeit the Gambit to come back to you. We couldn't let that happen."

"You lied to him," I said, a cold fury rising in my chest. "You let him walk into that valley thinking I was safe."

"He needs to focus," the healer insisted. "He is fighting three Alphas. He cannot be distracted by your... situation."

My situation. Being almost murdered in my bedroom was a "situation."

I swung my legs over the side of the bed. The room spun, then settled. My side was bandaged tightly, probably from a claw mark left by one of the Grimvales. It hurt, but it was a dull ache, already starting to heal quickly thanks to the wolf inside me.

"I need to go," I said, standing up. My knees wobbled, but I locked them.

"You can't," the healer said, stepping in front of me. "You are under lockdown. Roric's orders were clear. If the compound is breached, the Mate is to be moved to the deep cellar until the All Clear."

"The compound *was* breached," I snapped, moving past her to the table where my gear was piled. "Which means the cellar isn't safe. Nothing is safe. If they got in once, they can get in again."

I picked up the Karambit. The leather handle felt familiar now, comfortable in a sickening way. I clipped it to the reinforced belt at my waist of the fresh leggings someone had laid out for me. I pulled on my boots.

"Where do you think you're going?" the healer demanded.

"To the valley," I said, grabbing my tactical vest. It was Damien's vest, and I pulled it on. It smelled like him. It smelled like safety.

"That is forbidden!" she cried. "The Stone Circle is neutral ground, but it is a battlefield! No spectators allowed except the Seconds and the Arbiters. You will be killed!"

"I'm already being killed here," I said, turning to face her. "Elford sent assassins to my bedroom *before* the fight even started. Do you think he's playing by the rules in the valley? He's cheating. And Damien doesn't know."

"You can't help him," she argued. "You are untrained. You are injured."

"I am his Second," I said, my voice dropping to a growl that wasn't entirely human. "He named me. He trained me. And I am not going to sit in a cellar while he dies for a lie."

I walked to the door. It was a new door, a heavy steel-reinforced slab that had replaced the splintered wood of the old one. It was locked from the outside.

"Open it," I ordered.

"I can't."

"Open it," I repeated, "or I will shift and tear it off the hinges. And then I will tear through anyone who tries to stop me."

The healer looked at me. She saw the gold bleeding into my blue eyes. She saw the blood of the Draven that I had washed off my hands, but still carried in my soul.

She pulled a key card from her pocket and beeped the lock.

"There is a truck by the loading dock," she whispered, looking down. "The keys are in the ignition. It's the supply truck for the perimeter guard."

"Thank you," I said.

I didn't run. I walked. I walked through the halls of the Alpha's lodge, ignoring the stares of the few guards who remained. They saw the vest. They saw the look in my eyes. They stepped aside.

The compound felt like a ghost town. Most of the fighters were with Damien, and the reserve force was patrolling the walls. I slipped out the back exit, moving through the shadows of the loading bay. The truck was there, a battered Ford rusted by the sea air.

I climbed in, started the engine, and drove toward the rear gate. The guard there hesitated, but when he saw who was driving, he opened the barrier. I was the Alpha's Mate. In his absence, my authority was absolute, even if Roric claimed otherwise.

I drove fast.

The road to the Neutral Valley was a winding, treacherous track that cut through the densest part of the forest. The mist was lifting, revealing a sky the color of a fresh bruise.

I gripped the steering wheel, my knuckles white.

I promised him I would stay in the room, that I would wait for the flare.

But he had promised me I was safe. And that promise was broken the moment Scar-face kicked down the door.

The bond was silent. Too silent. It terrified me. Either Damien was blocking me completely from focusing, or he was already...

*No.*

I slammed my foot on the accelerator. The truck shuddered as I hit sixty on a dirt road.

I wasn't going to interfere. I couldn't. The Gambit was sacred. If I stepped into the Circle, Damien would be disqualified and executed.

But I had to see. I had to be there. I had to be the anchor he talked about.

And if Elford tried to cheat... if a sniper appeared on the ridge, or a second wave of assassins tried to rush the ring...

I touched the handle of the knife.

I would be ready.

I parked the truck a mile from the valley entrance, hiding it in a cluster of spruce trees. I continued on foot, moving silently through the underbrush. The wolf inside me was alert, cataloging every scent.

*Pine. Damp earth. Ozone.*

And then, stronger than everything else: *Wolf.*

Hundreds of them.

I reached the ridge overlooking the Stone Circle just as the sun broke through the clouds.

The sight took my breath away.

The valley was a natural amphitheater, a bowl of green grass surrounded by steep, rocky cliffs. In the center stood the Stones, massive ancient monoliths arranged in a perfect ring and weathered by centuries of storms.

Surrounding the ring, on the slopes of the valley, were the packs.

To the west, a sea of grey and brown marked the

Grimvales. They stood silent, holding axes and clubs, a wall of muscle. To the east, the Shadowfangs moved like shadows in the daylight. They were quieter, less distinct, but their presence was a heavy, suffocating pressure. To the south, the Dravens formed a chaotic, jeering mob. They were drinking, shouting, treating this like a spectator sport.

And to the north... the Ashen Ones. My pack. Damien's pack. They stood in rigid formation, outnumbered but disciplined. Roric stood at the front, his arms crossed, watching the center.

I crept closer, staying low in the brush, finding a vantage point behind a fallen log on the ridge line. I was high up, looking down into the bowl. I could see everything.

And I saw him.

Damien stood in the center of the Stone Circle.

He looked small from this distance, a solitary figure against the monoliths. He had taken off his shirt, and his skin gleamed with oil and sweat. He stood perfectly still, his hands loose at his sides, facing the northern entrance of the stones.

He was alone.

The Arbiter, old Silas, stood on a raised dais outside the ring. He raised a staff, and silence fell over the valley. It was a heavy, unnatural silence, broken only by the caw of a crow circling overhead.

"The Gambit is invoked!" Silas's voice boomed,

amplified by the acoustics of the valley. "Damien Ashford, Alpha of the Ashen Ones, stands to prove his claim to the Wolf Throne!"

A roar went up from the Ashen Ones. A jeer from the Dravens.

"The terms are set!" Silas continued. "Three battles. Consecutive. No mercy. No quarter."

He pointed his staff toward the eastern entrance of the stones.

"First Challenger! Selene of the Shadowfangs!"

The eastern stones parted, or at least seemed to, a trick of the light and shadow. Selene stepped through.

She was in human form. She wore a skin-tight suit of dark, shimmering material that looked like liquid scales. She held no weapons in her hands, but I saw the glint of metal strapped to her forearms—blades hidden along the ulna bone.

She looked fast. She looked lethal.

She walked into the circle, circling Damien like a shark.

Damien didn't move. He didn't turn to face her. He stood like a statue, staring straight ahead.

*Disrespect,* I thought, remembering our strategy. *He's ignoring her.*

Selene stopped. She hissed something I couldn't hear. Damien didn't react.

The bell rang—a deep, resonant gong sound that vibrated in my teeth.

The fight was on.

My heart hammered against the dirt as I watched. This wasn't training. This wasn't sparring in the gym. This was death.

Selene moved first. She was a blur, too fast for human eyes, but my wolf vision tracked her. She launched herself at Damien's back, the blades on her arms extending.

Damien didn't turn. He dropped.

He hit the ground in a crouch, and Selene flew over him, her blades slicing empty air.

As she landed and pivoted, Damien exploded upward. He didn't shift. He drove his shoulder into her midsection, tackling her.

They hit the dirt.

The crowd roared.

I gripped the bark of the log, my nails digging in. *Get up, Damien. Don't grapple with her. She has poison.*

Selene twisted like an eel, slipping out of his grip. She slashed at his face. Damien jerked back, a thin line of red appearing on his cheek.

*First blood.*

The Shadowfangs howled.

Damien backed away, wiping the blood from his cheek. He looked at it, then looked at Selene.

He smiled.

It was the smile he had given me in the gym. The *I'm winning* smile.

Selene paused, confused. She had cut him. Why was he smiling?

Because he hadn't shifted. He hadn't used his strength yet. He was playing with her.

"Bait her," I whispered.

Damien opened his arms wide, exposing his chest. Exposing his throat.

Selene took the bait. Her ego couldn't handle the mockery. She shrieked, a high, piercing sound, and shifted.

A massive black panther appeared—no, it was a wolf that looked like a panther, sleek and furless. She lunged for his throat.

Damien shifted.

The Black Wolf appeared, twice the size of Selene. He didn't dodge. He caught her mid-air.

His jaws clamped down on her shoulder. Her momentum carried them both down, but Damien was on top. He shook her violently, like a dog with a rat.

Selene thrashed, her claws raking his sides, scoring deep furrows in his flank.

*The poison,* I thought, panic rising. *If she breaks the skin, the poison gets in.*

Damien roared, a sound of pure fury, and threw her.

She flew ten feet, hitting one of the standing stones with a sickening crunch. She slid down the rock, leaving a smear of blood.

She didn't get up.

The Arbiter raised his staff. "One!"

Selene twitched.

"Two!"

She tried to rise, her legs scrabbling for purchase, but her back leg dragged uselessly. Broken spine? Or just stunned?

"Three!"

She collapsed, shifting back to human form, naked and broken in the dirt.

"Winner of the First Round!" Silas shouted. "Damien Ashford!"

The Ashen Ones erupted.

I let out a breath I had been holding for five minutes. He did it. He beat her in under sixty seconds.

But as Damien shifted back to human form, I saw it.

He stumbled.

He put a hand to his side, where Selene had scratched him. The scratches weren't healing. They were turning black.

The poison.

He looked up at the ridge, scanning the crowd. He wasn't looking at Roric. He wasn't looking at Elford.

He was looking for me.

The bond snapped open.

*Jazz?* His thought came, weak and distorted by pain.

*I'm here,* I projected back, pouring every ounce of

strength I had into the connection. *I'm watching. You won.*

*Poison,* he thought. *Burns.*

*Fight it,* I commanded. *You have ten minutes. Metabolism. Burn it out.*

He nodded imperceptibly. He sat down in the center of the circle, closing his eyes, entering a meditative trance. Roric ran into the ring with water and towels, tending to the wounds.

I watched, helpless, from the ridge.

One down.

But Kane was sharpening his axe on the sidelines. And Elford was laughing.

I looked at Elford. He was scanning the ridge, too. He held a phone to his ear. He looked annoyed.

*He knows,* I realized. *He knows the assassins failed. He knows I'm not dead.*

He looked up, directly at my hiding spot. It was an impossible distance, but he looked right at me.

He smiled.

And then he drew a finger across his throat.

I didn't flinch. I touched the Karambit.

*Come and get me, you son of a bitch,* I thought. *But you'll have to go through him first.*

The ten minutes were up.

Silas banged his staff.

"Second Challenger! Kane of the Grimvales!"

The mountain of muscle stepped into the ring.

I watched Damien stand up. He swayed, then

steadied. He was paler than before. The poison was working.

But he stood.

I watched the battle begin, my hand on my knife, my heart in the Circle, and the awful certainty settling in my gut that the hardest part hadn't even started yet.

# CHAPTER 32

# JAZZ

The sound of an axe hitting stone is a terrible thing. It sounds like the earth itself is cracking open.

I hid on the ridge, crouched behind a rotting spruce log, and watched Kane of the Grimvales swing a weapon that could have come from a torture museum. His double-headed battle axe, heavy iron covered in runes, moved fast in his hands—shockingly fast for someone as big as a grizzly bear.

Damien was dancing.

He had no choice. Selene's poison was still in his system. I could feel his blood moving slowly and heavily through our bond, dragging at his limbs. He hadn't shaken it off yet. Now he faced a giant who wanted to crush him.

The bell had rung five minutes ago.

Kane swung again, a horizontal arc meant to

decapitate. Damien dropped to his knees, the blade slicing the air where his neck had been a microsecond before. He didn't just dodge; he rolled forward, coming up inside Kane's guard, and drove his ceremonial dagger into the giant's thigh.

It should have crippled him. Instead, Kane just grunted, swinging a massive fist that connected with Damien's shoulder.

I flinched like I'd been hit myself. The blow sent Damien flying back ten feet. He hit the ground hard, rolled to his feet, but I saw him stumble. I felt a sharp pain in his left shoulder. Was it dislocated? Bruised?

"Get up," I whispered, my nails digging into the bark of the log. "Move, Damien. Move."

The crowd below was screaming. The Grimvales were howling for blood. The Ashen Ones were silent, watching their Alpha get battered by a superior force.

Damien shifted.

It was a desperate move. His human form was taking too much damage. The Black Wolf burst forth, snarling, and launched itself at Kane's throat.

Kane didn't look surprised. He dropped the axe and caught the wolf in mid-air.

Caught him.

He grabbed Damien by the throat and the flank, lifting three hundred pounds of angry wolf like it was a stuffed toy, and slammed him onto the hard-packed earth of the Circle.

The sound was sickening. A wet thud that vibrated through the valley floor and up into my bones.

I clapped my hand over my mouth to keep from screaming. The bond between us burned with pure, blinding agony.

*Damien!* I projected the thought, screaming it into the psychic void.

He didn't answer. He was fighting for air, scrabbling with his claws against Kane's massive arms.

I couldn't watch. But I couldn't look away.

I tore my eyes from the Circle for a second, scanning the sidelines. I needed to see Roric. I needed to see someone stepping in. The Arbiter, Silas, was watching impassively. This was the Gambit. No mercy.

My gaze drifted to the southern section of the valley, where the Dravens were gathered.

Empty.

The chair where Elford had been sitting—lounging, drinking, laughing—was empty.

A cold prickle of dread crept up my spine, sharper than the wind.

I scanned the crowd. The Draven mob was still there, jeering. But their Alpha was gone. And his personal guard—the four massive brutes who never left his side—were gone too.

He had signaled me. He had drawn a finger across his throat.

And now he was gone.

*He's coming.*

The realization hit me with the force of a physical blow. Elford wasn't waiting for his turn in the Circle, for Damien to die by Kane's hand. He was coming to collect the prize he had promised to take.

Me.

I looked back at the Circle. Damien had managed to twist free, raking his claws down Kane's chest, creating distance. He was alive. He was fighting.

I couldn't help him. But I could ensure I wasn't the leverage they used to break him.

I had to move.

I scrambled backwards, keeping low to the ground, moving away from the ridge line and into the dense cover of the forest. My plan to watch the battle was dead. I needed to get back to the truck. I needed to get moving.

I turned and broke into a run, weaving through the trees. The underbrush snagged at my tactical vest, briars tearing at my leggings. I didn't care. I engaged the quiet, rhythmic breathing Damien had taught me.

*Silence is survival.*

But the woods felt wrong.

Usually, the forest was full of noise: birds, wind, squirrels. Now it was completely silent. That kind of silence only comes when a predator is near.

I stopped, pressing my back against a massive pine tree. I held my breath, listening.

To my left, a twig snapped.

To my right, the rustle of a fern.

They were herding me.

I dropped my hand to the Karambit. *Up and in.*

I wasn't going to make it to the truck. They were between me and the road.

I looked up. The tree I was leaning against was old, its lower branches thick and sturdy.

If I couldn't run out, I would go up.

I sheathed the knife and jumped, grabbing the lowest branch. I hauled myself up, scrabbling for purchase on the rough bark. I climbed fast, ignoring the scrapes on my hands, until I was twenty feet up, hidden in the dense canopy of needles.

I froze there, hugging the trunk.

Below me, shapes emerged from the mist.

Three men. Dressed in dark tactical gear. Not Dravens.

They moved with a fluid, silent grace that I recognized instantly.

Shadowfangs.

My blood ran cold. Selene had lost her fight. She was broken in the dirt below. But her pack... her pack was hunting me.

"She was here," one of them whispered. His voice was like dry leaves. "Scent is fresh. Snow. Fear. And Ashford."

"She didn't pass the perimeter," another said. "She's close."

"Elford wants her alive," the third reminded them. "If you damage the merchandise, we don't get paid."

Paid.

The Shadowfangs were mercenaries. Elford had hired them to flush me out while he waited.

I held my breath, praying the wind wouldn't shift. Praying they wouldn't look up.

But Shadowfangs were spies. They were trained to look where others didn't.

The first one stopped at the base of my tree. He touched the bark. He looked at the scuff marks my boots had made.

He looked up.

His violet eyes locked onto mine through the branches.

He didn't shout. He didn't alert the others. He just smiled, lips curving in a thin, cruel line, and pulled a small silver pistol from his belt. They weren't in the Circle's jurisdiction.

He aimed.

I didn't wait to see if it was a tranquilizer or a bullet.

I jumped.

I launched myself from the branch, aiming not for the ground, but for the Shadowfang.

I shifted in mid-air.

It was the most painful shift I'd ever felt. Gravity dragged me down as my bones changed shape. I screamed, the sound turning from human fear to a wolf's roar halfway down.

The White Wolf hit the Shadowfang with the force of a falling anvil.

He fired, but the shot went wide, cracking into the canopy.

We hit the ground in a tangle of limbs and fur. I snapped my jaws, catching his arm, crunching bone. He screamed.

The other two Shadowfangs spun around, drawing blades.

I scrambled off the fallen man, my claws digging into the loam, and bolted.

I was fast. I was a Ferrari. But the woods were thick, and I was panicking.

I tore through a thicket of thorns, bursting into a small clearing.

And stopped.

The clearing was full.

Standing in a semi-circle, blocking my path, were six Dravens. Big, ugly, and smiling.

And in the center, leaning against a tree, picking his teeth with a sliver of wood, was Elford.

He looked perfect. His suit was spotless. He seemed more like someone waiting for a bus than a man hunting an Alpha's mate.

I skidded to a halt, snarling, my hackles raised. I backed up, but the two Shadowfangs I had evaded were already behind me, blocking the retreat.

Surrounded.

"Good morning, Jazz," Elford said pleasantly. "Nice jump. Very dramatic. Damien taught you well."

I growled low in my throat, crouching, ready to spring. *Come near me, and I'll kill you.*

"Oh, I wouldn't do that," Elford said, shaking his head. "Look at the odds, sweetheart. Eight to one. And my boys? They aren't restricted by the rules of the Gambit. They brought toys."

The Dravens raised rifles. Dart guns.

"Tranquilizers," Elford explained. "Ketamine blend. Enough to drop a rhino. If you fight, we shoot you. You wake up in a cage in the marsh with a headache. If you shift back and come quietly... well, you still end up in a cage, but maybe I'll let you keep your dignity."

I snarled again. I wasn't going quietly.

"Have it your way," Elford sighed. He snapped his fingers.

Three darts hit me at once.

One in the flank. One in the shoulder. One in the neck.

The effect was instantaneous.

My legs went weak. The world tilted and blurred into gray. The wolf's roar in my mind faded to a confused whimper.

I collapsed.

The ground rushed up to meet me. The smell of damp earth filled my nose.

I tried to stand. I tried to bite. But my body was

gone. I was just a consciousness floating in a heavy, numb sea.

The last thing I saw was Elford's polished shoes walking toward me.

He crouched down. I couldn't move my head, but I could see his face. He was smiling.

"Shift back, darling," he whispered. "It's easier to carry you."

My body betrayed me. The survival instinct, sensing the incapacity, forced the shift to conserve energy. The fur receded. The bones snapped back.

I was human again. Naked and helpless, lying in the dirt at the feet of the man who killed the King.

Elford took off his jacket and draped it over me. It was a mocking gesture of chivalry.

"There," he said. "Can't have the prize catching a cold."

He stood up, looking at his men. "Grab her. And be gentle. She's worth more than all of you combined."

Strong hands grabbed my arms and legs. I was lifted into the air.

"What about the fight?" one of the Dravens asked. "Kane is still pounding on Ashford."

"Let Kane have his fun," Elford said, checking his watch. "He's wearing him down. Breaking his bones. By the time my turn comes up... Damien will be a crawling wreck."

He looked down at me, his eyes gleaming with malicious triumph.

"You see, Jazz," he said, leaning in close so only I could hear. "The Gambit was never about fighting. It was about distraction. Damien thinks he's fighting for the Throne. He thinks he's fighting for honor."

He laughed softly.

"He doesn't know that we already voted. Last night. At the lodge."

I tried to speak, but my tongue was numb. *Voted?*

"The Alphas," Elford explained. "Me. Kane. Selene. Even the Arbiters looked the other way. We decided that a contender who breaks the Codex by bedding a rival... he doesn't deserve a fair fight. He deserves to be made an example of."

He stroked my hair.

"We agreed to take you. Regardless of who wins in the Circle. Even if Damien kills all three of us... His pack is forfeit. And you belong to the Alliance."

He turned and started walking toward the road.

"Bring her to the ridge," Elford ordered. "I want him to see her."

*No,* I screamed inside my head. *No, don't let him see me. He'll break.*

"I want him to look up from the blood and the mud," Elford said, his voice carrying through the woods, "and see that he has already lost."

I was carried through the trees. The darkness of the drugs was pulling at me, trying to drag me under.

*Fight it,* Damien's voice echoed in my memory. *Stay sharp.*

I fought to keep my eyes open.

They brought me to the edge of the ridge—the same ridge where I had been hiding.

Below us, the Stone Circle was a scene of carnage.

Damien was on his knees. He was back in human form, covered in blood and dirt. His left arm hung uselessly at his side.

Kane stood over him, heaving, his axe raised for a killing blow.

"Look at him," Elford whispered in my ear. "The King."

"Damien!" I tried to scream, but it came out as a breathless moan.

Down in the valley, Damien's head snapped up.

He heard me. Through the bond. Through the pain. He heard me.

His eyes locked onto the ridge. He saw the Dravens. He saw Elford. He saw me, limp and captured.

The change in him was terrifying.

He didn't look defeated. He didn't look broken.

He looked like the end of the world.

He roared—a sound that shattered the air in the valley. It wasn't a wolf roar. It was a demon's scream.

He lunged upward, ignoring Kane's axe. He drove his good shoulder into Kane's knees, toppling the giant.

But he didn't stay to finish the fight.

He turned toward the ridge. Toward me.

"Oh," Elford said, sounding genuinely delighted. "Now it gets interesting."

He keyed his radio.

"Execute Plan B," he ordered. "Bring the rain."

From the tree line behind the Stone Circle, where the Grimvales were gathered, muzzle flashes lit up the shadows.

Gunfire.

They were shooting into the Circle. They were shooting at the Alpha.

The rules were gone. The Gambit was dead.

"Watch closely, Jazz," Elford whispered, his hand tightening on my shoulder. "This is how you break a legend."

I watched as bullets kicked up dirt around Damien. I watched as he shifted into the Black Wolf, zigzagging through the hail of fire, trying to reach the cliff face. Trying to reach me.

But he was hurt. He was slow.

A bullet caught him in the flank. He tumbled, rolling, and came up snarling.

"Take her away," Elford ordered, stepping back. "I have a fight to finish."

I was dragged back into the trees. The last thing I saw was the Black Wolf, bleeding and surrounded, throwing himself against the impossible cliff, clawing his way up toward the sky, roaring my name into the indifference of the wind.

Then the drugs won.

And the world went black.

CHAPTER 33

# DAMIEN

The valley was a bowl of shadows, the sun still struggling to crest the eastern cliffs. The Stone Circle waited in the center, ancient and indifferent, a ring of monoliths that had tasted the blood of kings and cowards alike for three centuries.

I stepped out of the truck, my boots sinking into the damp, semi-frozen mud. The air was thick with the scent of gathered wolves—hundreds of them. It smelled of wet fur, woodsmoke, and the sharp, metallic tang of aggression.

Roric stood beside me, handing me a towel and a water bottle. He looked haggard, his uniform slightly disheveled, sweat drying on his brow despite the chill in the air. He had arrived only minutes before me, racing from the compound.

"Status?" I asked quietly, keeping my voice low so the gathering crowds couldn't hear.

Roric hesitated for a fraction of a second—a micro-expression of guilt that vanished as quickly as it appeared.

"Secure," Roric lied. "She's locked down tight. Guards on the door. No one gets in or out."

I nodded, letting out a breath I hadn't realized I was holding. "Good. If I know she's safe, I can do this."

"She's safe," Roric emphasized, though his eyes didn't quite meet mine. "Focus on the fight, Damien. That's what she wants."

I turned my attention to the arena.

I scanned the ridgelines. To the west, the Grim-vales were a wall of silent muscle, their axes gleaming dully in the low light. To the east, the Shadowfangs moved like oil, fluid and indistinct. To the south, the Dravens were a riot of noise and jeers, a mob waiting for an execution.

I looked for Elford.

He was sitting in a high-backed camp chair, elevated on a small wooden platform his men had erected. He was wearing that pristine suit, looking like a spectator at a polo match rather than a participant in a death match. He held a crystal tumbler in one hand.

He saw me looking. He raised the glass in a mock toast.

I didn't return the gesture. I turned my attention to the northern entrance of the stones, where the Ashen Ones were gathered. My pack. They looked grim. They knew the odds. They knew that if I fell today, their history ended.

"The Arbiter is signaling," Roric murmured, checking his watch. "Two minutes to the bell."

I stripped off my leather jacket, handing it to Roric. The cold air bit at the scars on my chest, tightening the skin. I rolled my neck, feeling the tension coil in my muscles. I was ready. The doubt from the night before was gone, replaced by a cold, hard clarity.

*She is safe,* I told myself, repeating the mantra I had been chanting since I left the room. *Roric has the perimeter. The tunnel is sealed. She is waiting for the white flare.*

I reached out with my mind, trying to touch the bond. I wanted one last hit of her presence before I shut it down for the fight.

Silence.

I frowned. Usually, the bond was a hum in the back of my head, a sense of direction and emotion. Today, it was a void.

*She's sleeping,* I rationalized. *Or the stress has caused her to wall off. Or maybe the distance is just too great.*

But the silence felt heavy. Cold.

"Alpha," a voice interrupted.

I turned. A Lone Shifter, one of the neutral arbiters, was standing there. He held a small, folded piece of heavy cream paper.

"Message for the Challenger," the wolf said, his

face impassive. "Delivered under the flag of the Gambit."

"From whom?" Roric demanded, stepping forward to intercept it. "There are no messages in the Circle."

"It pertains to the terms," the Shifter said, handing the note to me before Roric could grab it. "From Alpha Draven."

I took the paper. It felt expensive. Thick.

I unfolded it.

There was no letterhead. No seal. Just a single sentence scrawled in elegant, looping handwriting that I recognized from the few treaties Elford had bothered to sign.

*You thought she was safe in the tower, Damien. You forgot that curiosity kills the cat.*

My heart skipped a beat.

I read it again.

*You thought she was safe in the tower.*

He knew. He knew I thought she was at the compound.

I looked at the next line.

*Did you check under the bed, Damien? I hope you said goodbye properly. My men say she screams beautifully. I wonder if your guards were fast enough? Or perhaps I have her right now, waiting for you to die.*

The world stopped.

The noise of the crowd, the wind in the trees, the thrum of my own heart—it all vanished into a vacuum of absolute, ringing silence.

The image of Jazz under a ceiling that hid a door—under a bed that wasn't safe—flashed through me like a blade.

I looked at the note again. At the bottom, in smaller script:

*Step out of the Circle, she dies. Lose the fight, she dies. Entertain me, and maybe I let you say goodbye.*

A sound tore out of my throat—a low, broken noise that sounded like something dying.

"Damien?" Roric touched my arm. "What is it?"

I shoved the note into his chest.

Roric read it. The color drained from his face, leaving him grey and aged.

"No," Roric whispered. "I left her in the infirmary. She was sedated. I put two guards on the door."

"She woke up," I rasped, the realization hitting me like a physical blow. "She woke up and she came. Roric... she followed me."

I handled it!" Roric stammered, desperation in his eyes. "The tunnel breach was contained. I doubled the guard. I didn't tell you because I knew you would forfeit!"

"The tunnel?" I snapped my head toward him. "What tunnel breach?"

Roric froze. He had slipped.

"They tried to take her," Roric admitted, his voice hollow. "Before you left. Shadowfangs in the bedroom. We stopped them. She made me promise not to tell you so you wouldn't forfeit."

The rage hit me then.

It wasn't the hot, fiery anger of a fight. It was cold. It was absolute zero. It froze my lungs. It shattered the careful walls I had built around the bond.

She had been attacked. She had protected me by lying. And then, driven by that same insane loyalty, she had come here.

I slammed my mental shields down, reaching for her, screaming her name in the psychic void.

*JAZZ!*

Nothing. Just a dull, drugged haze. She was unconscious again.

I looked at the southern ridge. At Elford.

He was watching me. He had binoculars raised to his eyes. He wanted to see the moment I broke. He wanted to see the exact second the realization hit that he had already won.

He lowered the binoculars. He smiled. A slow, cruel stretching of lips.

He tapped his wrist, miming a watch. *Time to fight.*

I took a step toward him.

"Damien, no!" Roric grabbed me, locking his arms around my waist. "If you step toward him, you forfeit! The snipers on the ridge have orders to fire if you break the perimeter! She dies if you run!"

"He has her!" I roared, struggling against Roric's grip. My Alpha strength surged, throwing him off balance, but two Ashen enforcers jumped in, holding me back. "He has her, Roric! The challenge is a lie!"

"If you leave the Circle, the Gambit ends!" Roric shouted in my face, desperation in his eyes. "If the Gambit ends, Elford kills her legally! He executes a rogue trespasser! You have to fight! It's the only way to buy time!"

I stopped struggling. I stood there, panting, my chest heaving as if I had run a marathon.

Roric was right. The trap was perfect.

If I ran to save her, I forfeited my life and hers.

If I fought, I was dancing to Elford's tune while he held a knife to her throat.

*Entertain me,* I whispered, repeating the note.

He wanted a show. He wanted to see me bleed. He wanted me to fight for the hope of seeing her one last time.

I looked at Elford again.

*You made a mistake,* I thought, the cold rage crystalizing into a blade of pure intent. *You think this makes me weak. You think fear makes me slow.*

I turned to Roric.

"Let go."

Roric hesitated, then released me. "Damien..."

"Clear the field," I said. My voice didn't sound like mine. It sounded dead. "I'm going in."

"Strategy?" Roric asked weakly.

"No strategy," I said. "Slaughter."

I walked toward the Stone Circle.

The Arbiter, Silas, was already on the dais. He looked at me, frowning. He sensed the shift in the air.

He smelled the murderous intent rolling off me like smoke.

"The Gambit is invoked!" Silas boomed.

I stepped between the monoliths. The ground was hard-packed earth. The arena of my ancestors.

I stood in the center. I didn't look at the crowd. I didn't look at the sky. I stared at the eastern gate.

*Selene.*

She knew. She was part of it. The note implied capture. Shadowfangs were the capturers.

She stepped out. She was wearing that liquid skin suit. She looked confident. Smug. She thought she was fighting a distracted, heartbroken man.

She walked into the circle. She circled me.

I stood still. I let my arms hang loose.

*They came from underneath.*

The bell rang.

Selene moved. She was fast. A blur of motion.

I didn't dodge.

I watched her come. I saw the blades on her arms extend. I saw the triumph in her violet eyes.

She launched herself at my back.

I dropped.

It wasn't a defensive crouch. It was a coil.

She flew over me. As she landed, I didn't reassess. I didn't wait.

I exploded.

I drove my shoulder into her gut. We hit the ground.

She tried to twist away, slippery as an eel. She slashed at my face. I felt the skin split. I felt the burn of the poison.

I didn't care.

I laughed.

It was a broken, jagged sound that made her freeze for a fraction of a second.

"You took her," I whispered, my face inches from hers.

Selene's eyes widened. She saw it then. She saw that the distraction hadn't worked. It had just removed the last vestige of my humanity.

She screamed and shifted.

The panther-wolf materialized. She bit my shoulder.

I didn't shift to defend. I shifted to kill.

The Black Wolf tore out of my skin. I caught her mid-air. I slammed her into the ground.

I wanted to tear her throat out. I wanted to shred her until there was nothing left but wet ribbons.

*Entertain me.*

If I killed her too fast, it was mercy.

I threw her. She hit the stone. She broke.

Silas counted.

I stood there, panting, the poison burning in my veins. It felt like acid. It felt like justice.

"One! Two! Three!"

She was down.

I shifted back. I stood in the center of the ring, bleeding, poisoned, and empty.

I looked up at Elford.

*Are you entertained?*

He wasn't smiling anymore. He was on his phone.

Ten minutes. I had ten minutes.

I sat down in the dirt. Roric ran in.

"The poison," Roric said, pressing a towel to my cheek. "It's neurotoxic. You need to purge."

"Leave it," I said. "The pain keeps me awake."

"Damien, Kane is next. He will crush you."

"Let him try."

I closed my eyes. I reached for the bond again.

Still silence.

*Hold on, Jazz,* I begged. *Just hold on. Two more.*

The ten minutes vanished.

"Second Challenger! Kane of the Grimvales!"

Kane entered the ring.

He didn't look smug. He looked wary. He had seen what I did to Selene. He smelled the poison on me, but he also smelled the death.

He swung the axe.

I moved.

The fight was a blur of impact and agony. The poison made my limbs heavy. Kane was a mountain. Every time he hit me, something broke.

But I couldn't go down. If I went down, Jazz died.

He hit me with a fist that felt like a sledgehammer. I flew back. I hit the ground.

My shoulder screamed.

*Get up.*

I rolled. I stabbed him in the leg.

It wasn't enough.

He grabbed me. He picked me up.

For a second, I was airborne, suspended in his grip. I looked at his face. I saw the rune etched into his axe.

He slammed me down.

The world went white.

I lay there, staring at the sky. I couldn't breathe. My ribs were powder.

*Is this it?*

I turned my head. I looked at the ridge.

And I saw her.

They had brought her out.

She was limp. Unconscious. Elford was holding her up like a rag doll.

He wanted me to see.

He wanted me to die seeing her captured.

The rage that had been cold suddenly turned hot. It turned into a supernova.

*NO.*

I roared.

I didn't feel the broken ribs. I didn't feel the poison.

I surged up, shifting into the wolf, driving my shoulder into Kane's knees.

He fell.

But I didn't finish him.

I looked at the ridge.

Elford was smiling. He keyed a radio.

Plan B.

Gunfire erupted.

The dirt kicked up around me. They were shooting.

The Gambit was over. The rules were ash.

I ran.

I ran through the bullets. I ran toward the cliff. I ran toward her.

A bullet hit my flank. It burned.

I tumbled. I got up.

I threw myself at the rock face, clawing for purchase.

*I'm coming, Jazz. I'm coming.*

But the cliff was too high. The bullets were too thick.

I fell back.

I looked up one last time.

Elford was dragging her back into the trees.

And I was bleeding out in the dirt of the Circle, surrounded by traitors, listening to the laughter of the man who had taken my heart.

Darkness edged my vision.

*Not like this,* I thought. *Please, not like this.*

But the darkness didn't care. It swallowed the valley. It swallowed the rage.

And then, there was nothing.

# CHAPTER 34
# DAMIEN

The dirt of the Stone Circle tasted like iron and failure.

I lay face down in the mud, the cold seeping into my chest, listening to the chaotic symphony of my own destruction. The gunfire was a rhythmic, popping thunder that echoed off the valley walls, punctuated by the wet thuds of bullets hitting flesh and earth.

My flank burned, a deep, searing line of fire where the bullet had torn through muscle. My ribs felt like a cage of broken glass, grinding with every shallow breath. The neurotoxin from Selene's claws still moved through my veins, trying to shut down my lungs.

I was dying.

And up on the ridge, disappearing into the dark tree line, was the only thing that tethered me to this world.

*Elford has her.*

The thought wasn't a panic. It was clear. It cut through the pain and the poison like a scalpel.

I pushed myself up. My arms trembled, threatening to collapse, but I forced them to lock. I vomited —a splatter of bile and blood—and wiped my mouth with the back of a mud-caked hand.

"Stay down!" Roric's voice screamed over the din.

My Second slid into the mud beside me, grabbing my shoulder and trying to force me back into the cover of the earth. Bullets kicked up geysers of dirt inches from our heads.

"They have the high ground!" Roric shouted, his face pale and streaked with grime. "The snipers are pinning us! We have to crawl to the rocks!"

I shook him off. I didn't crawl.

I stood up.

It was the hardest thing I had ever done. Every instinct told me to hide, to curl up, to die quietly. But the Alpha, the monster Jazz had feared and loved, refused to bend.

I stood in the center of the Stone Circle, bleeding from three different wounds, swaying like a drunkard.

The shooting stopped for a fraction of a second. The snipers paused. Maybe it was shock. Maybe they were reloading. Maybe they just wanted to see if the corpse would walk.

At the ridge, Elford was gone, taking Jazz with him.

I looked at the dais where the Arbiter stood. Silas

was dead. A stray bullet, or maybe not so stray, had caught the old wolf in the throat. He lay draped over his staff, his white robes stained red.

The law was dead. The Codex was a corpse.

"Damien!" Roric pulled at my belt. "We have to go! The Grimvales are rushing the field!"

I looked to the west. Kane's pack was pouring down the slope, a tide of grey muscle and steel axes. They were howling, a sound of pure bloodlust. To the east, the Shadowfangs were moving like smoke, picking off my perimeter guards with silenced weapons.

The Gambit was over. It wasn't a duel anymore. It was an extermination.

I looked at Roric. I looked at the fifty Ashen Ones who had formed a desperate shield wall at the northern gate, trying to hold back the Draven mob.

"The Throne is gone," I rasped, my voice sounding like gravel grinding in a mixer.

"Forget the Throne!" Roric yelled. "Save the pack! Save yourself!"

"No," I said.

I reached down and ripped the ceremonial dagger from my thigh. I held it up, the blade catching the weak morning light.

"LISTEN TO ME!" I roared.

The sound tore my throat raw, but it carried. It carried over the gunfire, the screams, and the howls. It was the voice of the Ashen Alpha, driven by pure, reckless rage.

The battlefield seemed to hesitate. Even the Grimvales slowed their charge.

I pointed the dagger at the empty chair where Elford had sat.

"The Challenge is broken!" I bellowed. "The Arbiter is dead! The Truce is ash!"

I turned, scanning the ridgelines, addressing the hidden enemies, the traitors, the cowards.

"You want a war? You want to turn this valley into a grave?"

I slashed the air with the dagger.

"Then come and take it! But know this!"

I paused, letting the silence stretch, letting them see the blood dripping from my flank, the fire burning in my gold eyes.

"I renounce the Throne! I renounce the Codex! I am no longer a contender!"

Roric stared at me, horror dawning in his eyes. He knew what I was doing. I was stripping away the legal protection of the Gambit. I was stripping away the goal.

"I am the Warlord of the Ashen Ones!" I declared, my voice dropping to a terrifying, resonant low. "And I declare a Blood Hunt! On Elford Draven! On Kane of the Grimvales! On Selene of the Shadowfangs!"

I raised the knife high.

"Any wolf who harbors them dies! Any pack that

aids them burns! There is no quarter! There is no surrender! I will kill you all until the rivers run black with your blood!"

"KILL THEM!"

The command broke the spell.

The Ashen Ones roared. It wasn't the disciplined shout of a pack protecting a challenger. It was the primal scream of a pack unleashed. They had seen their Alpha cheated, shot, and poisoned. They had seen the law murdered. Now, they were off the leash.

The shield wall at the north gate broke. My wolves didn't retreat. They charged.

Fifty Ashen warriors threw themselves into the Draven mob. It was a collision of hate. Teeth met throat. Knives met ribs.

"Roric," I said, grabbing my Second by the vest. "Get me to the truck."

"You need a healer," Roric argued, eyeing my bleeding flank.

"I need a weapon," I snarled. "And I need to get to the ridge."

"We can't get to the ridge," Roric said, pointing. "The Grimvales cut us off. If we try to go up that slope, we're dead."

I looked at the wall of Grimvales advancing. Kane was at the front, limping from the stab wound I had given him, but still swinging his axe.

"Then we go through them," I said.

I shifted.

It was agony. My body fought me, broken ribs shifting and the bullet wound tearing wider as I grew. But the Black Wolf came anyway. He had to. The man was too broken to fight.

I hit the ground on four paws, snarling. I couldn't run fast. My back leg was dragging. But I was huge, and I was filled with a hatred so pure it felt like power.

*Follow,* I commanded the pack through the bond.

I charged Kane.

The Grimvale Alpha saw me coming. He laughed, raising his axe. He thought he had me. He thought the injured dog was coming to be put down.

He swung.

I didn't dodge. I didn't have the speed.

I took the hit.

The flat of the axe handle caught me in the shoulder, knocking me sideways. Pain exploded in my head, white and blinding.

But I used the impact. I let it spin me. I snapped my jaws, catching his ankle—the same leg I had stabbed earlier.

I crunched down. Bone shattered.

Kane screamed, toppling like a felled tree.

I didn't stay to finish him. I scrambled over his thrashing body, using him as a stepping stone.

*Move!* I roared at my pack. *To the trucks!*

The Ashen Ones formed a wedge around me. We forced our way through the Grimvale line. It was brutal, messy work. I saw my friends fall. I saw

Thorne, the young guard, take a spear to the chest. I saw old Silas's body trampled into the mud.

We reached the trucks.

"Drive!" I shifted back to human form as I threw myself into the passenger seat of Roric's SUV. I couldn't maintain the wolf. The blood loss was too great.

Roric gunned the engine. We peeled out, mud spraying, just as the Shadowfang snipers adjusted their aim. The back window shattered.

"Where are we going?" Roric shouted, swerving to avoid a Draven roadblock.

"The ridge," I gasped, pressing a towel to my flank. "Elford's extraction point. We have to catch them before they get her to the marsh."

Roric shook his head. "We can't, Damien! Look!"

He pointed through the windshield.

On the ridge road, a helicopter was rising. A sleek, black civilian chopper, unmarked.

Elford's Plan B.

I watched, helpless, as the helicopter banked and turned south, toward the wetlands.

She was on it. I knew it. I could feel her terror fading into the distance, a signal growing weaker and weaker until it was just a static hum.

"No," I whispered. I slammed my fist into the dashboard, cracking the plastic. "NO!"

"We can't catch a chopper," Roric said gently. "We have to regroup. If we chase them into the marsh now, in this state... we all die. And she dies with us."

I stared at the retreating aircraft. I wanted to shift. I wanted wings. I wanted to tear the sky apart.

But Roric was right. I was bleeding out. My pack was scattered. We had lost the battle.

"The compound," I said, the words tasting like ash. "Pull back to the compound."

"And then?"

"And then we barricade the doors," I said. "We arm everyone. Even the pups. And we call the Snows."

"The Snows?" Roric glanced at me. "Damien, the Snows are civilians. This is a war zone now."

"The Snows are the only reason we're not dead already," I said. "They have the town. They have the intel. And Elias... Elias will want blood."

We drove in silence for a mile, the sounds of the battle fading behind us. The Grimvales and Shadow-fangs wouldn't pursue us too far. They had won the field. They would be busy looting the dead and cele-brating the fall of the Ashen King.

I leaned my head back against the seat and closed my eyes. The pain felt alive, eating at me.

"I lost her, Roric," I whispered.

"We'll get her back," Roric promised. But his voice lacked conviction. He knew Elford. He knew what happened to wolves who went into the Draven marshlands.

"He's going to break her," I said, a tear leaking out

of my closed eye. "He's going to use the bond to hurt me. He's going to make me feel every second of it."

"Then you block it," Roric said. "You put up the wall."

"I can't," I said. "If I block it... I might miss the moment she needs me. I have to stay open. I have to take it."

We reached the compound. The gates were open, guarded by the terrified remnants of the reserve force. They saw the shattered trucks, the wounded wolves, the blood on their Alpha.

They went silent.

I climbed out of the truck. I refused the stretcher. I refused the help.

I walked to the center of the courtyard. I stood there, swaying and bleeding, looking at what was left of my kingdom.

"Listen to me!" I shouted. My voice was weak, but they heard me.

"The Throne is a lie!" I told them. "The Alliance is a lie! They cheated! They killed the Arbiter! They stole my Mate!"

A murmur of anger rippled through the crowd.

"We are not fighting for a crown anymore!" I said. "We are fighting for survival! Elford declared war on us! He thinks we are broken! He thinks we will scatter!"

I drew the dagger again. It was shaking in my hand.

"Are we broken?"

"NO!" a few voices shouted.

"Are we scattered?"

"NO!"

"Then arm yourselves!" I ordered. "Fortify the walls! Call in every favor! Call in every rogue! We are the Ashen Ones! We do not die quietly!"

I collapsed.

Roric caught me before I hit the ground.

"Get him to the infirmary!" Roric shouted. "Get the healers! Now!"

I was dragged into the medical bay. The smell of antiseptic replaced the smell of mud. Hands were on me, cutting away my clothes, pressing gauze into my wounds.

"He's lost a lot of blood," someone said. "BP is dropping."

"Get the IV," another voice ordered. "Stitch the flank first. Check for internal bleeding."

I stared at the ceiling lights. They were too bright. They hurt my eyes.

"Jazz," I murmured.

"She's not here, Alpha," a healer said softly. "Rest now."

"Phone," I rasped. "Give me... the phone."

"You need to sleep."

"GIVE ME THE DAMN PHONE!" I roared, grabbing the healer's scrub top.

Roric stepped in. He handed me my cell phone. The screen was cracked and smeared with blood.

My fingers fumbled with the keys. I dialed the number.

It rang once.

"Hello?" Elias Snow's voice. Anxious.

"Elias," I wheezed.

"Damien? Where is she? Where is Jasmine? The news is reporting gunfire in the valley. What happened?"

"He took her," I said. The words tore my heart out. "Elford took her. They put her on a chopper."

Silence on the line. A terrible, heavy silence.

"You promised," Elias whispered. "You promised she was safe."

"I failed," I admitted. "But I'm not done. I'm going to get her back. I'm going to burn the marsh down."

"You failed," Elias repeated, his voice turning cold. "You played your game, and you lost my daughter."

"Elias, listen to me. I need the Snows. I need you to find out where that chopper landed. I need you to track the Apex trucks. I need—"

"You need nothing from me," Elias cut in. "You have done enough."

"Don't hang up," I begged. "If you cut me off, she dies. We have to work together."

"I am done working with Ashfords," Elias said. "I am going to find my daughter. My way."

The line went dead.

I dropped the phone. It clattered to the floor.

"He hung up," I told Roric. "The alliance is broken."

"We'll fix it," Roric said, pressing a mask over my face. "Breathe, Damien. Just breathe."

The gas hit me. The world started to fade.

But I fought it. I had to stay awake. I had to find her.

*Jazz?* I sent the thought out, a desperate ping into the darkness.

Faintly, so faintly it might have been my imagination, I felt a pulse.

Fear. Pain. Motion.

She was still alive.

*I'm coming,* I promised her, as the darkness finally took me. *I'm coming.*

I woke up hours later. Or maybe days.

The room was dark. Roric was sleeping in a chair by the door.

I sat up. My body screamed in protest. I was bandaged from chest to hip. An IV line ran into my arm.

I ripped it out.

I stood up, holding the wall for support.

I walked to the table where my gear was piled. I picked up the dagger. I picked up the tactical map of the Dravens' territory.

I wasn't going to wait for my army. I wasn't going to wait for the Snows.

I was going to the marsh.

Roric stirred. "Damien?"

"Don't try to stop me," I said, my voice quiet in the dark room.

"I'm not going to stop you," Roric said, standing up. He looked exhausted, but his eyes were clear. "I'm going with you."

"It's a suicide mission," I said.

"I know," Roric said. He picked up his rifle. "But the pack is ready. We fortified the perimeter. We sent the pups to the safe houses. The warriors... they want blood, Damien. They want to finish it."

I looked at him. My Second. My brother.

"We're not fighting for the Throne anymore," I reminded him.

"I know," Roric said. "We're fighting for the girl."

He opened the door.

The courtyard was full.

Two hundred wolves. Ashen Ones. Rogues who had heard the call. Even a few lone shifters were disgusted by the murder of the Arbiter.

They stood in silence, waiting.

I walked out onto the porch. I didn't have a speech. I didn't have a crown.

I just had a knife and a map.

"The marsh," I said.

A low growl rippled through the crowd.

"We kill everything that stands in our way," I said. "We burn every building. We sink every boat. And we don't stop until we find her."

I limped to the truck.

"Mount up!" Roric shouted.

Engines roared to life. Headlights cut through the night.

The Ashen Ones were going to war. Not for a king, but for a mate.

And God help anyone who stood between us and the water.

# CHAPTER 35
# JAZZ

I woke to the sound of dripping water and the smell of ancient, fermented decay.

Consciousness came back slowly, pushing through the heavy fog of ketamine. My limbs felt heavy, like they were packed with wet sand. My head throbbed, pounding in time with a slow, distant clank-clank-clank.

I opened my eyes. The world was a blur of rust and grey.

I was suspended.

That was the first realization. I wasn't lying on a floor. I was hanging. My wrists were shackled above my head, the metal cuffs digging into my skin. My toes barely brushed the metal grating beneath me.

I tried to shift, to pull my arms down, but the movement sent a jolt of nausea rolling through my stomach. I gagged, dry-heaving into the empty air.

"Awake already?" a voice echoed from the shadows. "Good metabolism. Must be the Alpha blood rubbing off on you."

I blinked, trying to clear the grit from my eyes. The room came into focus. It was an industrial nightmare: a huge space with corrugated metal walls, rusted by salt and damp. The floor was a metal mesh grid, and below it, dark, oily water churned slowly.

We were in the marsh. More exactly, we were inside one of the abandoned canneries scattered across Draven territory. These were the skeletal remains of an industry that had died fifty years ago.

Elford stepped into the light.

He had left the suit behind. Now he wore dark fatigues, sleeves rolled up to show his muscular forearms. He looked less like a businessman and more like a warden. In his hand, he held a long, thin metal rod: a cattle prod.

"Where is he?" I croaked. My throat felt like I had swallowed glass.

"Damien?" Elford smiled, tapping the prod against his thigh. "He's coming. He's as predictable as the tide. He declared a Blood Hunt, did you know? He gave up the Throne. He gave up the Codex. All just to come for you."

He walked slowly in a circle around me. I felt exposed and vulnerable. I still had my leggings, but they had taken my boots and tactical vest.

And the Karambit.

I checked my waist with a subtle shift of my hips. The knife was gone.

"Looking for your toy?" Elford asked, stopping in front of me. He pulled the curved blade from his belt. "It's a nasty little thing. Cold-forged iron. Illegal in three states. Did he teach you how to use it?"

"He taught me how to kill you," I whispered.

"He taught you how to try. But you're a librarian, Jazz. You record history. You don't make it." Checking his watch. "The Ashen Ones are moving fast, but the marsh slows them down. They have to stick to the causeways. Which is exactly where Kane and Selene are waiting."

He stepped closer, grabbing my chin and forcing me to look at him. His eyes were muddy, devoid of the gold that made Damien's gaze so compelling.

"You're going to watch," he said. "I've set up a nice view. I want you to see exactly what your love has cost them."

He hit a button on the wall. A section of the corrugated siding groaned and slid open on rusted tracks, revealing a wide, jagged opening that looked out over the marshlands.

The view was desolate and terrifying.

Miles of sawgrass and black water stretched under a heavy sky. Thick, unnatural fog rolled in from the coast, clinging to the water like a shroud. The only landmarks were the rotting pilings of old piers and the causeway, a single narrow strip of paved road cutting through the swamp like a scar.

"That road," Elford pointed with the prod, "is the only way in for heavy vehicles. Damien will come that way. And when he does... the Grimvales will close the trap from the rear, and the Shadowfangs will hit them from the water."

"He knows it's a trap," I said. "He's not stupid."

"He's desperate," Elford corrected. "Desperation makes geniuses into idiots. He thinks he can power through. He thinks if he just hits hard enough, he can reach you."

He leaned in, his breath smelling of mint and rot. "He's wrong."

I stared out at the fog. It was moving strangely. Fog usually drifted with the wind, but this... this felt purposeful. It was swirling, thickening, obscuring the coastline to the east.

East.

The direction of Tallow. The direction of the Snow territory.

A chill that had nothing to do with the damp air raced up my spine.

"The fog," I whispered.

Elford glanced at it, frowning. "Sea fret. Common this time of year."

"No," I said, a realization blooming in my chest—a spark of hope so bright it hurt. "That's not sea fret. That's cover."

Elford looked at me sharply. "What are you talking about?"

"My father," I said, a smile touching my cracked lips. "He used to tell me stories about how the Snows survived the Great Purge. They didn't fight. They vanished. They used the weather. They summoned the mist."

Elford snorted. "Fairytales. The Snows are cowards. They're hiding in their gym."

"Are they?"

I looked back at the fog bank. It was rolling over the water, swallowing the pilings. And inside the grey wall, I saw movement.

Not one boat. Dozens.

Small fishing skiffs. Pleasure crafts. Zodiacs. They were moving silently, engines cut, drifting on the tide, hidden by the unnatural density of the mist.

And on the bows of those boats stood figures in grey. Elford followed my gaze. He squinted.

Then, a flare went up. Not red. White. It burst over the marsh, illuminating the fog with a stark, blinding brilliance. The mist seemed to explode.

From the fog bank, the Snow fleet emerged. They weren't landing on the causeway. They were landing everywhere—on the mudflats, on the rotting piers, crashing directly into the pilings of the cannery itself.

"What the hell?" Elford breathed, stepping back.

He keyed his radio. "Perimeter! Report! We have boats!"

"Sir!" a voice crackled back, panicked. "It's a fleet! It's the civilians! It's the Snows!"

"Sink them!" Elford roared. "They're fishermen! Blow them out of the water!"

But it was too late. The first wave of Snows hit the mud.

They didn't shift immediately. They were armed. My father, the pacifist history teacher, was leading the charge. He leaped from the bow of a trawler, a hunting rifle in his hands. He fired, taking out a Draven sentry on the perimeter walkway.

Beside him, Mrs. Henderson, the baker, was throwing Molotov cocktails. Bottles of high-proof alcohol with burning rags smashed against the wooden pilings, setting the rot on fire.

"They're attacking," I whispered, tears streaming down my face. "They came."

Elford stared, his mouth slightly open. He couldn't process it. The sheep had grown fangs.

"This is impossible," he muttered. "They're neutral. They don't fight."

"They're horrified," I said, watching my cousin Sarah shift into a grey wolf and tear into a Shadowfang mercenary. "Look at them, Elford. They're terrified. But they're doing it anyway."

It was chaotic and messy. The Snows didn't fight with the military precision of the Ashen Ones. Instead, they fought with frantic, desperate brutality. They swarmed. If one Snow fell, three more took their place. They were driven by a deep, primal need to protect their own.

And then, from the causeway, the second hammer fell. An explosion rocked the building.

I looked to the west. A fireball was rising from the roadblock Elford had set up. Through the smoke, a black truck smashed through the burning wreckage. It was battered, riddled with bullet holes, and running on rims. It skidded to a halt, and the door flew open.

Damien.

He was a mess: bandaged, bloody, and limping so badly, it should have stopped him. But he kept moving. He roared—a sound that carried over the water, over the gunfire, straight to me.

Behind him, the Ashen Ones poured onto the causeway. The alignment was complete.

To the east, the Snows rose from the sea like ghosts. To the west, the Ashen Ones burned a path of vengeance. In the middle, the Dravens, Grimvales, and Shadowfangs were trapped between them.

Elford turned away from the window, his face a mask of fury.

"They want a war?" he snarled. "I'll give them a massacre."

He turned on me.

"And you," he hissed, marching toward me. "You're the ticket out of here."

He hit the release on the shackles.

I dropped, landing hard on my knees. Before I could scramble away, he grabbed a handful of my hair and hauled me up. He jammed the cattle prod into my ribs.

"Move," he ordered. "Upstairs. To the roof."

"No," I gasped, digging my heels in.

He triggered the prod. A jolt of electricity slammed into my side, convulsing my muscles. I screamed, my legs giving out.

He dragged me out of the room, down a metal corridor that vibrated with the sounds of the battle below.

We passed windows. I saw glimpses of the fight.

I saw a Grimvale—huge and lumbering—swing an axe at a grey wolf. The wolf dodged, and another Snow jumped on the Grimvale's back. It was Mr. Henderson. He was biting and clawing, holding on for dear life while the giant thrashed.

I saw my father. He was surrounded by three Dravens. He wasn't shifting. He was using the rifle like a club, swinging it with a grim, horrified expression on his face. He looked sick. He looked like he wanted to vomit. But he didn't stop swinging.

"Look at them," Elford spat, dragging me up a metal staircase. "Look at your family. They're monsters now, just like us. You think they can go back to baking bread after this? You broke them, Jazz. You turned them into killers."

"I turned them into survivors!" I yelled, clawing at his hand.

We burst onto the roof.

The wind whipped the fog around us. The roof was flat and metal, slick with rain and oil. In the center, a black helicopter waited, its rotors spinning slowly.

"Get in," Elford shouted over the noise of the engine.

"I'm not going with you!"

"You don't have a choice!" He shoved me toward the chopper. "We're going to the secondary site. And if Damien follows, I'll drop you from a height. I looked at the open helicopter door. If I got on that helicopter, it would be over. I would never see Damien again.

I looked at the stairwell door.

It burst open. It wasn't Damien. It was Kane.

The Grimvale Alpha stumbled onto the roof, covered in mud and blood. One of his arms hung uselessly at his side. He was retreating.

"They broke the line!" Kane roared, his voice filled with panic. "The Ashen Ones... they aren't stopping! They're killing everyone! We have to go!"

He ran for the chopper.

Elford cursed. "Get back! There's no room!"

"I'm taking the seat!" Kane snarled, shoving Elford aside.

In the chaos, Elford's grip on me loosened. This was it. I didn't run. There was nowhere to run. We were on a roof surrounded by water. I turned to Elford. He was distracted, trying to pull his gun on Kane.

Up and in.

I didn't have the knife. I didn't have the strength. But I had the secret. I stepped forward. Elford saw the movement. He turned back to me, sneering. "Stay put, bitch, or I'll—"

I dropped my weight. I slid down, just an inch, changing the angle. I formed the claw. I didn't hesitate. I didn't think about the library. I didn't think about pacifism. I drove my rigid fingers into the hollow of his throat. I twisted.

Elford's eyes went wide. His mouth opened, but no sound came out. He grabbed his chest. He dropped the gun. He dropped the cattle prod. He fell to his knees, gasping, clutching at a heart that had just received a kill signal.

Kane stopped at the helicopter door. He looked at Elford, convulsing on the ground. He looked at me, standing over him with my hand still formed in a claw. The huge Grimvale looked terrified.

"Witch," he snarled.

He jumped into the helicopter. "Go! Go!" The pilot didn't argue. The helicopter lifted off, and the wind from the rotors knocked me flat, wet metal, watching Kane fly away.

Elford was still on the ground next to me. He was turning blue. His eyes were rolling back in his head.

He wasn't dead. Damien said it would take the system three minutes to restart. Elford was paralyzed, trapped inside his own body.

I scrambled away from him, backing up until I hit the parapet of the roof.

I looked down. The battle was raging. But at the causeway entrance, the fighting had stopped. A circle had formed. In the center stood Damien.

He was looking up. He was looking at the roof. He roared—a sound of victory and question. I pulled myself up, leaning over the edge. I waved my arms.

"I'm here!" I screamed, though I knew he couldn't hear me over the battle. "I'm here!"

He saw me. He broke into a run, sprinting for the building.

I slumped back against the wall, shaking uncontrollably. I looked at Elford. He was starting to twitch. The paralysis was fading. I looked around for a weapon. The cattle prod was lying in a puddle of water. I picked it up.

Elford gasped, sucking in a desperate breath. His eyes focused on me.

"You..." he wheezed. "How...?"

"The King's Fang," I said, my voice trembling but hard. "Damien sends his regards."

He tried to sit up, reaching for his gun. I jammed the cattle prod into his chest and hit the trigger. He screamed.

"Stay down," I ordered. "The King is coming."

The stairwell door banged open again. Damien burst onto the roof.

He stopped. He took in the scene. The retreating helicopter. Elford was twitching on the ground. I, holding the cattle prod, battered but alive.

# CHAPTER 36
# DAMIEN

The steel door to the roof didn't simply open. It broke apart under the force of my shoulder.

I burst into the storm, my lungs burning like I'd breathed in broken glass, my body aching everywhere. Climbing those metal stairs had been a fight against gravity and blood loss. The bullet wound in my side burned, and my ribs scraped together with every breath.

But none of that mattered.

All that mattered was the bond. It screamed in my head, a sharp alarm that pushed me through gunfire and up three floors of a burning building.

*She's here. She's here. She's here.*

The wind hit me first, a powerful gust carrying the smell of salt and the sharp tang of ozone. Rain poured down in sheets, turning everything into streaks of gray and black.

I scanned the roof, my weapon raised, my heart hammering a frantic rhythm against my ribs.

The first thing I saw was the helicopter, a sleek black shape turning away into the mist, its rotors beating the air. Kane was on it. I was sure. He had run away.

Then I looked down.

And my heart stopped.

Elford Draven was lying on the wet metal deck. He wasn't standing in triumph. He wasn't holding a gun to my mate's head.

He lay on his back, shaking. His hands gripped his chest, his face twisted in pain, his eyes rolling back. He looked like his own body was attacking him.

And standing over him was Jazz.

She was the most beautiful, terrifying thing I had ever seen.

She was soaked, her hair stuck to her face, her clothes torn and muddy. She shook with full-body tremors I could feel through the bond. But she stood, holding a cattle prod like a spear, staring down at the man who tried to break her.

"Jazz," I breathed. The sound was torn from my throat, raw and broken.

She looked up. Her eyes were wide, dark with adrenaline and fear. For a moment, she didn't seem to know me. She was still fighting, still in survival mode.

Then, the recognition slammed into her.

"Damien," she sobbed.

She dropped the prod. It clattered on the metal.

"I promised," she gasped, her voice thin in the wind. "I promised I'd survive."

I closed the gap between us in a heartbeat. I didn't care about Elford or the war. I pulled her into my arms and held her tight.

I pressed my face into her wet hair, breathing in her scent—rain, fear, and life. She was real. She was solid. She was warm.

"You did," I whispered in her ear, my hands moving over her back, checking for wounds, needing to make sure she was okay. "God, you did."

She held onto me, her fingers gripping my vest, as if I was the only thing keeping her grounded. I felt her heart racing against mine, a wild beat that slowly matched my own.

"He tried..." she stammered against my chest. "He tried to take me."

"I know," I soothed, rocking her slightly. "I know. I've got you. You're safe."

A sound cut through the moment—a wet, gurgling cough.

I tensed. The Wolf inside me wanted blood.

I pulled back from Jazz, keeping one arm wrapped tightly around her waist, and turned to look at Elford.

The Draven Alpha struggled to breathe. The paralysis from Jazz's attack was fading, but his body still wasn't working right. His limbs twitched. He looked up at me, his eyes finally focusing.

Hate. Pure, undiluted hate stared back at me.

"You..." Elford wheezed, blood bubbling at the corner of his mouth. "She... used the Fang."

I looked at him, then at Jazz. A fierce pride filled me, stronger than the pain in my side.

"You taught her well," Elford spat, trying to push himself up on one elbow and failing. He collapsed back onto the wet metal. "But it changes nothing. You are still... weak."

"I'm standing," I said, my voice cold. "And you're dying on your own roof."

"He was distracted," Jazz whispered, her voice trembling but fierce. "He thought he had won."

"He thought wrong," I said.

Elford laughed. It was a hideous, bubbling sound. "Did I? Look at you, Damien. Look at your pack. You bled for this. You broke your precious Codex. You became... me."

"I will never be you," I snarled.

"You killed for her," Elford rasped. "You started a war for her. That is what Vargas would have done. That is what I did."

He coughed again, his body arching as his nerves misfired.

"I killed him," Elford whispered, his gaze drifting to the grey sky. "Your father. He begged, Damien. He begged for your life. He traded his crown for your breath."

His confession hung in the cold air, heavy and final.

I had known it. I had felt it for ten years. But hearing him say it, knowing my father's mercy led to his death, made the cold in my veins turn to stone.

"I know," I said softly. "And that is why you die."

I let go of Jazz and stepped forward. I drew the ceremonial dagger from my thigh. The steel slid against the leather. It was my father's blade, the one that had spared Vargas thirty years ago.

It was poetic. It was justice. It felt right. He didn't look afraid. He looked... expectant.

"Do it!" Elford screamed, his voice cracking. "Prove it! Prove you are a killer!"

He tried to shift. I saw his skin ripple, bones cracking, jaw stretching. In his last moments, he wanted to become a weapon. He wanted me to kill him as a beast.

I raised the dagger.

I was ready. The Wolf in me wanted to tear. The man in me wanted to finish it.

But then, a hand touched my arm.

Small. Warm. Firm.

I froze. I looked down.

Jazz had stepped forward. She wasn't looking away. She wasn't asking me to stop. She was looking at the knife, and then at me.

Her eyes were clear. The fear was gone, replaced by a calm that took my breath away.

"Together," she whispered.

I stared at her. "Jazz, you don't have to..."

"He hurt us," she said. "Both of us. He burned my home. He killed your father. He tried to break us."

She reached out and placed her hand over mine on the hilt of the dagger.

"We finish it together."

I looked at our hands. My large, scarred hand wrapped around the leather grip. Her smaller, pale hand covering mine.

It was the answer. It was the only answer.

If I killed him alone, it would be revenge. If she did it alone, it would be pain.

But together, it was justice. It was the pack cutting out a disease. He was half-shifted now, a grotesque mix of man and wolf, snarling up at us. He saw our hands on the knife. He saw the unity.

For the first time, I saw fear in his eyes. He realized he hadn't broken us. He had made us stronger.

"No..." he gasped.

I tightened my grip. Jazz tightened hers.

We drove the blade down.

There was no struggle. Gravity and justice did the work. The blade sank deep into Elford's chest, piercing the heart that had poisoned our lives for years.

Elford gasped—a sharp, wet intake of breath.

His body arched off the deck one last time. His eyes

met mine, then Jazz's. The hate faded, then disappeared, leaving only emptiness.

He slumped back. His half-shifted features relaxed, sliding back into human form.

The King of the Dravens was dead.

We didn't let go of the knife right away. We stood over the body, our hands still on the hilt, breathing together.

The silence that followed was complete. Even the wind seemed to pause. The rain slowed to a drizzle. The weight lifted from my shoulders. The shadow that had hung over the Ashfords since my father's murder—the shadow of Elford Draven—was gone.

I looked at Jazz.

She stared at the body. She didn't cry. She looked solemn. She looked ancient.

"It's done," she whispered.

"It's done," I let go of the knife, leaving it in his chest. It belonged to him now, a marker for a legacy of hate.

I pulled Jazz into my arms again. This time, I held her because I needed her. I needed to feel her life against mine, to remind myself we were still here.

She pressed her face into my neck. I felt her shaking as the adrenaline finally wore off.

"I killed him," she murmured against my skin.

"We killed him," I corrected, smoothing her wet hair. "We survived, Jazz. We won."

I looked around the roof. The cannery below was

quiet. The gunfire had stopped. The sudden silence from the command center, from Elford, must have meant it was over. The pack would be waiting.

I looked at Jazz. She was battered, bruised, and exhausted.

"Are you okay?" I asked, pulling back to look at her face.

She took a deep, shuddering breath. She wiped the rain from her eyes and nodded.

"I'm tired," she admitted. "And I want to go home."

"We will," I promised. "But first..."

I looked toward the edge of the roof, overlooking the courtyard.

"We have to finish the job. We have to claim the peace."

She understood. She straightened her spine, lifting her chin. Despite the mud, despite the blood, she looked regal.

"Okay," she said. "Let's go."

I took her hand. Her grip was firm.

We walked to the edge of the roof together.

Below us, the fog lifted. The war was over. A new world waited.

# CHAPTER 37

# DAMIEN

The rain had stopped, but the world was still dripping.

I stood on the cannery roof, my boots slipping on the wet metal, holding Jazz's hand so tightly my knuckles turned white. Below, the courtyard was full of mud, debris, and faces looking up. The silence after the battle felt heavy, almost louder than the gunfire from before.

They were waiting.

Hundreds of wolves from the Ashen, Snow, Draven, and the last of the Grimvales and Shadowfangs stood frozen in the mud. They had heard the silence from above. They saw the helicopter leave. Now, they needed to know who had survived.

I looked at Jazz. She was pale, her hair plastered to her skull, shivering slightly as the adrenaline began to bleed out of her system. But she didn't look away from the drop. She squeezed my hand, a silent signal.

*Tell them.*

I stepped to the edge of the parapet. I didn't need a microphone. The shape of the valley and the Alpha projection I had learned would carry my voice all the way to the trees.

"THE DRAVEN IS DEAD!"

The words came out raw and rough. They echoed off the cannery's rusted walls and rolled across the marsh like thunder.

A ripple went through the crowd below. I saw weapons lower. I saw heads turn.

"ELFORD DRAVEN HAS FALLEN!" I roared, raising my free hand—the one not holding Jazz. "THE WAR IS OVER!"

For a moment, nothing happened. Then a sound began at the eastern edge of the courtyard, where the Snows stood. A cheer started, rough and unsure, but it grew. The Ashen Ones joined in, adding a deep, powerful roar of victory.

I watched the Dravens. They didn't cheer. They slumped, not in defeat, but in relief. The tyrant was gone. The fear that had controlled them for years vanished with his last breath.

"We need to go down," I said to Jazz, my voice dropping back to a normal register. "We need to finish this face-to-face."

She nodded, leaning heavily against me. "I don't know if my legs will carry me."

"I'll carry you," I offered.

"No," she said, straightening her spine with a visible effort. "The Queen walks."

A fierce pride filled my chest. That was my mate.

We turned and went into the stairwell. Going down was a blur of gray concrete and steel. The adrenaline that got me up here was gone, replaced by the pain of my injuries. My side burned with every step, and my ribs ached, but I couldn't show weakness now.

We reached the ground floor. The heavy steel doors to the courtyard were battered, scarred by bullets and claws. Roric was waiting there, along with a squad of Ashen enforcers.

Roric looked at me, his face streaked with soot and blood. He looked at Jazz, battered but standing. He let out a breath he seemed to have been holding for days.

"Alpha," he breathed. "Is it...?"

"He's dead, Roric," I said. "It's done."

Roric closed his eyes for a second, a silent prayer of thanks. Then he snapped back to attention. "The Grimvales are confused. Kane fled on the chopper, but he left half his berserkers behind. They don't know whether to fight or surrender. The Shadowfangs have melted into the shadows, but Selene... we have Selene."

"Alive?"

"Broken," Roric said grimly. "But alive."

"Open the doors," I ordered.

Roric signaled the enforcers. They hauled the heavy doors open, the hinges screaming in protest.

Light filled the dark corridor. I breathed in the cool, damp air. It tasted like mud and freedom.

"Ready?" I asked Jazz.

"Ready," she whispered.

We walked out.

Stepping from the dark cannery into the open courtyard was a shock. The sky was clearing, with clouds parting to show patches of pale blue. The low sun cast long shadows over the mud. The crowd parted as we advanced. Wolves stepped back, creating a wide corridor leading to the center of the yard.

I walked with my head high, ignoring the pain. Jazz matched me step for step.

We reached the center. The place was wrecked, but the packs had already grouped themselves apart from each other.

To my left stood the Ashen Ones and the Snows, my people. To my right, the Dravens huddled together, unsure what to do. In front of me, the Grimvales, left behind, held their weapons low and waited for orders that would never come. Guarded by two massive Ashen warriors, was Selene.

The Shadowfang Alpha looked nothing like the terrifying creature who had poisoned me in the Circle. Her liquid-armor suit was torn. Her face was pale, her violet eyes dull. She looked up as I approached, a flicker of fear crossing her features.

I didn't stop at her. I walked past her, toward the center of the gathering.

I needed something to stand for this moment.

I spotted the old cannery signpost, a thick wooden beam set in the concrete. I took the ceremonial dagger from my sheath. It was still stained with Elford's blood. The steel was dull in the flat light.

I looked at the Grimvales. I looked at the Dravens. I looked at my own pack.

"The Throne is empty!" I declared, my voice booming across the silence. "The Arbiter is dead! The Codex is ash!"

I raised the knife.

"But the Law remains!"

I slammed the dagger into the wooden post. It sank deep, vibrating with the force of the blow.

"The Law isn't in a book," I said, turning to face them. "It isn't in a stone circle. It's in the blood! And today, the blood has spoken!"

I paced the small circle I had claimed.

"Kane of the Grimvales ran," I spat, pointing to the sky where the helicopter had vanished. "He left you! He abandoned his pack to save his own skin! Is that an Alpha?"

The Grimvales shifted, a low angry murmur passing through them. They valued strength most, and to them, cowardice was the worst sin.

"No!" a few of them shouted.

"Elford Draven is dead!" I continued. "He died trying to cheat! He died begging!"

I turned to Selene.

"And the Shadowfangs... they poisoned the well. They turned war into murder."

I stopped pacing and stood tall. The Alpha power rolled off me, a force that made the weaker wolves lower their heads. "Son of Marcus. Slayer of Elford. Warlord of the Coast."

I looked at Roric. I looked at Elias.

"I claim the Wolf Throne!"

The silence lasted for a moment. This was the turning point, the moment when everything could change.

Then, Roric knelt. He dropped to one knee in the mud, bowing his head.

"Hail the King!" Roric shouted.

The Ashen Ones dropped as one. The sound of hundreds of knees hitting the mud was like a drumbeat. "Hail the King!"

Elias Snow watched me. He didn't kneel immediately. He looked at his daughter, standing beside me. He saw the fire in her eyes, the strength in her stance. He smiled, a small, proud thing.

He lowered his rifle and knelt. The Snow pack followed him.

"Hail the King!"

Now it was up to the others.

The Dravens looked at each other. They were leaderless. Broken. They saw the Ashen Ones, the people they had tormented, now holding the power. They saw me, the man who had killed their tormentor.

Slowly, raggedly, the Dravens knelt. They exposed their throats in submission. They wanted mercy.

The Grimvales hesitated. They were proud. They were warriors.

"Your Alpha abandoned you," I said to them, my voice hard but not cruel. "But I will not. If you stand with me, you stand with strength. If you stand against me, you stand alone."

The Grimvale lieutenant, a massive wolf with a scarred snout, looked at the dagger in the post. He looked at the helicopter's vanishing point.

He threw his axe into the mud.

He knelt.

The rest of the Grimvales followed. The sound of weapons dropping was the best music I'd ever heard.

The courtyard was a sea of bowed heads.

I was King.

But I wasn't done.

I turned to Jazz. She was the only one still standing. She looked around at the kneeling army, her expression stunned.

I reached out and took her hand. Her fingers were cold, but her grip was strong.

"A King is nothing without his heart," I said, my voice carrying over the bowed heads.

I pulled her into the center of the circle, right next to the dagger.

"This is Jasmine Snow," I announced. "She fought when you hid. She bled when you ran. She entered the lion's den and came out with its teeth."

I looked at her, putting all my love, gratitude, and devotion into our bond. I wanted everyone to feel it. I wanted them to know that hurting her would be like attacking the ground we stood on.

"And she is your Queen."

"Hail the Queen!" Roric shouted, his voice cracking with emotion.

"Hail the Queen!"

The roar was deafening. It shook the rust from the cannery walls. It sent the birds fleeing from the wires.

Jazz looked at me, tears spilling over her lashes. "You crazy bastard," she whispered, a watery smile breaking through. "You actually did it."

"We did it," I corrected.

I leaned in and kissed her. It wasn't a political kiss. It wasn't a show for the packs. It was a seal. A promise that whatever came next. Whatever wars, whatever politics, whatever ghosts came back to haunt us, we would face them together.

When we pulled apart, the sun had come out from behind the clouds. Light shone on the puddles in the courtyard, making the mud look like gold.

"What now?" Jazz asked, looking at the army waiting for orders.

"Now," I said, feeling exhaustion finally pull at my bones, "we go home. We heal. And then, we build." I then turned to Roric. "Secure the prisoners. Treat the wounded—all of them, Draven and Grimvale included. We start as we mean to go on."

"Yes, Alpha. Your Majesty." Roric grinned.

I looked at Elias. He nodded to me, a silent acknowledgement of the shift in power, and then moved to embrace his daughter.

I stepped back to give them a moment. I glanced at the dagger in the post one last time.

It was done. The long night of the Ashfords was over.

I looked up at the sky. *I didn't become you,* I told my father's ghost. *And I didn't become Vargas.*

I had become something else. Something new.

I walked back to Jazz. She let go of her father and took my arm. She leaned on me, and I leaned on her. Together, we held each other up, both tired and hurting.

"The truck is over there," she said, pointing to the battered black pickup Roric had driven.

"Can you make it?" I asked.

"Watch me."

We walked through the open ranks of our new kingdom. We left the cannery, the marsh, and the ghosts behind us. With the engine roaring to life, I reached over and took her hand again.

"First rule of the new kingdom," Jazz said, resting her head back against the seat, her eyes closed.

"What's that?"

"Nap time is mandatory."

I laughed. It hurt my ribs, but it felt good. It felt like hope for the future.

"Agreed," I said.

I put the truck in gear and drove us out of the valley's shadow, toward the light, toward Tallow, and toward the start of our new life.

# CHAPTER 38
# DAMIEN AND JAZZ

The silence of the forest was different now.

For months, the woods around Tallow felt tense, like a battlefield waiting to happen. Twigs snapped underfoot, the wind carried the scent of enemies, and the birds stayed quiet out of fear. But as I walked through the deep pines, holding Jazz's hand, the forest felt peaceful, almost sacred. The wind whispered through the needles, the stream bubbled over the rocks, and a hawk cried out high above, owning the sky.

It sounded like peace.

We left the cannery about an hour ago. I gave a command to Roric and Elias, asking them to handle the prisoners and care for the wounded. I was the King, and I had the right to lead. But at that moment, the only thing that mattered to me was the woman by my side.

Jazz stayed quiet. She still wore the clothes she had fought in: mud-stained leggings and my torn flannel shirt. But she walked with her head held high. She was no longer the shy librarian who once came into my garage looking for a mechanic. Now, she was the Queen who had ended a tyrant.

We reached the clearing where I had first taught her to shift. The old mill ruins stood watch, softened by the afternoon light filtering through the canopy.

"We're here," I said softly.

Jazz stopped. She looked around, her blue eyes taking in the mossy stones, the rushing water, the circle of trees where we had trained, fought, and fallen in love.

"It feels different," she said.

"That's because we're different," I answered. "We don't have to hide here anymore. We don't have to watch the perimeter."

I turned to her and pulled her into my arms. The bond between us felt strong and bright, filled with relief, exhaustion, and a deep love that almost overwhelmed me.

"Are you okay?" I asked, brushing a strand of hair from her face. I traced the small cut on her lip, a souvenir of the war.

"I'm tired," she admitted, leaning into my touch. "My body aches in places I didn't know I had muscles. But..." She looked up at me, a smile breaking through the grime on her face. "I feel light. Like gravity, just let go."

"That's freedom," I said. "It takes some getting used to." I kissed her forehead and breathed in her scent: pine, rain, and the sweet, snowy musk that was hers alone. Hers.

"I want to wash it off," she whispered. "The blood. The marsh. Elford."

"The stream is cold," I warned.

"I'm a wolf," she countered. "I don't mind the cold."

She stepped back and started unbuttoning the flannel shirt. She undressed slowly and without shame or rush, letting her ruined clothes—the tactical vest, the shirt, the leggings—fall to the forest floor.

When she stood naked in the dappled sunlight, she took my breath away. Her pale skin was marked with bruises from the battle, but she stood tall. The sun high-lighted the curve of her hip and the slope of her shoul-der. She looked like she belonged to the forest itself.

I took off my own clothes: the blood-stiffened pants and heavy boots. I left the ceremonial dagger on the pile. I didn't need it here.

I followed her into the stream. The icy water shocked my system, washing away the last traces of poison and pain. We waded out until the water reached our waists.

Jazz turned to me. She cupped water in her hands

and poured it over my chest, washing away the blood. She traced my scars, both old and new, with gentle fingers.

"You're healing," she murmured, touching the bullet graze on my flank. The skin was already closing.

"Fast metabolism," I said, my voice thick.

"No," she said, looking into my eyes. "It's the bond. You're healing because I'm safe."

She was right. As soon as Elford died and the threat was gone, my body started to heal. I felt strong and whole again.

And I felt hungry.

I reached for her and pulled her wet body close to mine. The touch sent a jolt through me. The cold water and her warm skin made my nerves come alive.

"Jazz," I groaned, burying my face in her neck.

"Damien," she breathed, wrapping her legs around my waist. The buoyancy of the water held us up.

I kissed her. This wasn't desire, nor was it desperate or fearful like the night before. It was a promise, a claim. I took her as my Queen, not out of duty, but because nothing else felt possible.

**Jazz**

When he pulled me close, all I could feel was his skin on mine. The fear I'd carried for weeks—of the Dravens, the Codex, of losing him—finally faded, replaced by a warm feeling deep inside me. I ran my hands over his wet shoulders, feeling the power in his muscles. He was a weapon that had been sheathed, a storm that had found its calm.

"Make me forget," I whispered against his lips. "Make me forget the roof. Make me forget the knife."

"I'll make you remember this," he vowed. "Only this."

He guided us to the bank, where the moss was thick and soft. He lay me down and covered me with his body, keeping me warm from the cool air.

His hands were gentle. He touched me like I was something precious he had nearly lost. He kissed the bruise on my hip and the spot where my pulse beat in my throat.

When he entered me, it was slow and deep. It felt like he filled every empty space inside me.

I gasped and arched to meet him. The bond between us flared, not with pain, but with pleasure. I felt his love so strongly that it seemed to wash away all the darkness from the war.

"I love you," he rasped, his eyes locked on mine. The gold in his irises was swirling, hypnotic. "I love you, Jasmine. My mate. My wife. My life."

"I love you," I sobbed, the emotions overwhelming me.

We moved together in a rhythm that felt timeless. It felt like a ritual, the final step in joining our lives. Right there on the mossy bank, we started a new legacy.

The climax, when it came, was overwhelming. It

felt like everything shifted. I called out his name, and he answered with mine, both of us lost in the moment. Afterward, tangled together, listening to the water and the wind. The sun began to dip lower, painting the sky in shades of violet and gold—the colors of the Shadowfangs and the Ashen Ones, now united under one banner.

Damien rolled onto his side, propping himself up on one elbow. He looked down at me, tracing the line of my nose with his finger.

"What are you thinking?" he asked softly.

"I'm thinking about my dad," I said, a smile tugging at my lips. "He led a charge, Damien. Elias Snow, the pacifist, led a naval invasion."

Damien chuckled, a low rumble in his chest. "He did. I think we might have to make him the General of the Snow Division. If he'll accept the title."

"He won't," I said. "He'll want to go back to teaching history. But he'll teach it differently now. He won't teach about how we hid. He'll teach about how we fought."

"And you?" Damien asked. "What do you want to do? The library is still there."

"The library is too quiet," I said. "I think I have work to do here. With you."

I sat up, pulling his flannel shirt—which I had rescued from the pile—over my shoulders.

"The Codex needs to be rewritten," I said. "The packs are broken. The Dravens need leadership, not punishment. The Grimvales need to learn that strength isn't just about violence. And the Snows... the Snows need to know they matter."

I looked at him.

"I want to help you build it, Damien. The new world you promised me."

He sat up and took my hand, kissing the knuckles.

"Then we start tomorrow," he said. "Tomorrow, we call the Council. We draft the new laws. We tear down the walls between the territories."

"But tonight?" I asked.

"Tonight," he said, pulling me back into his arms, "we stay here. Tonight, the King is off duty."

# EPILOGUE

T hree Months Later

The great hall of the Ashen Ones' compound looked completely different. Heavy, dark timbers were now covered in banners: not just the black and grey of the Ashen Ones, but also the white of the Snows, the grey of the Grimvales, the violet of the Shadowfangs, and the brown of the Dravens. In the center was a round table now. No head. No foot.

I stood by the window and watched the courtyard, which was full of wolves. Grimvale pups chased Ashen pups, tumbling in the grass. Draven teenagers learned to fix an engine from one of Damien's mechanics. My father sat on a bench, deep in conversation with a Shadowfang elder about the Treaty of 1912.

It wasn't perfect. There were still arguments. There was still mistrust. But there was no war.

The door to the hall opened.

Damien walked in.

He looked different now. The tired lines on his face were gone. He moved with a relaxed, powerful grace, his limp completely healed. He wore a simple black shirt and jeans, but he still had an undeniable presence.

He walked over to me, wrapping his arms around my waist from behind.

"They're waiting for us," he murmured into my ear.

"Let them wait," I said, leaning back against him. "It's good for them."

"You're enjoying this," he teased. "The power has gone to your head, my Queen."

"Someone has to keep you in line," I countered, turning in his arms to face him.

He smiled the same slow, dangerous smile that first caught my attention in a dusty garage. "You ready?" he asked.

"For the Council meeting? Or for the rest of our lives?"

"Both."

I reached up and straightened his collar. I saw the faint scar on his throat where I had struck him during our training. It was a reminder of how close we had come to losing everything, and how hard we had fought to keep it.

"I'm ready," I said.

He offered me his arm.

"Then let's go," he said. "The pack is waiting."

We walked out of the hall together, stepping into the sunlight of the courtyard.

The chatter stopped. The wolves turned. They didn't bow out of fear. They bowed out of respect.

We looked into each other's eyes. The bond between us radiated, a sense of unity that everyone could sense.

We were the King and the Luna, the Warrior and the Pacifist, the Black Wolf and the White. We were the balance. As we walked into the crowd, hand in hand, I realized the throne wasn't just a chair in a hall. It wasn't a title or a crown. The throne was this: peace, family, and the future.

And we had claimed it all.